continued . . .

"In this darkly fanciful take on the Houdini legend…the magician's life is recounted through the damaged memory of the fan who killed him with a punch to the stomach in 1926. . . . [Galloway's] his explorations of the relationships between truth and illusion, fiction and reality, need and conscience are stimulating and affecting. . . . An entertaining fictional reflection on the twentieth-century's most famous magician."

—*Kirkus Reviews*

"A brilliant novel, and one that virtually demands multiple readings to pick up all the subtleties (especially concerning the end of the book, and enough said about that)." —*Booklist* (starred)

"*The Confabulist* is a historical novel that is more relevant than ever today. What begins as a playful, mind-teasing mystery about Harry Houdini, the greatest magician who ever lived, turns subtly, brilliantly into a beautiful elegy on love and loss, identity, and self-deception. Galloway, who is fast emerging as one of our finest young writers, has produced another novel to linger over, read and re-read, in order to glean all that it has to offer." —Kevin Baker, author of *The Big Crowd*

"Galloway has always been an uncommonly gifted storyteller, and this is very much a novel about storytelling. It's also a haunting exploration of sorrow and identity and illusion—and a beautifully calibrated full-length magic act." —*The Vancouver Sun*

"Vancouver author Steven Galloway created literary magic with *The Cellist of Sarajevo*. . . . Now in his new novel, *The Confabulist*, Galloway makes magic again, this time of the literal, stage-show variety. . . . He takes fascinating true-life aspects of Houdini, mixes them with speculation, and creates a memorable though not always likeable character. . . . Galloway has created ideal conditions for the exploration of reality vs. illusion, of real vs. false memories. . . . With Galloway's elegant sleight-of-hand, [*The Confabulist*] is as finely crafted as the most intricate magic trick, right to the revelatory conclusion. Whether or not it's the ending you anticipate, you're likely to think, after any clever illusion, 'Amazing. How did he do that?'" —*Toronto Star*

"[Houdini is] the star of the book. . . . He is such a fascinating individual, well described in Galloway's novel. . . . Galloway is naturally drawn to real figures or the 'real-life moment.' And to realize his work he did a lot of research."
—*Ottawa Citizen*

"Memory, which is at the heart of [Steven] Galloway's new novel, is perhaps the most remarkable magic trick there is. . . . *The Confabulist*, Galloway's eagerly anticipated fourth novel, is itself a trick, too, an impressive feat of close-up magic from one of the country's most talented young literary conjurors. . . . It's a delightful, delirious narrative that hinges on a kick-ass supposition…that, once started, is as difficult to escape from as one of the straitjackets used in [Houdini's] death-defying stunts."
—*National Post*

"A fantastical new tale that interlaces history with imagination."
—*The Globe and Mail*

"Colourful . . . Galloway builds intrigue by mixing the personal and the political. . . . Readers looking for the innocent pleasures of a good smoke-and-mirrors mystery will be amply rewarded."
—*Quill & Quire*

PRAISE FOR

THE CELLIST OF SARAJEVO

"An exquisite novel of war and loss…The book feels vividly created… an elegant and ever fragile work of art."
—*O, The Oprah Magazine*

"Compelling."
—*Entertainment Weekly*

"Elegant."
—*Los Angeles Times*

"Indelible imagery and heartbreaking characters."
—*Kirkus Reviews* (starred review)

continued . . .

"Tense and haunting."   —*Publishers Weekly*

"Though the setting is the siege of Sarajevo in the 1990s, this gripping novel transcends time and place. It is a universal story, and a testimony to the struggle to find meaning, grace, and humanity, even amid the most unimaginable horrors."

—Khaled Hosseini, author of
The Kite Runner and *A Thousand Splendid Suns*

"I cannot imagine a lovelier, more beautifully wrought book about the depravity of war as *The Cellist of Sarajevo*. Each chapter is a brief glimpse at yet another aspect of the mind, the heart, the soul—altogether Galloway gives us fine, deep notes of human music which will remain long after the final page."   —ZZ Packer, author of *Drinking Coffee Elsewhere*

"A grand and powerful novel about how people retain or reclaim their humanity when they are under extreme duress."

—Yann Martel, author of *Life of Pi*

"A gripping story of Sarajevo under siege."
—J. M. Coetzee, author of *Disgrace* and *Diary of a Bad Year*

"Steven Galloway's *The Cellist of Sarajevo* is a wonderful story, a tribute to the human spirit in the face of insanity."

—Kevin Baker, author of *Dreamland* and *Paradise Alley*

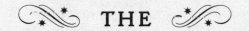 THE

CONFABULIST

STEVEN GALLOWAY

RIVERHEAD BOOKS
New York

RIVERHEAD BOOKS
An imprint of Penguin Random House LLC
375 Hudson Street
New York, New York 10014

The Library of Congress has catalogued the Riverhead hardcover edition as follows:

Galloway, Steven, date.
The confabulist : a novel / Steven Galloway.
p.   cm.
ISBN 978-1-59463-196-2
1. Houdini, Harry, 1874–1926—Fiction.   2. Magicians—Fiction.   I. Title.
PR9199.3.G265C66   2014   2013046178
813'.54—dc23

Riverhead hardcover edition: May 2014
Riverhead trade paperback edition: May 2015
Riverhead trade paperback ISBN: 978-1-59463-385-0

Printed in the United States of America
1   3   5   7   9   10   8   6   4   2

BOOK DESIGN BY MEIGHAN CAVANAUGH

for Diane Martin

Every man's memory is his private literature.

Aldous Huxley

THE
CONFABULIST

THERE'S A CONDITION CALLED TINNITUS WHERE YOU hear a ringing that isn't there. It's not a disease itself, merely a symptom of other maladies, but the constant hum of nonexistent sound has been known to drive the afflicted to madness and suicide. I don't suffer from this, exactly, but I have a strange feeling now and then that something wrong is going on in the background.

Today's meeting with Dr. Korsakoff is a good example. He's a strange little Russian who looks as though he's never let a ray of sunlight touch his skin, and when he speaks of the human body, I begin to drift. I don't see how he expects a man of my age to understand him. Thiamine, neurons, gliosis—all of it coated in his throaty accent, well, it goes right by me. I wonder if this is the point of such talk—a reminder that he has completed medical school and I have not. It seems to me that point was ceded upon my arrival in his office months ago. Did I tell him that as a young man I entertained notions of becoming a doctor? I can't remember. I was not at all paying attention to him, that much I know. But then, out of nowhere, he said something that was impossible to miss.

"You will in essence, Mr. Strauss, lose your mind."

I'd been staring at a potted philodendron placed in an awkward corner of his office. The room was even drabber than the hospital as a whole, but the philodendron was exquisite. As he droned I resolved to devise a plan to steal it. But then this "lose your mind" business caught my attention.

"The good news is that it will be gradual, and you likely won't even notice." He stared at me. He was probably worried I was going to start crying. I imagine a person in his situation is required to deal with a wide variety of unpleasant reactions.

"How does a person unknowingly lose his mind?"

"Yours is a rare condition," he said, seeming almost excited, "in which the damage that is being done to your brain does not destroy cognitive function but instead affects your brain's ability to store and process memories. In response to this, your brain will invent new memories."

All I could do was sit there. Everything seemed louder and slower. The fluorescent lights were a hive of bees, and footsteps in the hallway thunder-clapped toward the elevator. Somewhere down the corridor a telephone rang a fire alarm. Eventually I was able to ask how long I had.

He shrugged. "Months. Years, even. While you may have some associated difficulties, your condition is not life threatening. You're not a young man, so it's possible you might die of something else before it becomes a problem. Although it does appear that other than this you are extraordinarily healthy."

"Thank you," I said, which immediately seemed stupid.

"It is a degenerative physiological condition, and there isn't anything at this time that can be done about it. You might not even realize it's happening."

He kept talking, but that tinnitus feeling kicked in. Imagine if your mind was making a noise, not an actual noise but whatever the mental equivalent is. Then add a little fogginess and you have a pretty good idea of where I was. I realized the doctor had stood and moved from behind his desk. It seemed our appointment was over, so I stood too, but I felt that I couldn't leave the conversation where things were, with me as some sort of dumbstruck simpleton.

"I really like your philodendron." I stopped myself from mentioning that he should be careful because variegated philodendrons can be highly toxic to dogs and cats. I don't know how I know this, or if it's even true, and anyway you don't see many dogs and cats in a doctor's office so it didn't seem like useful information.

He smiled. It didn't suit his thin lips. "Thank you. I find it very calming."

We both observed the plant for a moment. One of its fronds fluttered in the breeze from the air-conditioning vent. "So do I."

"Would you like me to take your photograph with it?"

I would have, but his eagerness unnerved me and I refused. He hid his disappointment well.

And now I'm sitting outside on a bench by the main doors of the hospital. I could go straight home—there's no one waiting for me, no one whose feelings I need to concern myself with. I can stew away as much as I like in my one-room apartment, and I probably will later on. Right now I can't find the energy, and anyway I have a feeling I'm supposed to be somewhere this afternoon. If I can't remember where, then I'll have to go home and see if it's written down in the notebook resting on my bedside table, but at the moment it doesn't seem particularly important, and if it is I'll remember soon.

Watching the various people go in and out of the swishing automatic doors is soothing. They all have problems too, or else they wouldn't be here. Different problems than I, some more serious, some less serious, but problems all the same. One man in particular catches my attention. For some reason the sensor on the door doesn't register his presence. He continues forward and very nearly collides with unyielding plate glass. He steps back, startled, and waits for admittance. When it's not forthcoming, he waves his arms above his head and, as though recognizing him from across a crowded room, the hospital swings open its doors and the man ventures through them, appearing afraid they might close at any moment. I know how he feels.

Okay then, what is to be done? I am, apparently, going to lose my mind. Not all of it. I will still know how to tie my shoes and boil water and read and speak. But I won't remember my life. I don't know what to make of this. My life has been a mixed bag. I've spent much of it trying to atone for a mistake I made long ago as a young man. It was a stupid mistake and I often think that in attempting to settle my debts I've fouled things up even more. Other times I think I did the best I could. Likely I'll never know for certain which is right. But what if all that is gone, if each memory that is mine alone slips away forever? Will my burden be lifted or will it increase? What is a memory anyway, other than a ghost of something that's been gone for a long time? There are secrets I've kept. Maybe they should stay secrets.

No. I will have to tell Alice what has happened, explain myself, clarify what has been left obscure. She deserves to know the whole story. It has been a mistake to keep it from her for all these years. But I'll have to tell her properly, or it will only make things worse.

Alice knows most of the story already, but in any story there are details that can be pushed one way or another, and I have definitely pushed them in my favor. There are other details that can be left out entirely, which I have also done when it suited me. The only way is to start at the beginning and tell it as I believe it to be, not as I want it to be. I no longer have the luxury of time. My mind will soon become another door that is no longer open to me.

I deprived her of a father. This she has long been aware of. I could tell her all about him. The whole world knows me as the man who killed Harry Houdini, the most famous person on the planet. His story is complicated, though most of it is widely known. What no one knows, save for myself and one other person who likely died long ago, is that I didn't just kill Harry Houdini. I killed him twice.

HOUDINI

⌬ *1897* ⌬

EVERY SEAT IN THE OPERA HOUSE IN GARNETT, KANSAS, was filled. Any free place to stand was occupied. The electric lights hummed and radiated heat, every particle of dust in the room whirling as though alive. From where he stood at center stage Houdini, already a veteran performer at twenty-three, could feel the crowd breathe as a single organism. The room was his to do with as he pleased.

His wife, Bess, sat in a chair to his right, shrouded by a sheet. It was for effect—the spirit reading they were doing required no such concealment, but a little misdirection never hurt. These parlor tricks were all about the showmanship. He disliked them. There was no point to it if there wasn't any skill involved.

Three years earlier, when his new bride had still been superstitious and ignorant, he had begun to teach her the tricks of a false medium. Her sister's fiancé had died as a result of what Bess believed was the evil eye. At first he'd thought she was joking, but when he'd realized the extent of her belief he'd decided to show her what a simple matter deception was.

He waited until it seemed that Bess had cried herself out, and then smiled at her. "You've never told me your father's first name," he said. She opened her mouth, but he hushed her. "Write it on a piece of paper and fold it up."

As she wrote he paced away, appearing lost in thought. He couldn't understand how people believed such things. No, he could. There was a time he believed as she did. Maybe he still did a little.

He'd been gutting it out in the low-end museum shows of vaudeville for years without success. His brother Dash had been his partner, but once Houdini married Bess there wasn't room in the show for three people. The act could barely support two— their one-room tenement was evidence of that. It pulsed with smoke, rats, and clamor. In a few days they'd give it up to go back on the road.

He turned back to her. She was trying to act calm, but he could tell she was nervous. She held a folded square of paper.

"Burn it on the stove," he said.

She did as he directed, and he rolled up his left sleeve.

"Very few things in this world are as they seem," he said. "But that doesn't mean there isn't an explanation for them. We are surrounded by what we do not understand. We will always be surrounded by what we do not understand. The mind plays tricks on us, makes connections that aren't there. We must remain on guard against the deception of our own minds. If we can stop our minds from deceiving us, then we can stop the treachery of others."

Houdini went to the stove and put his fingers in the burned remnants of the paper. He rubbed the ash from the paper between his thumb and fingers, and then briskly up and down his forearm. He extended his arm toward her. Her face went from grief to rage and then, unexpectedly, to fear. Bess slowly backed away from him, hands outstretched, until she reached the door and ran from the room. On his forearm the name Gebhardt rose from his skin.

Houdini lowered his head and closed his eyes. Bess was prone to these sorts of outbursts, but he hadn't intended for this to happen. So often this was the case; he thought he was being reasonable and full of sense but now he'd only made things worse.

He caught up to her on the street. Where she was going he had no idea, but when he finally stopped her they were both panting.

"The devil, you are the devil—my husband has been taken!" She kicked at him, and tried to bite him as he embraced her.

"It's me, Bessie. I'm no devil. Come back and I'll show you how I did it. It's just a trick."

She didn't believe him, but she came with him anyway. Her eyes flitted from left to right, plotting escape. But he could see her realize that if he was the lord of darkness, then escape was not possible. If the devil asks you to dance, you dance as well as you can. He could feel her resignation and fear.

With his arm around her they walked back up the street and ascended three flights of fetid stairwell, stepping over a man passed out on the second-floor landing. Back in their room he sat her down in the chair by the stove.

"Look here," he said. He rolled up his left sleeve and took a vial of clear liquid and a toothpick from his pocket. "When you were writing down your father's name, which I have known since a few days after we first met, I was doing this."

He opened the vial and poured the liquid on his forearm. "Salt water," he said. He breathed hard on his arm and the water evaporated. Then he took the toothpick and scratched out a message on his skin. "You have to wait until the initial redness fades," he said. "It only takes a minute or so."

There was nothing visible on his arm now. "It will bear inspection. It's key to know just how hard to press into your skin. Too hard and your markings will be visible. Too soft and the effect won't work."

He took some ash from the stove and rubbed it over his arm. "You can use varnish thinned with turpentine and paint the name on your arm—then the ash will stick only to the varnish, but I find the effect lesser." She read what he had written and held out her hand.

He placed the vial of salt water and toothpick in her palm. She did as he had instructed, waiting for the water to disappear and then etching into herself with the toothpick. She refused to look at him. It seemed to him that much more time than was necessary went by before she dipped her hand into the ash and moved it over her arm. She hid her arm from his view and looked at him. His arm read

Forgive me

The fear and skepticism left her face. Her shoulders dropped and her whole body seemed to slacken. She stepped toward him, her arm extended.

I do

She'd lost her sense of superstition after that, becoming a valuable part of his show. Their modest act took them from shabby dime museums into larger theater engagements, though they were still living hand to mouth. Houdini now felt sure he was on the verge of a breakthrough. He signed on with Dr. Hill's California Concert Company, but soon heard rumors it was about to go bankrupt. In Garnett, Kansas, Dr. Hill asked Houdini for an act that would fill the house. So Bess agreed to another séance, even though it was risky.

From behind the sheet, Bess spoke, her voice high and ethereal.

"Is there a Harold Osbourne present here tonight? And his wife, Mary, as well?"

There was a rustling sound as people looked around to see who among them was being summoned.

Houdini stepped forward. "Is there anyone here who wishes to receive this message?" He made a show of peering out like a man looking through fog for a ship.

A couple in their late twenties and modestly dressed stood up. The man held out his arm to support his wife, and Houdini couldn't tell if they were afraid or excited. "I'm Harold Osbourne, and this is my wife," he said, firm and clear.

Bess waited for the crowd to quiet. "I have a message from little Joe."

"Is this message for you?" Houdini asked, pointing at the couple. The man tried to speak, but either changed his mind or was unable. After a moment he nodded his head.

"Ladies and gentlemen," Houdini said, "please give your full attention to the stage, as the spirit world has a message for our dear Osbournes. It is of utmost importance that you allow the spirits to speak now, for the sake of both the spirits and these good people."

Bess didn't move. People whispered, shifted in their seats. The tension in the room reminded Houdini of holding a wishbone with one of his brothers, each pulling it apart, knowing it would snap but not when. Bess remained quiet until the theater was completely silent. "Little Joe says he's in a happy place," Bess intoned. "And he says, 'Don't cry, Mama. There will soon be another to take my place.'"

Those in the room who knew the Osbournes gasped, and the woman lost hold of her husband's arm and slumped back. Word circulated that the couple had recently buried their six-year-old son, Joe, and that Mrs. Osbourne was two months pregnant. Slowly the furor rose, with cries of "Can you get a message from my father?" and "My wife, is she there?"

Houdini let this go on for a while, and when the crowd reached a frenzied pitch, he announced that the medium was spent and would rest for the night. He thanked the audience and made a pretense of removing the shroud and helping an exhausted Bess from her chair. She looked out into the theater at the parents of the dead boy, her face blank. She didn't resist him as he guided her offstage, nor did she go of her own accord. Her body remained stiff to the touch, like an overstarched collar, until she could no longer see the couple; then he felt her relax. The curtain fell and they stood there, listening to applause punctuated by desperate shouts. After ten minutes there was still no sign of anyone leaving.

Dr. Hill, fat, white-bearded, and professorial, ushered them down the hall, breathless and grinning.

"It'll be full houses from here on in," he chortled, his jowls rolling. Bess glanced at Houdini and he knew that look, fuming and inflexible. He worried she was about to go off on Dr. Hill, so he stepped between them and put his arm around the promoter.

"I'm glad, Doctor. We did our best."

Down the hall Houdini could hear a commotion, at first indistinguishable from the raucous crowd but gradually becoming distinct. He turned his attention from Dr. Hill to see the dead boy's father hurtling down the hallway, closely followed by a pair of theater attendants who had been roughed up.

"Houdini!" the man shouted. Dr. Hill shrugged off Houdini's arm and stepped away. Mr. Osbourne was much larger than he remembered. His bulky hands were in tight fists. He stepped into Houdini and swung at his head. Houdini ducked and slid to the side. He struck back at the man's stomach, connecting hard. The man fell to his knees, gasping, as the attendants and a few others caught up and stood around him.

"Let him alone," Houdini ordered. He took a moment to prepare himself for what was about to happen. Once the man regained his wind he got to his feet and brushed the dirt from his clothes. None of his rage had lessened, but the fight was out of him.

"Why did you say those things? Why would you put my wife through all that again?"

"Look, Mr. Osbourne. May I call you Harry?" Houdini smiled.

Osbourne clenched his fists. "No, you may not."

Houdini took a step forward, keeping his palms open and visible. "That's fine, Mr. Osbourne. I just thought I'd call you Harry because that's my name too. But it's okay. I understand how you feel, about the name and about what happened just now."

Osbourne shook his head. "I don't think you do."

"You'd be surprised. A lot of people, myself included, are taken aback when the spirits speak to them. It's a common reaction."

"No!" shouted Osbourne. "You don't understand at all. I came tonight because my wife believes in all this nonsense. I know it's all malarkey. But she believes. And now she thinks that our son, Joe, has spoken to us."

Houdini saw Bess out of the corner of his eye. She was about to speak. "Mr. Osbourne," he said, quickly, "what if I could prove to you that there is no deceit behind my wife's words?"

"I doubt very much that you could." Osbourne was becoming more and more agitated. Dr. Hill and the theater attendants had backed off. A crowd of other members of the California Concert Company had gathered down the hall. This type of encounter had never happened to the Houdinis before.

"Have a seat here beside me," Houdini said, motioning toward a row of chairs set outside a dressing room.

Osbourne reluctantly sat. Houdini sat beside him. Bess stayed off to the side.

"I readily admit that there is an element of showmanship in what we do," he said. "The sheet covering my wife or me, depending on who is contacting the other side, for example, is completely unnecessary. But people pay for a show, and we feel compelled to give them one. Will you allow me to dispense with all theatrics for the moment?"

Osbourne's shoulders were set and stiff. "I wish you'd ditch both the theatrics and the false hope you give people."

Houdini smiled, placed his hands on his knees, and closed his eyes. He counted to twenty, exhaled, then opened his eyes and stared at Osbourne.

"You were born in Tennessee but moved to Kansas when you were still an infant. Your father and mother died ten and twelve years ago, respectively. You had a twin brother named Alphonse who died when you were six. Your son, Joe, died of a fever and your wife stayed in bed for three months afterward. There is a scar on the back of her leg from a burn she received from the fire poker. You have an older brother whom you haven't spoken to since your father passed, whose wife died this past winter, and your mother says you should give him back your father's watch, as it belongs to him as the oldest son."

Osbourne jumped out of his chair, shaking. "How do you know all this?"

Houdini rose as well, placing a hand on Osbourne's shoulder. "They told me. How else could I know?"

"You can really speak to them?"

The disbelief drained from Osbourne's face. He slumped back into the chair, put his head in his hands. No one said anything. Osbourne looked up at Houdini, his face wet. "My son. He is happy?"

Houdini paused for a moment. "Very. He misses you and his mother, but he is happy and knows he will see you again someday."

Osbourne began to weep again, and Houdini sat beside him and offered his handkerchief. Osbourne took it and after a while managed to pull himself together. He gave Houdini his hand. "I'm sorry about before. But you don't understand. When our son died, my wife . . . it was like she was gone too. And then, slowly, things began to get better. She began to recover. We're having a new baby. I didn't want to come tonight. Joe is dead, and there's nothing to be done for that. But he's not, not really. I see that now. Thank you. Thank you."

Houdini saw Bess turn and leave.

He started after her, leaving Dr. Hill to deal with Osbourne. She retreated to their dressing room at the back of the building. They were one of only a few acts to have their own room—a recent development that Houdini was very happy about. He and Bess argued often, and it disturbed him to do it in front of others. A magician should cultivate a certain air of mystique.

He reached their room just behind Bess, in time for the door to slam shut in his face. He did not hear the lock click into place behind her—she knew that a lock was no impediment to him—but he knew her temper well enough. It would be best to wait until she had calmed herself somewhat.

Houdini didn't dare risk leaving the theater yet—people would be waiting for him at all exits, anxious for a reading or a favor. Possibly one or two might even be planning to give him a battering, as Harold Osbourne had been.

As he climbed the back stairs to the catwalk that ran above the stage, he wondered what exactly he had done. When people went to see a magic show, they knew the magician didn't have supernatural powers, and that nothing they saw was real. If he passed it off as such, it was nothing more than showmanship, which they'd paid to see. If he offered them anything less, he'd be cheating them.

He chose a perch on the catwalk with a view of the stage. The theater was empty now save for a couple of custodians sweeping up. In a few moments the stage and back of house would be broken down and hauled to the train station, where in the morning they would depart Kansas for an engagement in Cedar Rapids.

Tonight's endeavor was little more than the culmination of some clever research and bribery. All over North America traveling spiritualists could, for a few dollars, purchase tests from others in their trade. These shorthand logs about local individuals were dutifully maintained and circulated by a network of charlatans. It was amazing what could be overheard in a tavern, what a drink could buy from a man, what people said without realizing. A trip to the local graveyard, a few coins in the hand of the right person—like magic, most people's secrets were out in the open.

In the case of Harold Osbourne, a cursory examination of the family plot revealed a fresh grave for little Joe, and an overheard conversation between the town doctor and Osbourne's still bitter brother yielded the rest. It wasn't even the best test Houdini had, but it was the best of the people who showed up that evening. His local contact had, of course, informed him of Osbourne's presence before the show had begun. After he'd punched Osbourne, while he was down on the floor, he'd retrieved a square of paper from his coat pocket containing the relevant details, memorized them, and then palmed the paper. If Osbourne chose to believe he had supernatural powers, well, that wasn't his problem.

But he had the feeling, a feeling he often had, that his mother wouldn't approve. She might have viewed such things as dishonest. She was usually right. Her disapproval stung, no matter how implied or imagined it was.

Still, he had no choice. They needed this job. Signing on with Dr. Hill's California Concert Company represented the first real break he'd had in years. Hand-to-mouth—it was always hand-to-mouth, but this was the sort of show that could lead to bigger things. He had promises to keep, promises that a magician's poverty could never keep.

Below, the crew was beginning to break down the stage. He cradled his hat in his hands, turning it over and over, a habit he'd developed and continued to keep his fingers nimble. Most magicians he knew kept their hands in almost constant motion.

He'd never had any money. No one in his family had. His father worked all his life, and was honest and treated everyone square and still died poor. Rabbi Mayer Weiss came from Hungary to America to improve his lot but was reduced to menial jobs for most of his later years. He never stopped believing that riches were right around the corner.

When he was nineteen, Houdini had been called to his father's deathbed. His father looked at him without recognition, his body worn out by its sixty-three years. "Who's there?" he called.

"It's me, Ehrich." Houdini moved closer so his father could see him.

"My boy," he said. "Good, good." He held out his hand, and Houdini took it. It felt like paper.

His mother came up behind him. "See? He's here. I told you he'd come straight home."

"I came as quick as I could," Houdini said. He'd been working a sideshow in downtown Manhattan, barking people in. A kid came up to him and told him his father was dying. "Go home, magician," the kid said. He'd had to borrow money for the cab uptown, took the steps three at a time for five flights, then stopped outside his door and almost couldn't go in.

Inside, he found his brothers and sister waiting. He'd fix it, and if he couldn't, then it couldn't be fixed. He smiled at them and walked into their parents' bedroom as though nothing was wrong.

His older half brother Herman had died of consumption seven years earlier. His brother Nathan should have taken on the role of oldest son, but he was quiet and weak, and Houdini assumed the role, to Nathan's relief.

His father's eyes were glassy, betraying none of the sharp intelligence that had once been ever present. He was gazing at an empty space between Houdini and his mother.

"Ehrie," he said, so quietly Houdini could barely hear him, "you must promise to look after your mother."

Houdini leaned in, his mouth close to his father's ear. "Of course I will. You have my word."

His father smiled and motioned for Houdini to pass him the glass of water sitting beside the bed. Houdini held the water to his lips, cracked and nearly white, and his father drank. His mother could not prevent a sob.

When his father spoke again his voice was stronger. "You hear that, Cecilia? It's going to be all right. Ehrie will fill your apron with gold."

His mother shook her head. "It doesn't matter. All the gold in the world doesn't make a difference."

But his father continued to smile. He died three hours later.

All Houdini could remember now was his promise, a promise he still hadn't made good on. He'd tried it all. He'd done card tricks, close-up magic, larger stage illusions. He'd been the wild man at a dime museum, done handcuff escapes. None of it had led anywhere. Dr. Hill's California Concert Company was almost a proper touring company. It could have been their break. It still might be.

He looked at the theater below him. He'd always thought a theater felt strange without people in it. With its seats empty, its lights up, and its air still, it reminded him of a dead body.

They were booked with Dr. Hill for fifteen weeks and were only halfway through their run. Two months earlier they'd nearly lost the job completely. They were due to join the California Concert Company in Omaha and needed to change trains in the middle of the night. But their train was late, their connection was an express, and there was no time to load all of Houdini's trunks. For Houdini, though, proceeding otherwise was impossible. A magician without his tricks is nothing.

"I must insist," he told the porter, a boy barely old enough to shave. "My baggage must be loaded."

The porter shook his head. "I'm sorry, sir. The train is leaving."

"No," Houdini said, "it's not."

He walked to the front of the train, stepped onto the tracks, and grabbed hold of one rail with both hands.

The porter gaped, then rushed off. He soon returned with another railwayman, a large fellow who stood six inches taller than Houdini and outweighed him by a good sixty pounds. "Get off of there, sir, or I'll move you myself."

"I'll get off when my baggage is loaded," he said, "and, no, you won't be moving me." Bess crossed her arms and then marched away; off, he presumed, to board the train.

The railwayman surged forward and grabbed Houdini's arm. He was strong, but Houdini didn't budge. The railwayman stepped back, seized Houdini by the back of his coat, and pulled, but still Houdini wasn't moved. The man took off his jacket and tried again, grabbing Houdini's arms and legs in several places without success. The porter tried as well, on his own at first and then together with the railwayman. Houdini had both hands gripped on one of the rails and his feet wedged into the other rail. It looked as though he were doing a push-up. He'd move slightly when one or both of them tried to pull him off, but was otherwise immobile. It was an old sideshow trick. They could bring out a dozen men and they wouldn't move him. All he had to do was move the fulcrum of his body against their efforts, and his strength was magnified a hundredfold.

Eventually the conductor came out to see what the commotion was. "Why are you on my rails?"

"I have a ticket for your train, but they won't load my trunks," Houdini said, shifting his weight to account for the railwayman's renewed efforts.

The conductor watched for a moment as the railwayman, red-faced and sweating, heaved away at Houdini with no effect. He turned to the porter, shaking his head. "For God's sake, load the man's damned bags and let's get moving."

Bess wouldn't talk to him for the rest of the trip, but they arrived on time for their first show, and by the end of the night it was like nothing had happened. That's how things went with her. He'd do something bold, brash, or possibly stupid, and she'd react by punishing him as if he'd failed. He ended up having to fight two fights—one with his task or feat or problem, and another with her afterward. It exhausted him.

It wasn't always this way. When they'd met, she'd reacted to his predilections with enthusiasm. That was part of what he liked about her. This tiny, beautiful woman, who looked as though a light wind could break her in two but who in reality was stronger than any man wedged onto railroad tracks. When his brother Dash had first suggested a blind double date with a couple of girls from the Floral Sisters, a song and dance act, he was reluctant.

He often told people that with Bess it was love at first sight, but that wasn't true. He had seen her several times before he ever really noticed her. But the night of the arranged date, sitting at a table with his brother, Dash's date, and Bess, there was an instant when he looked at her and recognized that she was the mirror image of himself. Not the opposite but a perfect complement; her strengths addressed all his weaknesses, and he knew he did the same for her. And then, as unbelievably to him then as it remained now, Bess looked at him, and he could tell that she had seen the same thing he had. It was as close to a moment of real magic as he would ever experience.

"Do you like our act?" Dash had asked.

"Yes," Bess said, "very much. I think you are destined for greatness." She looked at Houdini as she said this, and her girlfriend giggled.

A week later they were married.

He felt bad about Dash sometimes. He'd picked Bess over his brother, but he didn't really have a choice. It was the way he'd parted ways with Dash that troubled him—he had to concede he'd lost his temper.

Their signature trick at the time was the Metamorphosis. It was a standard cabinet switch where members of the audience would be invited to inspect a large velvet bag that Houdini would then get into. Dash would tie up and lock the top of the bag, and Houdini would be placed in a trunk. The trunk was inside a large cabinet, closed on three sides with the fourth side open to the audience. Once the trunk was securely locked Dash would address the audience, draw a curtain across the open side of the cabinet, and step inside, and in an instant the curtain would reopen and Houdini would appear in Dash's place. The trunk would then be unlocked and the velvet sack opened to reveal Dash.

It was a good trick, and they often performed variations on it, sometimes with Dash starting in the bag. One night, playing to a large crowd, they were doing the version where Dash went first. But Dash somehow managed to get stuck in the trunk, so when Houdini stepped into the cabinet he was alone.

He couldn't quite believe it. It was such a simple switch. You are out of the bag before the trunk is locked, and then out of the gimmicked back of the trunk before the curtain is even closed. Once the curtain closes the front man ducks behind the trunk and inside, wriggling into the sack while the reveal takes place. But there was no Dash.

Until the day he died Houdini would hear the jeers of the audience. Even after he freed Dash and eventually did the switch, it was clear to all that something had gone wrong. A dime museum crowd loved seeing a magician screw up. Sometimes he thought that's what people came for. To see the magician fail, to experience the thrill of seeing someone trapped just as thoroughly as they were.

He was so angry afterward that he could barely even look at Dash.

"I'm sorry," Dash said. "The gimmick jammed."

"Well then, that's fine, Dash. We'll just explain that to everyone. Once they hear that the problem is you're incompetent they'll understand." He looked at Dash, who was going to either start a fight or cry, then pushed him aside and stomped out. They were fired from the balance of the remaining shows, but he'd already decided to replace Dash with Bess. She was smaller, a woman, and more versatile, all of which made for a better show, plus she was his wife. He'd been foolish to wait this long to make the change.

The stage was fully struck now. He'd best return to Bess. He hoped enough time had gone by. The duration of her anger was not something he could divine. He clambered down the stairs and made his way to their dressing room. On the way he passed several other performers, but none met his eye. They all knew what had happened between him and Harold Osbourne. No one wanted to become involved. That was how things worked. They were a troupe, but really it was every man for himself. Dr. Hill's California Concert Company wouldn't last forever, or likely much longer. Friendships were as much an illusion as any stage magic.

When he reached their room Houdini paused. He and Bess had a system for dealing with these matters, which he disliked but found necessary. He opened the door slightly, about a foot, and tossed in his hat. He then opened the door all the way but stepped out of view.

Almost immediately he heard a shuffling of feet, the snap of fabric, and his hat flew into the hallway. He closed the door and bent down to retrieve it. Fine. If that was how she was going to be, there were better things to do, even in this nowhere town, than sit and listen to his wife tell him all the many ways he was a failure.

He checked his watch. It was just after midnight. A walk was an idea. His overcoat was still inside the room but it wouldn't be cold out, and if he kept the brim of his hat low he wouldn't be recognized by the few who would be out at this hour.

The back door of the theater led into an empty lot. He could see his breath, and he walked briskly through the lot and down the street, away from town, his head down and his hands in his pockets.

He'd backed off doing the escapes for a reason. He doubted there was anyone around as good at them as he was, but escapes were difficult and dangerous. This worried Bess to the point of sleeplessness and he'd calculated that it was wise to appease her. Besides, escapes could quickly go wrong. When they did, the stakes were a lot higher than in tricks like the Metamorphosis.

The last time he'd done a handcuff trick was six weeks earlier in Halifax. It was a publicity stunt for that night's show, where in front of a crowd he was handcuffed and tied to a horse. The plan was to have the horse trot out of sight, where Houdini would free himself and ride back, triumphant. But the horse had other ideas. The second it was able, it took off at a full gallop toward the outskirts of town. Houdini managed to get himself free of the ropes, but he couldn't hold on to the horse and pick the cuffs, so he had no choice but to let it run itself out. It was a full half hour before he returned and most of the people had left, except for the newspapermen. Because of the amount of time he'd been gone, it was generally assumed that a confederate had freed him. He was about to explain the truth when he realized that what had happened was worse than what they thought. He'd been outsmarted by a horse, so it seemed preferable that they think him incompetent. His show that night was one of his best, but it didn't matter. The feeling of helplessness that over-came him while at the mercy of the horse was the worst thing he'd ever encountered, like a noose tightening around his throat.

A man passed by him on the street, and he worried that he might be recognized, but if the man knew him, he didn't show it. Houdini veered away and headed south, toward a small lake that was most likely deserted.

Since he was a boy he'd been good with locks, a talent discov-ered when his mother tried to prevent him and his siblings from eating a pie by locking it in a cupboard. He was so adept that at the age of eleven he'd been apprenticed to a locksmith named Hanauer in Appleton, Wisconsin. At first Hanauer wouldn't let him near anything but the simplest lock, and even then only to clean it. It seemed that all he wanted was someone to sweep up and watch the shop when he was out. Then one day the sheriff, a perpetually winded baby face named Shenk, came in with the largest man Houdini had ever seen. The giant was nearly seven feet tall and must have weighed at least two hundred and eighty pounds, most of it muscle. He was unshaven, his hair was mussed, and his hands were shackled in front of him.

"Afternoon, Sheriff. What can I do for you?" Hanauer asked, obviously nervous about the man Shenk had in tow.

Shenk leaned against the wall and picked at his thumbnail. "I need you to get the cuffs off this fella. Judge says he's innocent, though we both know that's not the case, don't we, Goliath?"

The giant said nothing, keeping his gaze on the floor.

"You lose the key again?" Hanauer moved to the drawer where they kept the master keys.

Shenk shook his head. "Worse. Key broke off in the lock."

Hanauer closed the drawer and took a closer look at the handcuffs. "You don't need a locksmith, Sheriff. You need a hacksaw. Ehrich, you get the saw and free this man while the sheriff and I get ourselves a beer." He turned to Shenk. "Should take him about an hour."

Houdini stepped back, bumping into the workbench. "You're leaving me alone with him?"

Shenk shrugged. "Sure, why not. Apparently he's done nothing wrong."

Hanauer let out a small chuckle and left with Shenk.

Houdini got the hacksaw from the back room. The giant stood immobile. He hadn't moved at all since entering the shop except to step aside and allow Shenk and Hanauer to leave.

There was a small vise attached to a workbench on the far wall, and Houdini motioned the giant toward it, but the man wouldn't go.

"I need you to put the cuffs in the vise so I can saw them."

The giant looked down at him and Houdini could see that he was afraid. "You'll cut me."

"I won't. At least not on purpose. I'll try to be careful."

"No."

Houdini put down the saw. "What do you want me to do?"

The man stared at him. "Dunno."

He was stuck for options. If Hanauer came back and the man was still in the irons, there'd be trouble. But Houdini would hardly be able to convince the behemoth to do anything he didn't want to. "Can I see?"

The giant held out his hands. Houdini stepped forward, then stopped. "What did they say you did?"

The giant looked down at the floor. "Stole."

"Did you?"

The giant looked at Houdini and smiled. "Yep."

Houdini smiled back, mostly because he didn't know what else to do, but he didn't move closer.

"I won't hurt you," the giant said. "I just want out of these cuffs so I can get far away from this town."

Houdini could relate. He'd twice run away, and twice returned to Appleton, not because he wanted to but because he had failed to make anything of himself. He stepped forward and examined the cuffs.

They were a fairly new pair of what he would later come to know was a Berliner figure-eight-style handcuff, shaped like a number eight that had been placed on its side and cut in half horizontally. On one side of the bisected eight was a hinge, and on the other side was the locking mechanism. Each loop of the eight encircled one of the giant's wrists.

The key had indeed broken off in the lock. If he was lucky, he could get it out and use the master. He fetched a pair of fine-point pliers and tried to grasp the piece of key. He succeeded in moving it around the keyhole enough so that the plug was partially exposed, but all his attempts to free it were fruitless. He'd have to pick it, though he wasn't sure if he could. The cuffs themselves were simple enough—a fairly standard pin and tumbler lock, probably with three pins. If he could get something past the broken key and into the plug he'd have a chance.

Although he'd never actually opened or even seen a pair of handcuffs up close before, he'd taken apart enough of these sorts of locks to know how they worked. A series of pins, in this case three, prevented a round metal plug from moving inside a larger cylinder. It was like he'd made a fist with a hole large enough to stick his thumb into, and then put toothpicks between the fingers of the fist and sunk them into his thumb.

So that the plug can turn and the lock will open, each pin is broken in two at a specific point. When a key is inserted into the keyhole, each pin is pushed upward a set distance so that the break is exactly between the plug and the cylinder, allowing the plug to turn and release the locking mechanism. If a little tension is applied to the plug, like a turning key, it creates a tiny ledge for the rising pin to rest on so that it doesn't fall back down into the plug. From there it is a relatively simple feat to push up on each pin until the point at which it cleaves is found. Get all three pins up and the lock opens. That was the theory, but he knew that what is simple in theory is not necessarily so in practice.

The broken key made using a conventional pick almost impossible, as it prevented him clear access to the plug. He fetched a piece of stiff wire he'd seen on the back workbench earlier that he thought he could bend to his purpose. But he needed some tension placed on the lock, and the broken key left nowhere to get a tension wrench into the plug.

He looked at the giant. "What's your name?"

"Jim Deakins."

"I'm Ehrich Weiss."

Deakins held out his arms and for a moment Houdini didn't know what to do. Then he realized that Deakins meant for them to shake hands. He let the giant grasp his right hand and was surprised when his grip was gentle. He had an idea.

"I need you to pull your hands apart. Not a lot. I just need a little force on the lock." He took back his hand. It was warm.

Deakins flexed his arms and twisted his hands apart.

"Easy. Not so much. Less." If there was too much torque the pins wouldn't move freely in their shafts.

"Sorry." Deakins relaxed a little.

Houdini worked the tip of the wire past the broken key and into the blank. He closed his eyes. It helped, he believed, if he visualized the inside of the lock. Nothing he could see was of any use anyway—everything of import was hidden to him.

He felt the first pin. With a light twist he eased the wire under it and pushed it upward. At first he felt no sign of any change. He raised the pin a millimeter, then another, and heard a small click.

"Did you hear that?" he asked Deakins.

"I didn't hear anything."

"Just keep your arms the way they are." If Deakins let off, the pin would fall and he'd have to start over.

He moved on to the second pin. The bend of the wire and the difficulty of access to the plug made this one more difficult, but eventually he got underneath it and brought it up. Again he heard a click.

"That's two."

Deakins looked at him, confused. "Two what?"

The third pin would be the hardest. The angle made getting the wire under it nearly impossible. He used a pair of pliers to bend a hook into the tip of the wire, hoping that would get him to the right spot, but it didn't work. After ten minutes it became apparent that the pin was not going to be raised. He took out the wire.

"Why are you stopping?"

"It's not working."

Deakins frowned. "It has to work. I get to go. The judge said so. I can't keep wearing these things."

Houdini stepped back. "Let me think. Don't move."

He closed his eyes. He visualized the plug, saw the small ledge the pins sat on when there was no key inserted, saw the pressure Deakins was applying create a slight twist between the plug and the cylinder that kept the top half of the pins up and open. And he saw the one remaining pin that was keeping the lock from moving. One tiny piece of metal sitting inside a shaft.

That was it. The shaft. All he had to do was move the pin in the shaft. He went into the back and returned with a ball-peen hammer.

"Hey, hold on," Deakins said.

"You're skittish for a giant," he said. "Hold still."

He held the cuffs at the lock with his left hand, and with his right he struck the underside of the plug with the hammer. Lightly at first, and then harder. On the fourth strike the lock sprung open and the cuffs fell to the floor.

Deakins stared, his mouth open. He looked at Houdini the way a man looks at someone who's just told him a lie. Then he rotated his hands, loosening his wrists, and stretched back his shoulders. He grinned.

Houdini bent down and picked up the handcuffs. They were

undamaged. Now he could remove the broken piece of key from the keyhole. He sat at the workbench and began to disassemble the cuffs.

"Thanks," Deakins said.

Houdini didn't look up. "You're welcome."

"What just happened?"

Houdini paused. He'd nearly got the cuffs apart. "I think I just discovered how to open handcuffs without a key."

He twisted out the broken key, put the cuffs back together, then went to Hanauer's drawer of master keys and handed the key to Deakins along with the handcuffs.

"Lock them on me."

Deakins shook his head. "I don't want to put anyone in these."

"I want to try something." He held out his wrists, palms down. "Please. Before Hanauer and the sheriff come back."

Deakins still appeared reluctant, but he reached out and snapped the cuffs onto Houdini's wrists. They weren't intended for a boy and were too large for him, but it didn't matter. Deakins locked the cuffs and Houdini walked across the room toward the workbench.

He closed his eyes and pictured the inside of the plug, the three pins, the cleave in the pins, and the cylinder. There was an angle he wanted to achieve, and after a moment he knew what it was. Then he opened his eyes, twisted his wrists in opposite directions to place some torque on the plug, and slammed the cuffs down hard on the workbench.

The cuffs leaped open and clattered to the floor. Both Houdini and Deakins stared at them. The hooves of a horse clopped by out on the street, and the wind creaked at the door. Deakins nudged the cuffs with his foot as if they were a dead animal. "Huh," he said.

Houdini didn't say anything for a while, unsure of what to do. "We shouldn't tell anyone how this happened," he said.

Deakins nodded. Houdini could tell that he would keep the secret. He picked the cuffs off the floor and returned the master key to its drawer. Deakins didn't move for a while, and then seemed to realize that he wasn't in anyone's custody.

"I guess I'll go then," he said.

The giant stared at the boy for a moment and then walked out into the street. Houdini took out a jar of polish and began to clean the handcuffs. He was finishing up when Hanauer and Shenk returned. It was obvious that they'd had more than one beer.

Shenk looked startled. "Where's the prisoner?"

"He's gone," Houdini said. "You said the judge let him go."

He handed the cuffs to Hanauer, who gawked at them in amazement. "How did you open these?"

"I picked the lock."

"Impossible."

"Not impossible, sir."

Shenk took the cuffs from Hanauer and slapped Houdini on the back. "Good work, boy. Saved me a pair of cuffs. Can you make me a new key?"

Houdini looked at Hanauer. So far he hadn't let him cut keys, though it was a relatively simple task. Hanauer nodded at the sheriff. "He'll bring it by later this afternoon."

After that Hanauer began to teach him. In less than a year Houdini had become a master locksmith. When he left Hanauer's employ the man actually wept.

.   .   .

Houdini smiled to think of it now. He hadn't seen Hanauer in years, and had learned more about locks than Hanauer could ever conceive of. He understood that he wasn't the only one who knew how to slam handcuffs, but he took pride in having figured it out on his own.

He reached the small lake. He'd visited here the last time they were in Garnett. It was during the day, and he and Bess had walked around the lake several times. There were a lot of people about, particularly children, and at one point a girl of about seven had come running around a corner fast, being chased in a game by some other children. She'd slammed into Bess, knocking her sideways into him. They'd both kept their feet but the girl tumbled over and skinned both her palms. As Bess rushed to her the child began to cry, apologizing through her tears.

"Don't worry, dear, don't worry. I'm fine, and you'll be all right too. It's just a little skin." She held the girl close and after a while was able to calm her, but Bess was quiet for the rest of the walk and that night in bed he heard her sob. He didn't let on that he was awake and eventually she fell asleep. He'd lain awake for the rest of the night with a dull ache in his stomach, and as he looked at the lake now it returned. He turned around and started back toward the theater.

They hadn't been married even a year when they found out they couldn't have children. Bess's ovaries were underdeveloped, the doctor said. It was all Houdini could do not to punch him in the face. He'd expected Bess to go into hysterics but she sat dead faced. Later when he'd tried to talk to her about it, she gave him that look again; and in the years since, they'd never spoken of that day or of children. But the memory was always there.

When he'd confided the news to his mother, she'd clutched him and wept with an unexpected ferocity.

"I'm so sorry, Ehrie. I can't imagine a life without my children." But when she'd stopped crying she'd told him that he would be fine, that there were many who loved him and many more who would love him.

"You are remarkable, my son. Your Bess knows it, and I know it, and that is enough. But in time many more will know it too." He could tell she believed her words, and the ache in his stomach lessened. What would he do without her?

And what would he do without Bess? It sometimes seemed a possibility. There were days he knew he could never be without her, and days he thought he could.

Before they'd found out they couldn't have children, they'd been working for the Welsh Brothers Touring Company. It was a shoddy setup. But it was there that he'd mastered the Needles.

Evatima Tardo was one of the other performers at Welsh Brothers. She was an arrestingly beautiful woman of no discernible ethnicity. Her act consisted of resisting pain and being immune to the bites of poisonous snakes, a popular attraction.

Evatima was watching from the back when he did the Needles for the first time. He could see her clearly, and while he was used to other performers watching him this was a new trick and there was something about her that was different.

He showed the audience a package of sewing needles and a length of thread. He then put the thread in his mouth and, one by one, the needles. Bess brought him a glass of water and he drank it and opened his mouth to show he'd swallowed the needles. Then he looked out into the audience as though something had gone horribly wrong, reached into his mouth, and slowly pulled out a bit of thread. He pulled the thread some more, and out came one, two, three, and eventually a fully threaded string of needles. He looked out into the crowd and saw Evatima smile, but the audience barely reacted. He was perplexed—it had gone off without a hitch, and he knew it was a good trick. When he and Bess moved on to the Metamorphosis, he saw Evatima leave.

Later he was sitting by himself on a crate, trying to figure it out, when he looked up and Evatima was standing in front of him.

"Your trick didn't play," she said.

He couldn't tell if her tone was sympathetic or lightly mocking. "No, it didn't."

"It's close-up magic. Won't work in front of a crowd. They all think you palmed the needles before they even went into your mouth."

Houdini said nothing. He wasn't about to tell her how the trick was done, even if she guessed correctly.

"I know you didn't," she said, as though reading his thoughts, "but for the trick to be impressive everyone else has to know it too." She gave him a long look and then smiled, just a little, her head tilted to the left. He could see her tongue between her teeth. She turned and walked away.

For the next show he tried something different.

"Ladies and gentlemen, may I please have a volunteer!" He chose a respectable-looking man in his early fifties. "You sir!"

The man appeared reluctant but was egged on by his wife and children. He stepped forward.

"Good sir, have we ever met before?"

"No, we have not."

"I am Houdini." He handed him a package of sewing needles. "Will you please examine this package and say what you find."

The man opened the package and removed the needles, a dozen of them. He took one, flexed it, and lightly pressed the sharp end into his palm. "They're needles. And they're sharp!"

The crowd laughed, a good sign. Houdini removed a spool of thread from his pocket, broke off a length, and handed it to the man for inspection. The man gave it a cursory look, pronounced it common thread, and handed it back.

Houdini then put the thread in his mouth. He held out his hand and the man passed him each of the needles, one by one, as he popped them into his mouth. He made sure that the man saw them go in. Then he called for Bess to bring him a glass of water. She came onstage and he mugged at her, which almost made her laugh. He drank half the water and contorted his face in agony the way a child does when taking medicine. He kept his hands in full view, knowing that people were looking for a switch, and handed the half-empty glass to the man.

"Sir, will you please examine my mouth to verify that it is indeed empty."

The man stepped close, and Houdini smiled. "Closer, sir. I realize we're not married and you're not a dentist, but the good paying folk out there are relying on you."

"Actually, Mr. Houdini, I am a dentist." The crowd laughed uproariously at this. Even Houdini cracked a smile.

"Most excellent, sir. I hope you'll excuse me for not having seen a member of your profession for quite some time." More laughter rolled toward them.

Houdini opened his mouth wide and let the dentist look at the back of his throat and the roof of his mouth. He raised and lowered his tongue several times to show there was nothing above or under it. He then hooked a finger into each cheek and pulled, showing that there was nothing between his bottom jaw and cheeks, repeating with the upper jaw. Then he pulled up his upper lip and, finally, his bottom lip.

"I apologize for making you work on your day off," he said. "Are you satisfied that my mouth is empty?"

"Absolutely."

"And what, in your professional opinion, is the likely outcome of having swallowed a packet of needles?"

The dentist stood up straight. "I would imagine you are soon to be in quite a bit of pain. You will require a doctor, not a dentist."

Houdini chuckled at this. "Most men would, good sir. But I am not most men." His face turned serious. He looked out into the crowd and stepped toward them, his body shifting from a casual pose to a stiff and declarative one. He removed his coat and dropped it to the floor, thrust his stomach upward, dropped and then raised his chin, and pursed his lips. He reached up with his right hand, pulled about four inches of thread out of his mouth, turned to the dentist, and gave him the end of the thread. He kept his hand on the dentist's wrist, and together they pulled the thread until his arm was fully extended and all twelve needles had emerged, dangling fully threaded from the dentist's hand.

He took the glass of water from the dentist's other hand and drank almost all of what remained, handing the rest to Bess as she returned to the stage.

This time the audience stood and clapped and shouted. And Evatima Tardo, in the back, stood looking at him with desire.

What happened after would happen numerous times with numerous women. This was the first time, though, and the only time when he'd revealed a secret. He had expected her to behave in bed the way she was onstage—erratic, dangerous, immune. But she was almost the opposite, cautious, almost tentative, and never once did he feel as though she was the one controlling them, though she was. Afterward she'd said something that had stuck with him all these years.

"You can't amaze anyone if you don't first make them believe," she said. "It's a simple trick, your needles. The simple tricks are the best, if you make them believe."

He opened his mouth to protest that the trick wasn't simple, though it was.

"Don't start with your nonsense. You had loaded needles, already threaded and tied off, in your mouth the whole time, between your lower lip and gum. You added the inspected needles, swallowed the thread, and spit the inspected ones into the water after you drank. Having the dummy hold the half-empty glass was a nice touch, but we both know that it's almost impossible to see needles in a glass of water, even if you know to look. When you showed your lower lip you swept the loaded needles into your cheek. Then you pulled the thread out and you were done."

He gave up. There's no cheating a cheater. "Yep."

Bess gave no indication whether she knew about the affair.

He'd immediately been overcome by guilt and avoided Evatima as much as possible. She seemed as though she'd expected this and aside from the odd disconcerting glance didn't approach him again. The Welsh Brothers job lasted only another few weeks, and then it was off to yet another dead end. People liked the Needles, they liked the Metamorphosis, and they liked his handcuff escapes, but none of it was getting him anywhere.

Houdini arrived back at the theater. It was very nearly two in the morning, and he was tired and freezing. They had an early train and he needed at least a few hours' sleep. The back door was locked, but a few seconds with a pick and tension wrench gained him entrance. He crept down the dark hallway. A light showed in the crack underneath their dressing room door.

He removed his hat, opened the door, and tossed it inside. Then he shut the door and waited. He thought about Harold Osbourne and his wife, and wondered what they were doing, what he'd done to them. He'd lied to them. They'd come to him for a show, but he hadn't given them the Needles or a gimmicked trunk. He'd used their pain against them, had taken advantage of them as surely as a doctor selling a false cure. You can't amaze if you don't first make them believe. That much was true. But there was more to it. You must make them believe the impossible, not simply prey on their fears and hopes. One was entertainment, gave people hope and brought relief from the pain of life, and the other was thievery at its finest.

The door opened. Upon entering the room he saw Bess seated

on the floor in the corner. Beside her was a half-empty bottle. He sat down next to her but didn't touch her.

"What we did tonight was wrong," she said.

"I wish you'd lay off this stuff." He moved the bottle out of her reach. She didn't react.

"They lost a child. It was just plain wrong."

"I know."

She turned and kneeled, facing him. She smelled of laundry soap and sawdust. "Do the escapes. I don't care how dangerous they are. I don't know what I'd do if you were hurt or killed. But we can't do this anymore."

He reached out and pulled her to him. "We won't. Don't worry."

"I'll always worry."

"And I'll always escape."

Once, not long after his father had died, Houdini had thought he'd seen him on the street. He looked at a man at a certain angle, mistook his identity, and for a fleeting moment he forgot that his father was dead—he was, if only briefly, still alive. And then Houdini remembered, and the pain of his father's death came back to him with a cruelty unique to an unwanted recollection.

This is what he'd done to Harold Osbourne. He had brought his son back, and then killed him again. Or, worse, he'd given him a false hope that his son was still out there, alive in some fashion. Sooner or later this hope would be unsustainable, and Osbourne would experience his son's death once again.

This was also, he knew, what Bess faced. They hadn't lost a child; they had lost a child who had never existed. And there was nothing he could do about that. He could not replace it with anything, and he could not mitigate it.

But he could offer escape. He could present to her a reality where she didn't have to think about that. If their lives were full everywhere else, if he directed her attention away from their vanished child, then maybe her pain would lessen. He could do this. He was sure of it.

He closed his eyes and saw the inside of a lock. Pins, plugs, cylinders, cams. He saw ropes and chains and irons, and he saw himself shrug them off as if they were nothing. He was Houdini, and he would mystify the world. He would fill his mother's apron with gold. He would keep Bess safe.

MARTIN STRAUSS

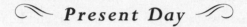

~ *Present Day* ~

"A MAGICIAN IS AN ACTOR PLAYING A MAGICIAN." JEAN-Eugène Robert-Houdin, Houdini's namesake, wrote this. I've read hundreds of books about magicians over the years. I feel like I know them better than some of the actual people I interact with, but this quote is my favorite by far. At first I thought he was merely talking about showmanship or stage presence, but it's a bigger idea. Unless the magician has actual supernatural powers, unless what he does alters the workings of the known universe, then all we witness is a man pretending to be a magician. Everything is an illusion.

This is what has always captivated me about magic—the idea that we can create something that seems both real and impossible. That we could be two things at once without fully knowing which is material and which is a reflection.

I want to get up from the bench, march back into the hospital and into Dr. Korsakoff's office. I want to demand that he do something. He's a doctor. Doctors are supposed to make you better, not tell you there's nothing they can do and then invite you to have your picture taken with foliage. But as I'm about to stand, I'm once again distracted by the swishing of the automatic doors. The man who was there before, the one the door sensor didn't recognize, has returned. This time the doors register his existence and swiftly part to allow his exit, and he walks with confidence and vigor into the world. What happened to him inside? He must have a good doctor.

The fight goes out of me. Of course if there were anything Dr. Korsakoff could do, he would offer it. I lean back into the bench and look out at the street. It's a warm day. The sun is strong, not so much that I could cook an egg on the sidewalk, which I have never tried, but enough to make the world seem cheerful and welcoming. The cars that drive by are clean and colorful, their drivers likely the sort of people who willingly let people pull in front of them and merge lanes with grace and optimism.

If I'd known it would have led to this, I would never have gone to the doctor. I realize that wouldn't have changed anything—I didn't get sick because I went to the doctor, I only found out about it. Still, I wouldn't have ended up on this bench, unsure of where to go or what to do.

It started innocuously. I was trying to unlock the door to my car, but the key wasn't working. No matter how much I tried it wouldn't fit the lock. I looked around the parking lot of the grocery store, wondering if it was possible there was another green Chevrolet nearby.

Then there was a woman standing behind me.

"Can I help you?"

"My key doesn't seem to be working," I said.

"That's because this is my car."

For some reason instead of protesting I stepped aside, and to my amazement she took a set of keys out of her purse and without resistance slid one into the lock and opened the door. She kept one eye on me as she slipped into the driver's seat and started the car. I stood, shocked, and watched as she pulled out of the parking spot and drove away.

My ears hummed and then I knew the problem was indeed that this had not been my car. I remembered that my car was in fact the blue Honda four or five spots down.

The more I thought about it, the more concerned I became. I had never owned a green Chevrolet. I knew this. How, then, was I to square this knowledge with the fact that I had a clear memory of pulling into the lot of the grocery store and parking that green Chevy? How was it I could feel the vinyl of the seats, hear it squeak as I eased out of it, hear the thud of the heavy door slamming shut behind me?

There were other, similar incidents. Small things. I tried to dismiss them, but each time they came with a memory, a recollection that I knew to be false but which seemed real.

When I told my regular doctor about it, he looked at me as though I were lying. "You mean you're remembering things that aren't true?"

Eventually, after numerous assessments that led nowhere, I was referred to Dr. Korsakoff. He ran a battery of tests. His office called me in for the results. And now here I am.

Substance and illusion. Knowing which is which is difficult, maybe impossible. The audience in a magic act knows it's a trick. They don't believe the magician has magical powers. But they want to. They want the illusion to have substance, even if it's a substance that's unknowable to them. The job of the magician is to nurture this desire, twist this desire, tease this desire. It must be made to seem impossible but also possible. There must be a moment when a logical outcome is made baffling and wondrous. If he fails to create this moment, then he is a failure as a magician.

One of my earliest memories is of being maybe five or six and going on a picnic with my parents. I remember my mother in the kitchen making sandwiches, and helping her pack a basket with sweets and bottles of soda. My father carried it as we hiked to a meadow a few miles from our house. A bee chased me for a while, buzzing in my ears as it careened by, and I hid behind my mother in an attempt to confuse it. She laughed at this while my father pretended that the bee was chasing him, dropping the picnic basket and waving his hands in the air, mimicking my childish hysterics.

We found a clearing and my father spread a blanket out on the ground while my mother unpacked our basket. The field smelled of dandelions, and above me there was one lone cloud that I tried to impose a familiar shape upon but it looked only like a cloud. I bit into my sandwich, the sharp tang of mustard on roast beef a puzzle in my mouth, and sat there warm and satisfied. I can still feel the cool breeze gliding across my forehead.

Years later, when I was about fourteen, I mentioned this day in passing to my father and he stared at me, his face blank, and said that we'd never been on any such excursion. As sure as I was that we had, I knew better than to argue with him. I asked my mother about it, and she couldn't remember that day either. "There's no meadow like that within walking distance of our house," she said, and the more I thought about it, the less sense it made. We'd never been on any other sort of picnic like that before or since. But I remembered it as clearly as I knew my own name. Over the coming weeks I spent my afternoons combing the surrounding land for a place that looked even remotely like the spot in my memory.

I still wonder if this memory is real or false, if it's me or everyone else who's wrong. Because that moment on the blanket is the happiest childhood memory I have. It has become the baseline from which I judge subsequent experiences. To this day the best thing I can imagine is sitting in the sun with your family, comfortably quiet and happy for the fleeting joy of being alive. Is this illusion or substance? What does it mean if this moment never happened?

I wondered about this even before Dr. Korsakoff's diagnosis, but now, obviously, it has taken on a new significance. If he's right, if there really is nothing he can do about my condition, then maybe I should start to keep progress reports, like Charlie Gordon in *Flowers for Algernon*. It might prove useful to document whatever is going to happen to me. Perhaps if I write things down, I can create a story for myself that, through rereading, will become a sort of new reality as my ability to distinguish between illusion and substance worsens.

And Alice. If there's any substance left of me, then I owe her the truth. I deprived her of a father. I can't even now explain fully why I did it. It all seems a lifetime ago, and from where I'm sitting now, it's easy to make excuses and justifications and hard to remember how it all felt at the time or exactly what happened. But I owe Alice something. An apology? It's a little late for that. An explanation is something I'm not sure I have to offer. All I can give her is the truth as I know it, or as I can recall it. If I've learned anything in my life it's that magicians aren't the only ones hiding their identities from the world.

A woman with a small child passes me. The child, a girl with curly brown hair tied into pigtails with red ribbons, looks unhappy. Her mother is holding her by the hand and pulling her along. The girl is lagging as best as she can, making it clear she doesn't want to go inside. I can't say I blame her one bit. I wouldn't want to go either. I feel a strange kinship with this sprite in her blue dress and knee socks. The doors open and admit first the mother and then the girl, her childish attempt to avoid the inevitable defeated.

None of us wants to go. And I don't mean inside the hospital, though that's true. What I mean is no one wants to die, but we each know that sooner or later it's going to happen to us. We tell ourselves that it's a long way off, and turn to notions of religion or spirituality or science to make sense of it, and for some that does bring some existential comfort, but still most of us lag as much as we can, just like this girl. No one gets to stay. Yet we live and act as though it is otherwise.

The magician trades in this human struggle. Magic that is not real magic affects us because it mirrors our existence. We know that what we see isn't as it seems, but we want it to be and want to understand it. We want to be fooled, and then want to know how we were fooled. We cannot prevent our minds from trying to figure out how the trick was done. I believe this is more than just intellectual curiosity. We strive for immortality in the face of its impossibility.

But magicians are clever. They understand that a magic trick is all about turning illusion into substance in such a way that we never fully comprehend what happened, or what we think happened. They know that a trick loses its power once we understand how it was done, and also that it loses its power once we no longer wish to understand how it was done.

There are four elements to this grand tug-of-war between substance and illusion. There is effect, there is method, there is misdirection, and finally, when it's all over, there is reconstruction. Magic is a dance between these four elements. The actor playing a magician seeks to choreograph a way through the trick with these component parts. If he does so, he will have achieved magic. If not, he is a failure.

Effect is the reason the trick exists. Without it there's no point. It's the rabbit coming out of the hat, the woman shown to be sawn in half, the ace of spades somehow inside your coat pocket. Often a good effect is kept secret until the moment of its reveal. You don't actually know what the trick is until it's finished. Other times the effect is announced at the start, and you're watching for it, waiting for it, but then when it happens, you're still amazed. Either way, the audience lives for the effect, we desire it more than anything, and if it pleases us we will believe, to a point, that the magician is not an actor but someone capable of altering the known laws of the universe.

Life is like this. Happiness is an extremely relative concept, but we will believe we are happy if the sum of daily effects is high enough. The more disappointments, bafflements, and failed outcomes we experience, the less likely we are to believe we are happy.

But of course it's not easy to achieve an effect. If it were, magicians wouldn't be extraordinary. Things we take for granted as everyday occurrences—like images on a television screen, telephones, electricity—would all have at one time been the most profound effects a magician could produce. The radio once worked people into a state of pandemonium, but over time we have become used to it. We don't know how these devices function, outside of a rudimentary understanding of technological concepts—certainly less than 1 percent of the population could actually explain how, say, a television works, let alone build one. We are, however, familiar with them. And so the things they do, however mystifying, no longer speak to us. We need to have the order of the universe tilted, and you can't do this with things you're used to.

Given that a magician isn't actually tilting the universe, he must somehow achieve his effect using the tools available to mere mortals. How he does this is the method. The wires, the doubles, the mirrors, the trapdoors—magical methods vary from deceptively simple to diabolically clever. A good method is one where as little can go wrong as possible and where all aspects necessary to create the effect are fully within the magician's control.

The problem with this is that the audience is on the lookout for the method. Because inherent in the wondrousness of the effect is the implication that if we could do it too, if the method were to become available, then we would also be magicians. We might shrug off the inexorable march of death.

So the audience must never be able to detect the method. If they do, the effect will be rendered meaningless. To keep this method secret, the magician employs misdirection. Misdirection can be as subtle as a tiny gesture, as obvious as an explosion, as expected as a curtain, or as coy as smoke. The audience is on the lookout for this, and the magician must be cunning about his use of misdirection. It is dishonest, and he knows it, but it is not malicious. It is in service of a greater truth.

The final element is the most complex. After the effect has been revealed, after the method has been executed and the misdirection has prevented its detection, the audience will attempt to reconstruct the trick. They will think back to what they saw and try to figure out how it was done. If they succeed, even after the fact, then the effect is ruined and the whole act was for naught. The misdirection and method must not be detectable, even in hindsight. For this reason, the magician will insert elements into the trick that are there for the sole purpose of confounding the reconstruction of the trick.

The magician knows that what happened and what we will remember having happened can be two entirely different things. If he shows us A and C, we will believe we saw B. If he does his job, we will swear that we saw the impossible with our own eyes. When we close our eyes, we will see things as we believe they happened, not as they actually did. This is essential for the effect. It is what carries it forward, what propels us to seek the next effect, to keep our mortality in abeyance.

If Alice were here and I were to tell her this, she would shake her head and smile. "Martin," she might say, "a magic trick is just a magic trick. Life is more complicated."

She'd be wrong, though. Effect, method, misdirection, reconstruction. For me, they explain everything.

The little girl and her mother emerge from the hospital and stop beside me. The girl releases her mother's hand while her mother searches through her purse. I smile at the child, but she doesn't smile back. She stares at me, her face impenetrable, as though she's not sure what she's looking at. I've never been very good with children—there's something about them that I can't connect with. I wish this were not the case, because I like children, or at least I think I could if I'd spent more time around them and gotten over whatever this barrier is between us.

I smile at the girl again and remove a coin from my pocket. I hold it out for her to see, let her eyes take in its shiny glint. I transfer the coin from my right hand to my left, toss it in the air, and we both watch it rise, stall, and tumble down to my waiting right hand. I nod and show her the coin. Then I pass it to the other hand and toss it in the air again, higher this time. The bright sunlight makes it sparkle as it once again tries to escape gravity, fails, and returns to my waiting right hand. I open my hand and we look at the coin even more closely. She's captivated, I can tell. I move the coin to my left hand and toss the coin in the air a third time, but this time I don't catch it. The girl watches as it disappears into thin air; my hand, waiting to catch the coin, sits empty. She looks at me, surprised, and I raise a finger to my mouth and curl my lips into a shush. Her mother finds whatever she was looking for in her purse and takes hold of the child's hand, pulling her away, unaware that anything has happened. As they depart the girl looks back at me and smiles. She has seen something unexpected and impossible.

And that's magic. She saw the coin vanish. Or at least she thinks she did. It was in my hand all along. Before each toss I visibly transferred the coin from my right hand to my left before throwing it, a casual and seemingly insignificant gesture that was, of course, not insignificant at all, because the final time the transfer never took place. My hand was empty when it mimicked its throw, and while she watched it my other hand dropped the coin into my lap and out of sight. But if you were to ask her, or most other people who witness this trick, they would swear they'd seen the coin tossed into the air.

I've thought a lot about this over the years. How is it we can be so sure that we've seen, heard, or experienced what we think we have? In a magic trick, the things you don't see or think you see have a culmination, because at the end of the trick there's an effect. Misdirection tampers with reconstruction. But if life works the same way, and I believe it does, then a percentage of our lives is a fiction. There's no way to know whether anything we have seen or experienced is real or imagined. The first two times the girl thought she saw me toss the coin in the air she was right.

This gives me pause. If I'm going to be able to convey to Alice all that I know, and exactly what happened, then how important is it for me to differentiate between what I saw and what I think I saw? Is it even possible?

I try to catch a glimpse of the girl and her mother, but they're gone. I wonder if she will remember this moment years from now, if she will wonder if it really happened. I think back to the picnic, feel the sun on the back of my neck, taste the roast beef sandwich my mother made, hear the buzz of the bee. Or is that my tinnitus? How long have I been seeing things that weren't there?

MARTIN STRAUSS

1926

IT IS A CONSTANT STRUGGLE NOT TO BECOME THE THING you hate most. When I left for Montreal to study at McGill, my father expressed the opinion that I'd be back soon enough, likely sooner rather than later. My mother thought she knew better.

My mother was the only one who ever believed I would amount to anything. She had always seen something in me that no one else, including me, saw. Whenever I exceeded expectations, she would act as though a positive outcome was never in doubt. I often regret that I never asked her what she based this outlook on. It seemed risky, as though she might decide it was a foolish attitude if she were to think about it too much.

"You will be back, Martin. To visit. I'll miss you," she said.

They were both wrong. I never set foot in my hometown again.

My studies proved far easier than I'd anticipated, though my problem had never been intelligence. I had a hard time caring about things. My father interpreted this as laziness, but it was more than that. Most tasks seemed so irrelevant and meaningless that it didn't seem worth doing them at all. I was smart enough that I didn't have to try at much but not smart enough to succeed at anything without effort.

Montreal was a lonely town. You didn't have to speak any French to survive, but it would have made life easier; my French was pretty terrible. I stayed in a rented room in a boardinghouse along with other students and the odd laborer.

My only real friend was a student across the hall, Will Riley. He never seemed to go to class or study. He had money, and I assumed he had family behind him, so how he did at McGill was mostly irrelevant. He always knew a good place to get a drink and liked to buy a round in exchange for company, so we ended up out together often enough for me to be drinking more than I should have. All my life this has been a weakness, but when I was younger I maybe didn't try to keep it in check.

By my final year I had my studies down to a routine. I'd go to class, do whatever was required to pass, and work odd jobs to supplement my income. At nights I'd go drinking with Will.

I'm not sure exactly what happened, but whatever anxiety I'd experienced growing up about who I was or what I would become seemed to lessen to the point that people probably couldn't tell it was there.

Perhaps this was the reason Clara took an interest in me. I never really understood why she wanted me, much as I never understood my mother's confidence.

It's inexplicable what causes a person to love someone. It is a feeling so irrational that it allows you to believe that the person you love has qualities they don't actually possess. And when someone loves you back, it's nearly impossible not to feel you must never let them see what you are really like, because you know deep inside that you are not worthy of their love.

But Clara chose me. She made an effort to be near me, and she made it clear that all I had to do was meet her halfway. I finally worked up enough nerve to ask her out, and she said yes. We saw each other a couple of times a week after that, and though I was always waiting for the moment when she'd decide that she'd had enough of me, she seemed content, even happy.

One of our favorite things to do was visit the vaudeville theaters. We'd seen Al Jolson, Eddie Cantor, Howard Thurston, Charles Carter, and a dozen others. We disagreed about the singers, but we both loved the magicians.

After seeing Howard Thurston, I was inspired to learn a couple of card tricks. The one I liked most was called the Memory Master. When I felt I had it down, I showed it to Clara.

I took a deck of cards and fanned it out on the table between us, faceup. "Ordinary cards," I said. I then broke the deck into two piles and combined them. As I was doing this I took note of the top card, the ace of spades, and the bottom card, the three of diamonds. I shuffled the cards a couple of times but maintained the two cards' respective positions at the top and bottom of the deck.

"Pick a card," I said, fanning them out in my hands, facedown.

Clara smiled at me. "Shuffle them again."

I feigned indignation. "Don't you trust me?"

She laughed. "Of course I do."

I shuffled them again—the way the trick worked, I could shuffle them as many times as I wanted so long as the ace stayed on top and the three on the bottom.

"Okay, pick a card and don't show it to me or tell me what it is."

She reached out and took a card, looked at it, and smiled. What a smile. I felt as if I'd fooled the world into believing I was capable of greatness.

"Put it facedown on the table." I broke the deck in half at the middle and placed her card in the break. I had swing cut the cards, which means that when you cut the deck you move the top half from one hand to another, so that the top card becomes the card in the middle, and the bottom card ends up next to it. I knew that whatever card Clara had chosen was now in the middle of the deck between the ace of spades and the three of diamonds.

I then broke the deck slightly above the middle and riffle-shuffled the cards. This might add a card or two between the ace and the three, but it wouldn't change the general ordering of the three key cards.

"Now for the hard part." I fanned the cards out on the table, faceup. "I will memorize the order of the entire deck of cards."

Clara laughed as I made a show of holding my thumbs to my temples and squinting. After a few seconds I said, "Got it."

"Really?"

"Absolutely. I'm going to turn around and close my eyes. I want you to move the card you selected to a different spot in the deck."

I turned away and waited for her. Between the ace of spades and the three of diamonds were two cards, the five of hearts and the ten of clubs. Whichever one of those two was missing would be the card she'd chosen.

"You can turn around," she said.

I turned around and looked down the entire length of the deck. I stopped when I got to the ace. Next to it was the five of hearts, then the ten of clubs, then the three of diamonds. None of the cards had moved. Something had gone wrong.

Clara watched me and seemed to understand that the trick had failed. I frowned and looked at the cards again, then up at her. "I think I screwed it up."

She leaned over the table and kissed me. I forgot about the stupid card trick. She tasted like lilacs.

"Who cares," she said. "I don't like you for your magic tricks."

The beer hall was poorly lit. Will was sitting at a small table in the back and was a couple of beers ahead of me. He grinned at me as I sat, and pushed a mug across the table.

"You look like a kid who's just seen his first naked lady," he said.

I hadn't been aware there was any look on my face. "Shut it."

He pretended to flinch. "This is how you treat me after what I've got for us?"

I drank a good third of the glass, set it down, and wiped my mouth on my sleeve. "What exactly is it you've got for us?"

He reached into his coat pocket and handed me four small pieces of paper. They were tickets to Harry Houdini's show the following night at the Princess Theater.

"How did you get these?" I'd tried all week to get tickets.

He shrugged. "They fell off a truck."

Houdini fascinated Clara. He'd performed earlier that day at

McGill, but the place was so packed we couldn't get in. I'd never seen such a crowd before—there were people up on ladders in the student union building. Clara and I had hung around for a while before giving up, and she'd been disappointed about it.

I stayed out drinking with Will for two or three more hours, celebrating our good fortune. It was too late to go to Clara's and tell her the good news unless I wanted to have a run-in with her father. Eventually I stumbled out into the street. It was a crisp October evening, but I had enough beer in me not to feel the cold.

After about a fifteen-minute walk, and some trouble getting my key into the lock, I wobbled my way up the stairs and made it into my room. On the desk was a stack of mail that I'd tossed there that morning. At the bottom was a letter addressed to me in my father's handwriting. My father wasn't one to write.

I sat down and opened the letter. The words made no sense. I understood each of them but couldn't string them together. I felt sick, and I could feel the blood pumping through my temples become a high-pitched whine. There was a glass of water on the nightstand and I drank it, lay down, and closed my eyes as tightly as I could.

I awoke the next morning with a roaring headache. My sheets were soaked in sweat and the room felt like a sauna. I opened the window and stuck my head out, but it made little difference. I sat on the bed, dizzy, and waited for the world to stop spinning. It didn't. I lay down and fell back asleep.

I awoke again around three in the afternoon feeling a little bit better. I washed and dressed as best I could and made my way outside. I had a flask for emergencies, and this felt like an emergency. Three long pulls of cheap whiskey seared my throat and things began to level out.

Clara's house was about a twenty-minute walk away. Winter was doing its best to gain a foothold, but for now the air was brisk and you could barely see your breath. I'd pulled on my coat and stuffed my pockets without thinking, and had to double-check I still had the two tickets Will had given me the night before.

The initial pain of the day had retreated to a general sense of numbness. It felt like an improvement, and I resolved to establish a more optimistic outlook. I was alive, had my life in front of me, and was on my way to pick up the girl I loved and see the world's greatest performer. What more could I possibly hope for in a day?

Clara lived in an upscale neighborhood with fashionable houses nestled back from tree-lined boulevards. Her father was in finance and had done well for himself as some sort of bigwig with the Bank of Montreal. They were wealthy, but she had never really let on exactly how well-off her family was. It didn't seem like she much cared about that sort of thing.

I'd met her father a number of times and was unable to tell whether he approved of me.

"What does your father do, Martin?" he asked the first time she brought me home for dinner.

"He's in shipping," I said, which wasn't technically a lie. My father worked part-time for the Canadian Pacific Railway.

Because today was Friday I thought it unlikely Clara's father would be home. Before climbing the stairs to her front door I took a quick slug from my flask and then stashed it in my pocket.

Clara answered the door, her hair flowing over her shoulders.

I wanted to bury my face in it but didn't. She smiled when she saw me, but her smile faded.

"What's the matter?"

"Nothing," I said. I reached into my pocket and retrieved our tickets. "Look what I have."

She took the tickets from my hand. "Where did you get these?"

"Will."

"Wow," she said. "I wonder who he had to kill." She laughed and got her coat and scarf. She held my hand as we walked back toward the theater, and she told me about an argument her mother and sister had had and the kind of dog she someday hoped to own. Then she talked about a mathematical theorem she'd been studying.

"How was your day?" she asked.

I didn't want to tell her that I spent it in bed. "It was fine. Not much happened."

The show didn't start until seven, so we got a table at a restaurant a block away and ate a leisurely supper.

"There probably won't be any crate escapes," she said. "He doesn't do those anymore. He's kind of gone off the audience challenges. I hope he does the Water Torture Cell, though. My cousin saw it in Philadelphia and said it was terrific. And the Needles. I have no idea how he does it."

I'd wondered that myself. In fact, I'd read about and heard his act described so many times that it felt like I'd witnessed it firsthand. I had in my mind a vivid image of a string of needles coming out of his mouth, pulled by an unbelieving member of the audience.

We finished our meal and strolled the rest of the way to the theater. The night was clear and bright. The streets were full of people, and as we got close to the theater Clara pulled me closer and squeezed my arm. I stopped walking, leaned over, and kissed her.

"This is going to be great," I said.

Will was waiting for us outside the theater. He had a woman with him who I'd never met before, though that wasn't unusual. He often showed up with women who were loud or drunk. I didn't mind so much but was concerned that Clara might be upset. She'd never said anything about it, but I didn't want to risk it. I'd tried to keep her as insulated from Will as much as possible.

Tonight's girl seemed all right. Will introduced her as Evelyn, and she smiled. Clara went right up to Will and gave him a hug.

"Thanks so much for getting the tickets," she said, and held on to him for what I perceived as a moment longer than necessary, if a hug was even necessary in the first place. He'd gotten the tickets for me, not her.

"Anything for Martin. You're a lucky girl," he said, and winked at me.

The Princess Theater was an impressive building. There were large murals of musicians and entertainers, and the seats were covered with velvet. It must have held over two thousand people if you included the box seats and twin balconies. Our seats were near the back on the ground floor, not the best but still pretty great. Evelyn sat next to Will, who was beside me, then Clara on the aisle. The room buzzed with excitement.

"We'll go to the Pig and Whistle after?" Will said. The Pig and Whistle was a bar in the basement of the Prince of Wales Hotel, a popular spot with students.

"Sure," I said.

The house lights dimmed and the theater manager came

onstage. "Ladies and gentlemen," he boomed in a throaty baritone, "it is my wondrous pleasure to introduce to you the one and only Handcuff King, the Great Mystifier himself, back from the grave a thousand times, Mr. Harry Houdini."

The applause was deafening. Clara was excited, more so than I'd ever seen her. We'd been to numerous shows but this was different. She looked over, bit her lip, and leaned into me.

Houdini was a short man, but you didn't notice at first. He was muscular, and though the hair at his temples had gone gray he seemed in excellent shape. He spoke in a commanding voice that demanded attention.

Houdini began by calling for a volunteer from the audience. Of course every hand in the theater went up. He picked a man from the front row and an assistant led him onstage.

"He's doing the Needles," Clara said.

She was right. We watched as the man inspected a package of needles. Houdini popped about thirty of them into his mouth, then some thread, chewed, and washed them down with a glass of water. He then looked sick, contracted at the stomach, reached into his mouth, and pulled out a piece of thread. The man took it and Houdini slowly backed away from him. From his mouth came a string of threaded needles that must have been six feet long. It was just as I'd pictured it. "Wow," I said.

He moved on to some conjuring of cards and other objects, some really great bits of magic. After these, the stage was cleared and there was a small musical interlude.

Will leaned in and whispered to me, "Your girl there seems to like the magic."

Clara was flushed and beaming. Her hand was on my knee, her index finger running back and forth on the fabric.

The show began again and Houdini invited a committee of audience members, selected at random from a glut of volunteers, onstage to fasten him into a straitjacket. "Nice and tight, gentlemen," he said. "We don't want anyone thinking you've let me off easy." Once he was fastened into it, he writhed and wriggled like a madman until he was free of it.

A group of assistants wearing rubber coats wheeled a large curtained object onto the stage. The curtain was moved aside to reveal the Water Torture Cell. It was a large box, about five feet high and three feet square. On the front was a glass window; the other three sides were enclosed wood.

Houdini addressed us. "Ladies and gentlemen, introducing my original invention, the Water Torture Cell. Although there is nothing supernatural about it, I am prepared to forfeit the sum of one thousand dollars to anyone who can prove that it is possible to obtain air inside the cursed cell when I am locked up in it after it has been filled with water. Should anything go wrong when I am locked up, one of my assistants will watch through the curtain, ready to demolish the glass with his ax, allowing the water to flow out in order to save my life."

Clara's hand had moved up my leg and was now resting at my midthigh. It was becoming difficult to concentrate. We'd kissed a bit, but that was as far as anything had gone. Her eyes were locked on every movement Houdini made.

"Let me first thoroughly explain the apparatus, and then I will invite a committee onstage to examine everything. The cover is a steel frame made to prevent it from being opened even if it were not locked. Padlocks will hold it in place once I am secured inside. In front, there is a glass plate for self-protection. I do not expect anything untoward to happen. But as we all know, accidents will happen and when least expected."

Houdini then invited a dozen men to inspect the cell. They came onstage and poked at the thing, examining it from top to bottom.

"Are you satisfied?" Houdini asked.

One man, an elderly fellow with a cane, was not. "How do we know there's not a trapdoor underneath?"

Houdini smiled. "An excellent question. Choose any portion of the stage you wish and I'll have the cell moved there."

The man took a few steps back, scuffed his foot on the floor, and pointed. Houdini's assistants pulled the cell to the spot he'd chosen, and with a hose and several large buckets they filled it with water.

An assistant locked Houdini into handcuffs. He lay down on the floor, and the lid was lifted off the top of the cell by a wire and pulley system. The lid had stocks that were fastened around Houdini's ankles before being pulled aloft, suspending him upside down in the air. He took one last deep breath before being lowered into the cell. Water sloshed over the side as he was submerged. His assistants fastened the hasps at the lid and snapped padlocks onto them. They then raised the curtain around them.

The band played while an assistant stood by with his ax, his gaze alternating between the curtain and the stopwatch in his hand. After two minutes everyone who had been holding their breaths to test him had given up. Another minute went by. The curtains fluttered. A few more seconds passed. Then the curtains flew open and Houdini staggered from the cell, dripping wet but unharmed. The cell was still full of water and the lid was intact, the locks undisturbed.

Bedlam followed. The audience vaulted to its feet and made the theater tremble under the weight of its admiration. The din was so loud that I couldn't distinguish my own voice from Will's or Clara's, though I cheered with the full force of my lungs.

It took some time for the racket to die down, but when it did the theater manager announced an intermission. We got up and went to the lobby. Clara and Evelyn went off to the washroom, leaving Will and me by ourselves. We found a spot in the corner and took turns with the flask.

"These tickets are going to pay off in spades," Will said, looking to see if Evelyn was on her way back.

I shook my head. "I doubt it."

"You're blind." He handed me back the empty flask. "You're a smart guy, Martin, but you don't get a lot. And Clara is one of those things. You treat her like she's some sort of saint, like she's above you. She's not. She's right down in the regular world just the same as you."

I put the flask back in my pocket. "I don't treat her like a saint."

"Really? You even do anything other than make eyes at her?"

I very nearly answered that I'd kissed her a number of times but realized that this was exactly his point. There was something about Clara that made her almost untouchable to me. Her faith in me had put her in the same camp as my mother. But she wasn't my mother, she was a twenty-three-year-old woman.

"Don't worry, Martin," Will said. "You'll figure it out."

Clara and Evelyn returned, making a response unnecessary.

Will became engaged in a conversation with Evelyn, and I took a few steps away from them, pulling Clara with me.

"Let's not go to the Pig and Whistle after," I whispered. "Let's go somewhere quiet, just us."

The lights in the lobby flickered on and off, on and off. The intermission was over.

Clara's lips lightly scuffed my ear. "Let's go somewhere now." I'd never seen her look at me the way she was, or maybe she had and I hadn't noticed.

"Are you coming?" Evelyn asked. "The show's going to start again."

"Go on ahead, we'll be right there," I said. Will was about to argue with me but changed his mind. I took Clara's hand and we went through the lobby to a side door that led up a narrow stairway. Off to the side was a coatroom. The door wasn't locked and the light was off. No one saw us as we snuck inside.

"Lock the door," Clara whispered.

I clicked the lock into place and reached for her. The room was windowless; the only light came through the crack under the door. We kissed, and it wasn't the same as any kiss we'd shared before. It was desperate and ambitious.

Clara's hands were at my belt. I lifted her skirt. She smothered a sigh as we surged against the wall. I was aware of how awkward we were, but it didn't matter.

She guided me into her, laughing as we knocked over what I think must have been a coat rack. She was the softest thing that had ever lived, and I felt for a moment like I might be invincible. The entirety of my life distilled itself to a girl and a coatroom.

I'm not sure how long we were there together. It seemed like a long time, and it seemed like it was over in the blink of an eye. As we pulled our clothes back into place, neither of us spoke, but when we kissed for the last time before opening the door, I knew that everything had changed.

There was a smile on Clara's face as we stole down the hallway, but by the time we were downstairs in the lobby it was gone.

"Are you all right?" I asked.

She didn't say anything, just gave me a small nod. We found our seats in the dark, as the show had begun again.

The third act of Houdini's show was a lecture on spiritualism. I hadn't much thought about it, though it was something people were very interested in. At that point in my life I had no inclination to consider life after death, whether it was real, whether those who were dead could be communicated with. Death had never touched me in a way that made it necessary to think about such things. For a great many others, however, particularly those who had been through the war and lost people, it was an unavoidable question. And the spiritualists claimed to have the answer.

"There is an adage that truth is stranger than fiction, but some of the miraculous things attributed to the spirits would not be told, could not be told, by even the most famous writers of wild fiction. The conglomerated things you are asked to accept in good faith are almost inconceivable, but under the projecting mantle of spiritualism these vivid tales are believed by millions."

Houdini had changed back into evening clothes, and the stage was empty save for a table and chair. He paced back and forth with purpose, his voice loud and zealous.

"We read in the newspapers of some payroll bandit who steals thousands of dollars, or of burglars entering homes and stores

and breaking open safes and taking valuable loot, but these cases
we read of are nothing in comparison to news of mediums who
have earned millions of dollars, blood money made at the cost of
torture to the souls of their victims. Folks who hear voices and
see forms should see their physicians immediately."

The audience laughed, but the energy in the room was different. Where before there was a tension between life and death,
a cultivated air of mystery, it now felt as if we were being let in
on a secret.

"I am familiar with a great many of the methods of these human
vultures. I think it is an insult to that scavenger of scavengers to
compare such human beings to him, but there is, to my mind, no
other fit comparison. Their stock-in-trade is the amount of knowledge they can obtain. It is invaluable and they will stop at nothing
to gain it."

Clara wasn't paying attention. She was staring down at her
hands, which were clutched on her lap. I put my hand on hers
and she looked up and smiled at me. The way she looked at me
was different, and I couldn't tell how. Had she seen something
in me up in the coatroom, a revelation of my nature she hadn't
known? I wondered if she regretted what we'd done.

"Mr. Bernard Delacroix, I have a message from the spirits
for you," he called. "Are you there?"

A man stood up in the audience.

"Your aunt Genevieve wishes me to tell you that she desires
for you to call on her son, your cousin, who has been unwell. He
has always been a sickly boy and wants to thank you for being so
good to him."

The man appeared shocked and sat down. Houdini called the

names of a half-dozen people and gave them messages from beyond. They each responded with disbelief, then confirmation that
the information was indeed accurate. I thought about what I
might say, if I were on the other side, that might be of any conse-
quence to those still alive. What would there really be to say? You
might describe what it was like, and maybe give some insight into
what it was like to die, but beyond that it was difficult to imagine
how death could fix whatever you'd done in life. If you were a fool
in life, why wouldn't you be one in death?

"Myra Goldfarb, your mother is here and tells me that her
leg no longer bothers her. She is dancing every night with your
father and brother."

A woman in the audience cried out, "Is she really here?"

"No, madam, I'm afraid she isn't. None of what I've said tonight was gained by any method beyond the ordinary ability of
man. Through spies, bought information, and trips to the graveyard I've been able to gather everything I need to convince you
I can speak to those who have departed. These mediums, these
bloodsuckers, do the same thing, but they do not tell you so. For
that they cannot be forgiven.

"Nor can those who support them, those like Sir Arthur
Conan Doyle, a man capable of creating a character as intelligent
and analytical as Sherlock Holmes but incapable of seeing through
the trickery of Margery Crandon, the witch of Beacon Hill."

He went on to show how mediums manipulated the tables
during a séance, how they manifested ectoplasm, how they rang
the bells and chimed the triangles and blew the trumpets. He
gave a demonstration of slate writing, showing us in clear view
how he did it. It was fascinating, I suppose—the entire theater

was riveted—but I had a hard time paying attention. I could not shake the feeling that I'd done something I could not take back. But I knew that everything had changed.

One summer morning when I was about ten I was in the kitchen with my mother. My father came in and announced that Charlie, the family dog, had died. That dog had been with us since I was born, and was as much a friend to me as anyone. A boy and his dog, that old story. My reaction to hearing this news should have been shock, grief, almost anything other than what happened.

"So what," I said, "he was a stupid animal."

This was something my father would have said, I thought, or maybe there is more of my father in me than I know. It is inexplicable to me why I said it. But I did, and an instant later I was on the floor with my head buzzing and a throbbing jaw. My father stood over me, his fists tight at his sides, as angry as I'd ever seen him. I didn't dare speak. I can't say how long he stood there. He breathed hard, and then my mother came over and touched him lightly on the arm. This made him look at her and she looked back at him, and his anger faded. Without speaking he turned and left the room. I lay on the floor a while longer and then sat up.

"I'm sorry," I said to my mother.

She looked down at me. "Your father loved that dog."

"So did I." My jaw was really starting to hurt now that the shock had begun to wear off.

"I know you did," she said, handing me a wet cloth. "But some things once said can't be taken back. Not everything is reversible, even if you're sorry."

Houdini's speech came to an end. He bowed to us as we rose to our feet, holding nothing back. He came back several times for encores, and then the lights came up and the Princess Theater reluctantly disgorged us into the street. We were tightly packed as we left, almost dazed, and somehow I became separated from the others. One second Clara was right in front of me and the next she was replaced by a woman with a feathered hat, who was an instant later replaced by a tall man whose overcoat smelled of pipe smoke.

Out on the street I searched for her, expecting to see her standing by a streetlamp, waiting for us. Waving when she saw me, a smile on her face. All I saw were the faces of strangers.

After a few minutes Will and Evelyn emerged from the theater, spotting me immediately and weaving through the throng.

"Was that a show. Wow," Will said, his face flushed.

"Where's Clara?" Evelyn asked.

I shrugged. "Wasn't feeling well." I felt sick. We shouldn't have gone to that coatroom. This wasn't how it should have been. None of what was happening was right.

"She seemed fine at intermission," Evelyn said. She scanned the street for her.

"I have to go," I said. "I should have walked her home."

Will, to his credit, seemed to know something wasn't right. "Go do what you need to do, and come by the Pig and Whistle afterward. We'll be there awhile." I could tell he wanted to say more but not in front of Evelyn.

I walked away. Moving fast, I took the route that seemed the most likely one Clara would choose. She only had a bit of a head start on me, and I should have been able to catch up with her. After ten blocks I began to run. It was the only way to stop from thinking. My lungs ached from the cold air and my feet hurt, but instead of stopping I ran faster.

When I reached her house, I stopped and, hands on my knees, fought the wave of fatigue and nausea that had been chasing me. The lights at her house were all off. If anyone was home, they didn't want it known or had gone to bed. I couldn't simply walk up and ring the bell—what would I say if her father was home? There was no way to explain my presence, even to myself.

I stood there in the night air, sweating, unsure of what to do next. She was gone. Where I didn't know. I pulled out my flask and unscrewed the stopper, tipping it to my lips. It was empty.

Wherever Clara had gone, she didn't want to be found. I turned away from her house and began a slow walk back into town. I tried to keep my mind still, wanting to do anything other than think. My brain, as usual, did not cooperate.

Was this how life worked? Were people there one moment, wound around you so tightly you couldn't distinguish what was you and what was them, and gone an instant later? This couldn't be how it worked. Could it?

In front of me was the Prince of Wales Hotel. Will and Evelyn were probably inside. I didn't feel very social, and certainly didn't want to have to talk about Clara, but I did want a drink. Maybe not just one.

An awful thought seized me. What if something had happened to Clara? What if she hadn't vanished of her own volition but instead someone had taken her? I had to find Will. He'd know what to do.

I went through the heavy door and into the lobby, feeling a blast of warm air as the door swung shut behind me. A small crowd had formed at the far end, and as I passed by I saw that Will was there, speaking with a man I couldn't quite see. I changed course toward

Will and stopped. He was talking to Houdini himself. There were ten or twelve others with him, a few I recognized, and they were all listening raptly to Houdini's response.

"He's staying in the hotel," Will whispered to me when he saw me standing beside him. Houdini seemed shorter up close, but it was immediately apparent how strong he was. He had a magnetism about him—even if you had no idea who he was, you would know immediately that he was someone important.

"Feel my forearm," he said to one fellow. He flexed his arm and held it out to him.

"It's like iron," the man said.

"It has to be," Houdini said. "Fools like Sir Arthur may say that the spirits help me in my work, but the truth of it is that I'm a mortal man, and all that keeps me alive is my wits and my training."

At that moment my attention veered toward the stairway leading down to the Pig and Whistle. I did a double take as I saw Clara and Evelyn climbing the stairs. Will whispered, "She was here waiting for us all when we got here. She's been wondering where you were."

It hadn't occurred to me that she'd wait for us here. Is that what had happened? It didn't make sense completely, but here she was.

I looked over to where Clara was, and she was staring straight at me. I realized that she wasn't the one who had been lost. I was. And I, or anyone, could see that she was relieved to have found me. I knew from the look on her face—this woman loved me.

"Is it true that your stomach muscles are strong enough to withstand any punch?" Will asked Houdini, but I wasn't interested in their conversation.

I was about to go to Clara when I put my hand in my pocket,

and it emerged holding the letter my father had sent me. I dropped it onto the floor as if it were on fire. I began to bend to pick up the letter. Instead, I stepped forward, toward Houdini. My hand tightened into a fist and I swung hard, transferring my weight from my back foot to my front foot and striking him squarely in the gut. It was nothing like iron. I felt the air pushed out of him and heard him exhale a grunt, and then the force of my punch took me into him. His hand grabbed at my coat as we both fell to the floor.

There was a moment while we lay there when our eyes met. His face was serene, not at all in pain. He looked, if anything, relieved. Content. He made no attempt to fight back. I didn't understand it.

Someone grabbed me by my shoulders and pulled me off him, though I wasn't hitting him anymore and had no intention of doing so. I was roughly pulled away, and the last I saw of Houdini was him being helped to his feet, looking a little winded but otherwise unharmed. I couldn't see where Clara was. I was ushered to the door and heaved onto the street. Will came outside and stopped a couple of meaty-looking guys from giving me a beating. I wished he hadn't—I had no intention of resisting. He spoke quietly to them, trying to defuse things, and I turned away and started toward home.

For days after I ignored all knocks on the door, all shouts at my window, barely ate, barely slept. Every crack on the wall was enumerated. Each scrape on the floorboards was tabulated. I wished the world stopped, frozen until I could make sense of it. I sent away all voices that came to me and sat in silence, paralyzed by my actions and an inability to respond to them. It felt as if a great pit had opened up beneath me, and if I were to make any move at all I would fall into it.

Eventually hunger drove me out of my room. I went to a nearby diner and sat at the counter, ordered a coffee and a sandwich. I ate in silence. There was a paper on the counter from the day before. I had to reread the headline to believe it.

Houdini was dead. He'd died in Detroit the day before, from what the paper described as "a burst appendix brought on by an unexpected blow." The paper went on to give a brief and vague account of what had happened in the lobby of the Prince of Wales Hotel. I wasn't named, but I knew I was the one who had punched him. I was the one who had killed Harry Houdini.

I staggered out of the diner and went straight to my room. A panic seized me. I was the cause of the death of the most famous man in the world. It was only a matter of time before the papers figured out who I was. There had been plenty of people there that night who knew me.

My palms were sweating. I wiped them on my coat and felt in its right-hand pocket an unfamiliar weight. I reached inside and discovered a small, leather-bound notebook I'd never seen before. Scrawled inside were a jumble of letters that made no sense whatsoever.

SDBDWWHQWLRQLDPWDNLQJBRXRQDKX-QWIRUWUXWK

There were about a hundred and fifty pages of this, and no clue as to what it all meant or how the notebook came into my pocket.

I set the book down and picked a letter off the floor. Someone had slipped it under my door while I was out. The envelope had no stamp or return address, only my name in bold lettering. I opened it. On a sheet of paper in the same handwriting was written

You need to leave. You cannot stay here.

Immediately I knew that whoever had written the note, whether it was a threat or a warning, was right. I had to go.

By nightfall I had packed my bags and emptied my room, sliding the key under the door as I left. I was operating on adrenaline, reacting to my situation without thinking. I had planned to go straight to the train station, but instead I turned toward Clara's house. I didn't know what I would do when I got there, and spent the walk in a half daze.

When I arrived there was a light on upstairs, and I knew she was home, but I couldn't make myself knock on the door. What could I possibly say to her? I'd sealed my fate the moment I'd punched Houdini, but for Clara that wouldn't matter. She had been wrong to love me. I had let her down, but if it hadn't been this, then it would have been something else. I couldn't even explain to her why I had punched Houdini—I didn't know myself. I wished I had time to figure it out, to enumerate my failings and repair them. But whoever had warned me to leave had made it clear I was in danger. I couldn't put Clara in danger too. As long as I was around, she wasn't safe. If I really did care about her, then the only thing left for me to do was disappear. I turned away and walked the long walk to the train station.

I would vanish as completely as any man had ever done, if I could. Disappearing was all that mattered to me now.

HOUDINI

∼ 1904 ∼

MORE THAN FOUR THOUSAND PEOPLE CAME TO LONDON'S Hippodrome that day. They didn't come to see the world's most opulent theatrical building. They didn't come for the stage large enough to present a circus complete with elephants or for the grand replica ship's saloon. They came to see only one thing.

Six performers opened the bill. The audience had no interest whatsoever in them. As three o'clock drew closer their fidgeting and whispering became louder. The ushers and attendants grew nervous, and the manager wondered aloud in front of the gallery of a hundred journalists whether this was a good idea after all.

The last act finished and the stage was cleared. Onto it was carried a wooden cabinet about three feet tall and equally wide. The front was covered with a red velvet curtain. At the sight of the cabinet, the crowd cheered, startling the stage dressers and nearly causing them to drop it.

A man came onstage. He was tall and thin with a pale face, his long charcoal coat unbuttoned. His shoes were a deep black and polished to a fine luster. The man walked with the confidence affected by someone who is in fact frightened. When he spoke, his voice was surprisingly deep—he appeared more the sort of man to have a thin, reedy voice.

"Good afternoon, ladies and gentlemen." The crowd applauded with limited enthusiasm. They weren't here for this man. "Please allow me to introduce to you Mr. Harry Houdini."

All eyes focused on the wings, but Houdini did not emerge. Then the doors at the back of the Hippodrome were thrown open, their weight echoing down toward the stage, and at once the entire audience turned to see Houdini, in a black dress coat and white high-collared shirt, stride down the aisle like a marching soldier. By the time he reached the front row, everyone was standing, and their ovation lasted long after he leaped to the stage. He bowed once or twice to acknowledge them, but his trademark ebullience was not on display.

He surveyed the crowd. These people were London's finest. The past four days had been a flurry of promotion and preparation. He had barely slept.

Houdini made his introductory remarks. There was no lock that could hold him. He was Houdini, the Handcuff King. He lauded the London public for their appreciation and dared all imposters to duplicate his feats. "I am ready," he said finally, "to be manacled by the *Mirror* representative if he be present."

The man who had introduced him, the only other person on the stage, stuck out his hand. "I am Richard Kelley. I represent the *Mirror*." Houdini shook his hand and smiled at the man. Of course he had known who he was. It was all a game. He could see Bess off to the side, watching him. She was wearing black knickerbockers, which he didn't like and which she wore, he suspected, to irritate him.

They each called on the audience for a committee of citizens to ensure fair play, and one by one nearly a hundred people came forward. Once the committee was assembled, Kelley brought out the handcuffs from his coat pocket. Houdini held out his wrists and Kelley fastened them. The key itself was over six inches long, and Kelley had trouble getting it into the keyway. He had to turn it a full six times to fully lock the cuffs. Houdini closed his eyes as Kelley struggled to lock the cuffs. The man was a fool, and he was showing himself as such to the world.

When the cuffs were locked, Kelley removed the key and placed it in his inside coat pocket. He moved a few steps away from Houdini, sweating, his hand routinely darting into his coat to verify the presence of the key.

"Ladies and gentlemen," Houdini said in his loudest voice, "I am now locked up in a handcuff that took a British mechanic five years to make. I do not know whether I am going to get out of it or not, but I can assure you I am going to do my best."

The cheers were cacophonous, and while various members of the committee examined his cabinet he heard shouts of encouragement. The enthusiasm of the audience amazed and frightened him.

Once all were satisfied that his cabinet was as it appeared, he entered it and drew the curtain. The sounds from outside were somewhat muffled, but the feeling of four thousand sets of eyes trained upon the curtain was ever present.

The cabinet was a tight fit and he had to kneel. In his opinion this made his escapes seem more dramatic—a large cabinet would have given the impression that he was free to do whatever he liked and also would have admitted into the viewer's mind the possibility that it held a confederate.

He inhaled until his lungs were as full as they could be. Tonight would be the culmination of his years of hard work. He had become Houdini, the Handcuff King, had escaped from every lock put before him. He'd toured America, Europe, and Russia with top billing, made more money than he'd ever dreamed of. After this challenge he planned to return to America and buy a fine house and pour gold into his mother's apron, as he'd promised his father he would. Things with Bess would settle down too—without the demands of the road for a few months they'd be able to get back to their old selves. She'd see that he had done what had to be done to succeed, and that any dalliances along the way were not really his fault but simply a result of the pressure he was under; none of them meant anything anyway. She would forgive him everything.

Today was a nasty piece of business. Four days ago Richard Kelley had brought these damnable handcuffs to his show and asked him, onstage, to open them. He'd tried to shrug him off— they weren't regulation cuffs, and the terms of the open challenge were that he would escape from any cuffs of regulation issue.

He had good reason to insist on these terms. Months earlier in Blackburn, a man named Hodgeson had fooled him and chained him up with plugged locks. There was no key or pick on earth that could open them—once they were closed, they were unworkable. It had taken him hours to free himself, tearing chunks of flesh off in the process. The show would have been a complete disaster, if not for a file passed to him by Bess.

Kelley hadn't been deterred by his insistence on regulation cuffs. Houdini had been fettered by three other challengers, and within moments had freed himself, to everyone's delight. Kelley then asked him for a pair of the handcuffs from which he'd just escaped. Houdini had assumed that Kelley wanted to see if they were gaffed, which they weren't, so he handed him a locked pair.

Kelley took the cuffs, walked over to the stage stairs, and slammed them on the tread. The cuffs fell open. "Regulation cuffs such as these?"

The audience jeered and hissed.

"Mr. Houdini, you claim you are the Handcuff King. Yet you refuse to wear these handcuffs, the result of five years' labor by Birmingham locksmith Nathaniel Hart using good British steel and bought with British gold. Hart says no mortal man can pick this lock. If you are unwilling to try, then you are not the Handcuff King."

He was trapped. Without examining the handcuffs closer he couldn't agree to the challenge—there were a hundred ways to make a cuff unopenable. But he couldn't very well refuse. He was lost for words and happened to look into the wings. Standing with his arms crossed, a cigar drooping from his lip, was Alfred Harmsworth. Houdini recognized him as the owner of the *Daily Illustrated Mirror*.

Harmsworth nodded at him just slightly, and Houdini knew that he had to accept Kelley's challenge.

"I am sure that you and the *Daily Illustrated Mirror* will

understand that a pair of handcuffs such as these will require me to prepare myself. I therefore agree to your challenge, set for four days from now. I will do my very best to open your handcuffs, Mr. Kelley. Houdini has never yet failed."

Harmsworth was waiting for him as he came offstage. He was a tall, heavyset man with a child's face and shrewd eyes. At thirty-eight years of age he was fast becoming the most powerful man in British publishing. He'd come from poverty and understood what the masses wanted and how to give it to them. He could control what people thought, how they remembered events, how history was written.

"Scared of a pair of handcuffs, are you?"

Houdini half smiled, unsure of what Harmsworth was up to. "They're not regulation cuffs."

"No, they're not. So we're on?"

Houdini paused. Harmsworth could be a dangerous enemy. "I don't see as how you've left me any choice."

Harmsworth laughed. "No, I don't suppose I have."

Houdini said nothing. He took a coin from his pocket and began to work it back and forth in his hand, starting at his thumb and progressing to his pinky finger and then back again with increasing speed.

"This will make both of us," Harmsworth said. "The publicity will solidify the *Mirror* as the foremost paper in London and you as the foremost performer. You should be thanking me."

The song the orchestra had launched into when he entered his cabinet was one of his favorite waltzes, "On the Beautiful Blue

Danube." Houdini listened to it in the dark, with four thousand people watching. He thought about all the challenges he'd faced and met with hard work and ingenuity. And luck. He hated the idea of luck, because luck allowed for the idea of chance, and chance admitted the possibility of failure. For every way most men knew to unlock a lock Houdini knew of three. He had backup methods for his backup methods. Only by killing chance had he been able to make this life for himself.

But he also knew that circumstances largely beyond his control had contributed to his success. It was six years since he'd broken out of a police holding cell in Chicago, engaged in what he often thought of as his greatest talent—publicity. One of the officers who handcuffed him was Lieutenant Andrew Rohan, who told Houdini to leave the station and never come back. "We don't want you in our jail," he'd said.

Two weeks later Rohan came to see him with a proposition. He took him to a nondescript building that could have housed an inept accountant or an unsuccessful lawyer or a clientless tailor. Once inside, he was taken up a side staircase to a sitting room with a large fireplace and several chairs positioned around a circular table. Rohan motioned for him to sit and then left. After a few minutes the door opened again and a tall man entered, wearing a pin-striped suit and spectacles. He was clean-cut with a well-waxed mustache, and walked across the room with a casual grace and confidence.

"Good afternoon," the man said, extending his hand for Houdini to shake and then sitting opposite him. "I'm John Wilkie."

Houdini knew the name. Years ago, as a reporter for the *Chicago Tribune*, Wilkie had written an account of having witnessed the apocryphal Indian rope trick. Every magician knew it was a trick that didn't exist and had never been performed, but which the more credulous members of the public read as fact. Multiple reports of seeing such a trick soon spread across the world, and the article became an object lesson, for magicians, of what, if properly convinced, people will say, and even believe, they have seen.

"You've become a magician?"

Wilkie shook his head. "Amateur, I assure you. I have turned my attention to other areas. I am the director of the Secret Service."

Houdini was speechless. He knew that Rohan had been upset with him, but it was all part of an act. "I haven't done anything illegal. The jailbreaks were approved by the police."

Wilkie smiled. "You misunderstand, Mr. Weisz. You're not in trouble."

"It's Houdini. Harry Houdini."

"Exactly. We know all about you. Born Erik Weisz on March 24, 1874, in Budapest. Interestingly, when you came to America the spelling of your name was changed and your date of birth is recorded as April 6. Why is that?"

"I don't know. My parents changed the spelling of all our names, and the birthday must be a mistake."

"But now Ehrich Weiss has become Harry Houdini. Born in Appleton, Wisconsin, on April 6, 1874." Wilkie reached into his pocket, pulled out an American passport, and slid it across the table toward him.

Houdini had never officially changed his name or applied for a passport. "I don't understand."

"I'm disappointed, Mr. Weisz. I've been under the impression that you are exceptionally intelligent. Do you know what it is the Secret Service does?"

"Vaguely. I know you're in federal law enforcement."

"That's correct. We're the enforcement branch of the Treasury Department. We were created on the day Abraham Lincoln was shot. Counterfeiting, bank robbing, illegal gambling, that sort of thing. We also protect key government officials and visiting dignitaries. And we could use a man with your particular set of skills."

"Are you asking me to work for you?"

"In a manner of speaking, yes."

"I'm a performer. I have no intention of becoming a police officer."

"And that's exactly why you are of interest to me. I have plenty of agents. And they think like agents and have the abilities of agents. You, on the other hand, have a range of abilities that they do not possess and that are of much use in our line of work."

"I find that hard to believe."

Wilkie smiled in a way that did not entirely reassure him. "There is a fine line between an escapist and a crook. They both know how to do things that lawmen don't. Lock picking; safecracking; escaping ropes, handcuffs, and chains—all your gimmicks and tricks. Everything you do, all the techniques you employ, are skills my agents require."

"You want me to quit and become a Secret Service agent?"

"No, absolutely not. I want to help you make better use of your skills. You've been stuck for some time, Mr. Weisz. I can assist with that. In return, you can share your knowledge with me, and occasionally perform a service for your country."

Wilkie held out his hands, palms up, to show they were empty, and then he clapped them together and produced a card. Houdini was somewhat impressed. Wilkie was more adept than the average amateur. Wilkie handed him the card. It read MARTIN BECK, ORPHEUM THEATER, 3 P.M.

"I believe you are aware of Mr. Beck's reputation in your business. You have an audition tomorrow at the indicated time. I have every reason to believe he will offer you a contract for the next season's circuit at rates you will find to be very attractive. I also believe that the police in the cities you will be visiting will be happy to allow you to break out of their facilities, which should provide you very good notices in the papers. I also anticipate that you will, from time to time, find a moment or two to assist my men and to teach them some of the more pertinent tools of your trade. And if and when we need something specific, we will call."

Houdini looked again at the card. Martin Beck was the owner of one of vaudeville's largest theater consortiums. He'd been trying for years to get someone like Beck to notice him.

"You have yourself a deal, Mr. Wilkie."

"I thought as much." He stood, they shook hands again, and Wilkie walked to the door. Before opening it he turned toward Houdini. "I trust that this conversation, and our arrangement, will stay between the two of us? It is, after all, called the Secret Service for a reason."

"Of course. I have never had any trouble keeping a secret."

As things turned out, however, he would have other things to worry about than the keeping of secrets. Wilkie kept up his end of the bargain: the next day Martin Beck signed Houdini on for the year at thirty dollars a week, and before long he was one of the biggest acts in vaudeville. His jailbreaks were set up by Wilkie's men, often against the wishes of the local police officials, who had no wish for their security to be exposed. After a while, though, their reluctance dissipated. Whether it was because word had gotten around that his visits were not optional, or because they warmed to the good publicity it generated, he didn't know. What he did know was that the newspaper accounts of his jailbreaks drove the crowds into the theaters.

The arrangement worked to everyone's benefit. Whenever he did a jailbreak at a police station, he'd give the police a cursory lesson on lock picking and safecracking, and every once in a while one of Wilkie's men would turn up at a show, wanting to know some detail of how a counterfeiter was producing a bill or the various techniques of cardsharps. He often got the feeling that they already knew the answers to their questions, but it hardly seemed prudent to point out how one-sided their arrangement was. Wilkie had provided him with an opportunity. He'd made the most of it. Without his skills, without his publicity and showmanship, he'd still be performing with the California Concert Company. He, not Wilkie, had invented Houdini, and he had become Houdini so well that there was no stopping him.

One afternoon in 1901, following a show in San Francisco, Houdini was approached by three men. Two of them were sharply dressed, and he could tell immediately upon shaking their hands that they were gamblers. They introduced themselves as Simpson and Wallace, and the third man, whose hand surpassed the other two's grace and dexterity, said his name was Findlay. He stood out from the other two, saying little.

Their proposition was simple. They wanted him to help them break into a casino—not to rob it but to plant marked cards. For this they offered him a hundred dollars. Wallace, who was the shorter of the two gamblers, did most of the talking. Simpson was an oddly shaped man of average height whose arms appeared too long for his body. He'd somehow managed to trim his mustache unevenly, so that one side of it curved upward. It gave him a look of perpetual mirth.

"We've seen your show, Mr. Houdini, and we know it'd be a quick matter for you to pop open the lock and get us in," Wallace said, his voice hushed. He looked around and produced a roll of money from his pocket. Findlay stood back a few paces and made a pretense of rolling a cigarette.

Houdini looked at the money. He didn't desperately need it. "You're right, gentlemen, what you propose would present little challenge to me." He had no issue with gambling—he had himself indulged more than once, and Bess had nearly killed him in his sleep one night after he'd lost sixty dollars in a game of craps. He knew enough about casinos to know they weren't on the level, and cheating a cheater was no problem to him. He almost relished the idea. But there was something about this he didn't like. It was, for starters, breaking and entering, even if he didn't go in, and he reasoned that if he were going to turn to crime it wouldn't be with these three men.

"I'm afraid, however, I can't help you. I only wish to break out of jail cells I've voluntarily entered."

Simpson chuckled and then stopped. He looked at Wallace.

"Is it an issue of money?" Wallace asked.

"No, it's an issue of morality. I don't mind you cheating a casino; in fact I wish you luck. But I do not use my abilities for criminal pursuits." Houdini tipped his hat to the men, wished them a good day, and began the short walk back to the hotel where Bess was waiting for him. As he passed Findlay, who hadn't moved since introducing himself, Findlay raised his eyes to meet his, and it seemed to him that something menacing was conveyed between them. On his walk back to the hotel he had the feeling he was being followed, but on the three or four occasions he looked behind him he could detect nothing out of the ordinary.

Just before midnight, he received a telephone call that there was an urgent telegram from New York at the front desk for him. His first thought was that his mother had fallen ill, and he dressed and left the room without hesitation. As he rounded the corner in the hallway, however, he saw the unmistakable bewildered smile of Simpson. He felt something hard and metal press into his back.

"That's a revolver, if you're wondering," Wallace said. "We've decided you've reconsidered our proposal."

There was no sign of Findlay, but Houdini was sure he was somewhere, probably stationed as a lookout. As they descended the stairs he felt a great sense of relief pass over him—the telegram was a hoax and his mother was likely safe in bed. She missed his father, he knew. She talked about him often, as though he was still alive. "Ehrie," she might say, "your father will like this a lot." But he could see her sadness. He would tell her that he would take care of her, but even he didn't really believe it. He mourned his father as much as she did.

They moved down the stairs and through the lobby of the hotel, and Findlay fell in step beside him.

"Is the gun really necessary?" he asked Findlay, even though it was in Wallace's possession.

Findlay didn't answer him. They kept walking in silence, Findlay on one side, Simpson on the other, Wallace behind him. Houdini ran through several possible escape scenarios. Each ended with him getting shot. He decided to remain calm and see what happened. He guessed that they would take him to unlock the casino and then let him go.

"I'm wondering, do I still get the hundred dollars?"

This seemed to confuse Simpson, but it brought a slight smile to Findlay's face.

"After all the trouble you've put us to? No, I don't think so," Wallace said.

"How about fifty?"

"How about you spring open the door and I don't shoot you?"

The cable cars had stopped running, and there were few people out. A man crossed the street, his path destined to intersect with theirs, and Wallace pressed his gun into Houdini's spine, a reminder to behave. The man nodded to them as he passed, and then appeared to recognize Houdini. Findlay saw this too, and slowed his pace to put himself between the man and Houdini. Houdini couldn't see if anything happened, but Findlay returned to his side quickly and they continued their walk.

They reached the casino after about twenty minutes. They stood across the street for a few minutes while Findlay and Wallace cased things out, then motioned him toward a wooden side door, leaving Simpson on the street as lookout.

Wallace shoved him toward the door. "Open it."

Houdini took a quick look at the lock. It was a standard pin and tumbler. He could open it in under thirty seconds. He reached his hand into his inside pocket for his picks.

Wallace raised the gun at him, which startled Findlay—his hand flew into his coat with a speed and precision Houdini hadn't expected, but stopped short of drawing what he assumed was a gun.

"Easy! I'm just getting my tools. You didn't think I opened locks with my mind, did you?"

Wallace lowered his revolver, though only slightly, and Findlay regained his stony visage. Houdini took out his picks and turned back to the lock. The way Findlay had gone for his gun made him suspect that he was exceptionally dangerous. Would they kill him after he opened the door? They wouldn't risk a gunshot here, but whatever else happened, he couldn't let them take him somewhere else. He needed more time to come up with a plan for escape.

Escape. Only this time there was no trick to it. To get out of this he would have to act quickly and improvise as he went. This made him nervous as the gun was pointed at him.

"What's the deal with your man Simpson?" he asked, placing his pick into the keyway.

"Simpson?" Wallace asked.

Houdini understood that the three of them were using fake names. "It's just that compared to you two he seems a bit of an amateur."

Wallace shrugged. "He's good with cards. And every army needs soldiers."

Houdini saw Findlay raise an eyebrow at this. Findlay was

clearly the man in charge, but he was content to let Wallace believe he was running the show.

A plan began to form. He would break into the casino and lock them out. They couldn't pick the lock—that was why he was here in the first place. For once, breaking into something would save him. As long as he was inside he'd be fine. It would require a little luck for Findlay to be distracted for a half second. He would have to wait for the right moment and hope that he would know it when it came.

He worked the lock and felt it give. He turned his tension wrench a little and the lock was defeated. But he didn't turn it all the way. Findlay was watching him intently, so he pretended to be having trouble with the lock. He took his pick out and stared at it as though it contained some great secret.

"Is there a problem?" Wallace asked.

"No, it's just giving me a little more trouble than I expected. I'll have it open in a minute."

There were footsteps on the street. Houdini waited until Wallace and Findlay shifted their attention, just for an instant. He torqued open the lock, shouldered the door open, darted into the casino, turned, and slammed it shut. The lock engaged behind him, and he smiled. The men outside tried the door. When it didn't open, there was a moment of silence.

"Sorry," he heard Simpson say. "I just came to say all's clear."

"What are we going to do now?" Wallace said.

"We're done," Findlay said. It was the first time he'd spoken since he'd introduced himself.

"No," Simpson said, and then Houdini heard a gunshot. Had Findlay or Wallace shot Simpson? He looked down at his left hand and saw a red hole in the flesh between his middle and ring finger, followed by tremendous pain. They'd shot him through the door.

"Goddammit!" Wallace shouted.

He began to panic. His hands were his livelihood. A magician with a crippled hand was finished. They might as well have shot him in the face. A rage began urging him to pull open the door, grab one of their guns, and fight the three of them. Someone pushed at the door again, but it held. More silence. Had they gone?

The casino had only a few lights lit, but he could see that there was no exit wound in his hand. It appeared to be a small-caliber bullet, and it hurt like hell. He moved each of his fingers, and everything seemed to be intact. The bullet was lodged in the fleshy crevice between the knuckles on his middle and ring finger. As long as it didn't become infected he'd probably be all right.

As a feeling of relief began to set in he thought of Bess. He could have died tonight. These were men with real guns that held real bullets, and it was clear that they had little regard for his well-being. His throbbing hand was proof of that. A slight difference in the shooter's aim might well have been the end of him.

And what would have become of Bess then? Without him she would have no way of supporting herself. She would be at the mercy of the world. As would his mother. The weight of this responsibility settled onto him, making him feel more constrained than he ever had inside a trunk.

He wanted to be gone from this place, but there was nothing to do but wait. He wrapped his hand in his handkerchief and sat down on the floor. If the casino had a night watchman, he hadn't come running when the gunshot went off. It would be difficult for him to explain his presence here, if found, as he had no way of proving anything except that he had a bullet in his hand.

At around five the sun began to come up. He walked through the casino to the front door, picked the lock securing it, opened the door, and stepped out onto the street.

There was no sign of Findlay, Simpson, or Wallace. He began to make his way back to his hotel. Several times he stopped, bending down to tie his shoe, looking for anything out of the ordinary. When he reached his hotel, he took the staff staircase to his floor, raced down the hall and into his room.

Bess was asleep in a chair facing the door. There was an empty bottle of gin on the floor. When he closed the door behind him she sat up.

"Where have you been?"

"Ssh," he said, keeping an ear at the door.

"Don't you shush me. I suppose you've been with one of your women."

He turned to her. "I was kidnapped by three men who wanted me to break into a casino for them."

Bess snorted. "That's a good one."

He held out his left hand and unwrapped his handkerchief. It was crusty with blood, and his hand was swollen. It looked worse than it was, he knew. "I suppose you imagine that I've shot myself in the hand?"

Bess's contempt washed away. She rushed toward him, taking his hand gently and examining it. "Oh God. What have you got yourself involved in?"

"Just a hazard of being Houdini," he said, and told her a version of the evening's events.

"Are you okay? We need to go to the hospital."

Houdini checked his watch. They were due to catch a seven o'clock train to Portland. "No time right now. I don't think it's serious. Just a scratch. I'll go later."

Bess protested, but Houdini wouldn't hear of delaying their departure. They made the train without incident. He kept a sharp eye the whole time, half expecting to see Findlay on every corner, waiting to feel a revolver pressed up against his back. Bess could sense his nervousness.

When he arrived in Portland, a doctor saw him and removed the bullet. It seemed insignificant once it was out of his body, nothing more than a small nub of metal. They had to modify their show slightly to account for his injury, but he counted himself lucky to have escaped more or less unscathed. That night, just as he was about to go onstage, he received a telegram.

Heard you had an incident with gamblers. You handled yourself well, as suspected. I am impressed. J. E. Wilkie.

Houdini placed the telegram in his pocket and sat down. How did Wilkie know? Was he watching him? He was caught up in something he couldn't see the whole of. And what did Wilkie mean by "as suspected"? This didn't sit right with him. He resolved to keep a sharp eye on his dealings with Wilkie and his men.

He hadn't told Bess about the deal he'd struck with Wilkie. If she ever did find out, she'd be beyond angry.

Two days later, President McKinley was shot by an anarchist named Leon Czolgosz, and two days after that he died. The assassin was caught and tried, and less than two months after firing two bullets into the president's abdomen he was executed in the electric chair. The day after the execution, Wilkie came to see Houdini. He did not look at all like a man who had just failed to protect the president of the United States from a disgruntled millworker—his appearance was every bit as natty as ever. But when he spoke Houdini could detect the strain he was under through the hoarseness in his voice.

After a few moments of cursory small talk, Wilkie said, "I want you to go to Europe."

Houdini shook his head. He was playing to packed houses, and every few weeks his salary went up. There was nothing in Europe that could be better than here.

"Do you know why Czolgosz shot the president?" Wilkie didn't wait for an answer. "He was inspired by the man who shot the king of Italy. Europe is a breeding ground for revolution. Something is going to happen. I don't know what, but we need to be prepared."

"What do you propose I do about this?"

"Do what you do. Travel, break out of prisons, talk to people. The same as you do here."

"If it's the same as I do here, then why can't I just stay here?"

"Because I don't need you here." Wilkie looked at his hand. "I see you've healed just fine."

"Yes, thank you. How did you know what happened?"

Wilkie smiled. "It is my job to know. Do you see now what I mean about you having a set of skills suited to this business?"

Houdini frowned. None of this made sense. "I'm not a spy." He had been pulled into something he couldn't see the whole of, and it had put him in danger. Real danger, which was not the kind he was used to. He needed to find a way to get the upper hand.

"Yes," Wilkie said, "you are. Not in a conventional sense but in a practical sense. Magicians watch, they gather information, and they act on that information. We aren't that different, you and I. Why not work together? I have given you a career. In return, I require you to help me. I intend to guard the stability of this country by whatever means necessary."

"You gave me a career?" Houdini choked on the words.

"You have performed admirably, Ehrich. In fact, you have exceeded my every expectation. This invention of yours, this Houdini, has done well for you. But I got you your bookings, the venues for your publicity stunts, and your favorable press coverage. And what has been given can be taken away."

The *Mirror* cuffs were the most formidable pair of handcuffs Houdini had ever encountered. They were made of solid steel and contained the most advanced lock ever made. In 1784 the locksmith Joseph Bramah had conceived of a new type of lock that he proclaimed could not be picked. He was so confident that he offered a large cash prize to anyone who could defeat this lock. The prize went unclaimed until 1851, when A. C. Hobbs defeated the lock at the world's fair in London. It took him more than fifty hours, an amount of time that struck Houdini as impressive.

A Bramah lock consists of a cylindrical shaft with a shear line ring around it. At the back of the shaft is one large spring, pressing down on any number of notched sliders. A tubular key is inserted into the keyway, and grooves in the key push each slider to its correct depth, at which point a notch in the slider allows the shaft to rotate free of the shear line ring. The problem with trying to pick a Bramah lock is that because there is only one spring pressing on all of the sliders it's difficult to tell when the pick is at the correct depth. Even if it is at the right depth, holding it there while you pick the other sliders is nearly impossible. In addition to this each slider has at least one false notch.

The only method Houdini knew to pick this lock was to use an extremely thin shim of metal to figure out where the notches in the sliders were, and then through trial and error make a series of duplicate keys with each possible variation until he found the right series of grooves. This was how he suspected Hobbs did it, and it explained why it took him so long.

The *Mirror* cuffs consisted of two Bramah locks, one nestled inside the other. The inside lock had six sliders and the outside lock had seven sliders. Houdini was confident that he could pick it, but it would take hundreds of hours.

The band had finished the waltz. He couldn't place the song they were playing now, which irritated him. It wasn't half bad, and he was sure he'd heard it before. His knees were getting a bit stiff, and he shifted his weight so his blood could continue to flow to his limbs. He hadn't been in the cabinet long—about fifteen minutes. The crowd still seemed engaged. He moved the curtain slightly and heard them react with gasps and shouts. They were worked up all right. He'd better get out of this soon or they'd lynch him.

He looked down at the handcuffs on his wrists. They were

solid steel, an exact fit. There'd be no wriggling out of them. The *Mirror* cuffs were an impressive piece of workmanship. It was an extremely good thing that he wasn't wearing them.

Harmsworth had laid the whole thing out for him. The handcuffs were as advertised, more or less. It hadn't taken anyone five years to make them, and there was no such person as Nathaniel Hart, but other than that they were the most sophisticated locks Houdini had ever seen. They had been proudly displayed to a panel of professional locksmiths the day before. A selection of these men were onstage now, waiting to examine the cuffs should he escape. He doubted that any man alive other than himself could pick them, but even he couldn't pick them here in this cabinet, and not fast enough to make a good show. But the cuffs that Kelley had locked on him were a replica, held on by a simple screw mechanism. Kelley had turned the key so many times because he wasn't engaging a lock, he was setting a screw. He'd been instructed to try to disguise this fact, a clear giveaway to anyone who knew what to look for, but instead he'd emphasized it.

Houdini hadn't wanted to do it like this. He didn't mind the occasional use of gaffed cuffs, but for something this high profile—this would surely rank as one of the greatest escapes ever—he preferred a little more art. Yet Harmsworth had insisted.

He pushed at the curtain and then opened it. Everyone expected him to emerge free at this point, but it was too soon. A show had to last for a certain length of time.

"Excuse me, ladies and gentlemen. I am unfortunately not yet free. I simply desire to get a better look at these fine handcuffs—the light in my cabinet leaves much to be desired."

He caught Bess's eye. She had been testy today, or perhaps it was just his imagination. Perhaps it was he who was testy. That was the thing with Bess. It was hard to tell who started things. Once they were both wound up it didn't really matter. She winked back at him, mischievous. He imagined them together, later that night, once he had escaped. They would go for a walk along the Thames, quiet but together. Or perhaps they would stay in and order a lavish dinner, talk about what they would do when they returned home. He was too hard on her. It was an offshoot of being hard on himself, but he had no right to be this way. He would make it up to her, be better. First, however, he had an escape to perform.

Bess had been, correctly, against the idea of going to Europe.

"We have a good life," she said. "We don't need to do this. Do you not remember the last time we went to Russia?"

Wilkie's threat had stuck, though, so they finished their bookings and sailed for London. A week after arriving, Houdini received an invitation to visit Scotland Yard, ostensibly to demonstrate his abilities with their finest handcuffs. The cuffs had produced little challenge, but afterward he was taken aside by the head of the Scotland Yard's Special Branch, William Melville. Melville was a severe-looking fellow, with a trace of an Irish accent and an obvious temper. He was the walking embodiment of a policeman, hulking and muscled and intimidating. It was a hot June day but he wore his coat buttoned all the way up and didn't appear to sweat at all.

"Wilkie tells me you're good," he said. "Are you?"

THE CONFABULIST   103

Houdini tried not to appear offended. "I just gave what I thought was a convincing demonstration."

"I don't trust Wilkie."

"Neither do I."

Melville laughed. The sound he made struck Houdini as comical, but the magician kept his face serene. "Good. Then we're in agreement."

Houdini suspected he knew where Melville was headed with this talk.

"I think you'll find Her Majesty's Great Britain very different from your United States of America," Melville said.

"I can assure you I've already discovered many differences."

Melville laughed again. "I'm sure you have. Here, though, I think you'll find that doors don't just open for you, no matter how good you are with locks. You will need them opened for you."

"I can assure you that no door has ever just opened for me, sir," Houdini said. He did not like Melville's implication.

"You misunderstand me. Or possibly you don't. No matter. I am aware of your arrangement with Wilkie. I would like to engage you in a similar arrangement. You are in a unique position, Mr. Houdini. You can travel to Germany and Russia and learn things that most men I employ cannot. Wilkie knows this as well as I. We have many enemies in common, and so we have many friends in common."

"And what's in it for me?"

This time, Melville didn't laugh. "Doors, sir. Like you, I am a man who can open doors."

"What, precisely, will I be doing for you?"

"Just keep your eyes and ears open for now. Should you find yourself breaking out of any prisons on your travels, I might like to know the particulars of their layouts and weaknesses."

While touring Germany and France for the next three years, Houdini sent both Melville and Wilkie regular reports. Descriptions of prisons he escaped from, information about military barracks he toured, profiles of politicians and police officers he met. It was unclear to him of what value this information was, and he rarely received acknowledgment from either of them. He began to imagine that they had lost interest in him. His fame was growing, and soon they would no longer be able to affect his career in any way.

This changed in the fall of 1903, when a promoter contacted him with an offer to tour Russia. He wasn't particularly eager to go—he'd heard from other performers that the Russian police had a way of getting their hands in your pockets. The sheer volume of paperwork required to ship his equipment, much of which technically qualified as burglary tools, was inhibiting. But both Wilkie and Melville insisted that he go, as Russia was on the brink of war with Japan.

His fears turned out to be right. He was under surveillance by the Okhrana, the secret police, and policemen or minor officials were everywhere, looking for bribes. He did not declare his religion on his entry visa. Jews were not permitted to perform onstage in Moscow without a permit, nor was it legal for any person of Jewish descent to reside overnight in Moscow. Should the Okhrana find out he was Jewish and hadn't declared it, there'd be trouble.

Nowhere had he encountered such a juxtaposition of wealth and utter poverty. Upon his arrival in Russia he caught a glimpse of a third-class rail car, and could hardly believe what he saw. People were stacked like firewood, their faces blank and vanquished. On the other side, the patrons at the Yar, a trendy upscale restaurant in Moscow, where his show ran each night from eleven until one in the morning, redefined the word "decadence." Money rained from them. Their clothes cost more than his mother could contemplate, and he'd never seen so many jewels in one place.

The Russians were a superstitious lot. It was almost like he'd gone back a century. He was very careful not to claim supernatural powers, but after a while his denials only served to strengthen people's belief that he was some sort of holy man or mystic.

After two weeks at the Yar the Okhrana finally acted. Houdini was taken by horse carriage to the Butyrskaya Prison, where the chief of the secret police, Sergei Zubatov, was waiting for him with half a dozen of his agents.

Zubatov was a thin man of average height, a smooth face that made him look younger than he was, and a somewhat poorly kept mustache. Houdini recognized a shrewd man who saw much and revealed little. He held his body in a casual pose, but Houdini could tell Zubatov was anything but casual.

Houdini sat opposite Zubatov on the hard wooden chair provided.

"We have a problem, Mr. Houdini," said Zubatov at last in surprisingly passable English.

"We do? I've been careful to break no laws," he said.

"That's true. You have been circumspect. But your escapes are causing trouble for me."

"I'm afraid I don't understand."

"Your escapes. There are those who believe that you are some sort of wizard or a holy man. And then there are those who believe that you are an ordinary man, like them. It is the latter who are a problem for us."

Houdini said nothing—it was clear that Zubatov had an agenda.

"It is all an act, yes?"

"Yes and no. I can escape from any restraints placed upon me. I use natural means to do so, and what's seen in my act is real enough."

Zubatov shook his head. "No, that won't do. I cannot have men believing that the locks in Russia, both real and symbolic, can be opened."

Houdini shrugged. "I'm no ordinary man. I can't help what people take from my show."

Zubatov stood and motioned for him to follow. The six other Okhrana officers smiled, just a little, and Houdini knew something was up. He cursed Wilkie and Melville for forcing him to come to Russia. What did they care if he spent the rest of his life in some Russian prison or ended up dead?

He was led down a narrow corridor, Zubatov in front of him and the six officers behind. At regular intervals there was a heavy metal door with a small window in it. From one of them a harried man peered out, his eyes bloodshot and beard ragged. He called out to Houdini in Russian, his voice high and pleading. One of the officers shut the window casually, the way a person might close a window to a disturbance on the street so as to not interrupt a conversation.

At the end of the corridor a door opened onto a large enclosed courtyard. There was a gate on the far wall. Between Houdini and the gate was a small wagon. Zubatov motioned at the wagon and, for the first time, seemed excited.

"This is the Black Maria."

It was a box made of some sort of heavily tarnished metal, with a small barred window in the door. On the door was a rudimentary lock. He opened the door. The floor was lined with zinc sheeting. There was some straw on it, but aside from that the cell was empty.

Houdini bent down to tie his shoelace, considering how to proceed, then stood and faced Zubatov.

"No one stays long at Butyrskaya. This wagon transports those exiled to Siberia. Many do not survive the journey. No one has ever escaped."

"It is a formidable construction."

"Can you escape from it?"

Houdini paused. He did not doubt he could, assuming all was aboveboard. But there was something about the way Zubatov was looking at him that made him suspicious. Still, he could hardly refuse. His reputation depended on it.

"Of course. I will return tomorrow and show you. The conditions are these. The wagon will not be modified from how it appears now, and no additional locks will be used. You may search me as you would any prisoner, but the wagon will be left over there, in the corner, and the courtyard will be empty while I make my escape. My methods are my own, and I will not allow them to be observed. Is this agreeable to you?"

Zubatov smiled. He looked to Houdini like a man whose trap had just been sprung.

"I will see you tomorrow, then."

That night at the Yar there were more Okhrana agents than usual, or so it seemed to Houdini. Something was amiss.

At the end of the show there was a knock on his dressing room door. Houdini was tempted to ignore it—he was busy assembling the tools he'd need for the escape. But the knock had a tone to it that compelled him to open the door.

A tall, blond, bearded man dressed entirely in black stood in the hall. He held his hands behind his back. He motioned with his head and Houdini nodded. The man stepped into the room, his footsteps nearly silent, and Houdini closed the door.

The man's eyes swept the room, pausing on the apparatus set out on the small worktable in the corner.

"I take it you have had an interesting day, Mr. Houdini," he said in unaccented English.

"I have. But I can often say as much." Houdini sat down and began to eat an apple.

"Forgive my rudeness. I come as a friend." The man introduced himself as Viktor Grigoriev, an attaché of the Romanov family. "As you may know, the czar and czarina have, shall we say, an interest in the occult." Grigoriev sat in the chair next to Houdini.

"I do as well."

"What, may I ask, is the nature of your interest?"

Houdini considered his answer. "I'm a magician. Much of what we do appears similar to what these so-called psychics or healers or whatever you want to call them do. I've yet to see an act of the spirits that I can't explain through natural means. But there's always doubt."

"I am correct that you make no claim to powers not of this world?"

"That is correct. I can do things that are extraordinary, but they come from skill and practice."

"That is as I suspected. I'm glad to hear it." He rose from his chair. "You would do well not to trust Chief Zubatov. I would in particular not make the assumption that the locks on the transport wagon will be as you found them today."

Houdini stood and extended his hand. He had suspected as much. "Thank you."

Grigoriev shook his hand. "I will be in touch, Mr. Houdini."

Houdini was getting hot. Normally he'd be out of the cabinet by now. He was a little bored as well. Sitting still was not in his nature. He'd been in the cabinet for thirty-five minutes. He may as well enliven the show a bit. He pulled aside the curtain and shook his head.

"Please allow me to stretch my legs, ladies and gentlemen. It is rather cramped in here, and I'm not use to being contained for so long." People laughed at this, and some shouted encouragement. In general it seemed to him that people were still in good spirits. He couldn't see Harmsworth, but assumed he was happy with the proceedings. He crawled out of the cabinet.

"Mr. Kelley," he said, as loud as he could so as to be heard over the crowd, "I wonder if I might have a glass of water?"

Kelley appeared flustered, even though Houdini had told him that this was something he often did. Sometimes, if things went badly, he'd code out to Bess that he needed a particular skeleton key from his trunk. She'd put the key in the glass and he'd get it in his mouth. As long as she held her hand the right way the key was impossible to spot.

Kelley got his wits about him and nodded, and someone brought water from offstage. One of the panel members, taking his job seriously, examined the water glass. It was empty, of course. Smart man, though, Houdini thought. Any other night and he might have found something.

The man, satisfied that the glass contained only water, allowed Kelley to bring it to him.

"How you holding up, Kelley?" Houdini whispered as he took the glass in his manacled hands.

Kelley's hands shook as he released the glass. "What's taking you so long?"

"Harmsworth wants a show. And that's what I'm giving him."

Houdini drank the water in three gulps and handed Kelley back the glass. He waved to the audience and walked back to his cabinet.

"Excuse me, if you will. I must return to my work."

He knelt down and pulled the curtain closed. Something seemed wrong. The man who'd inspected his water—he'd seen him somewhere before, and not in London. He was a shadow of memory, just a flicker, a tiny sliver that dug its way into his mind. Was it his face? The way he moved? He tried to place him but failed.

This was not good. He had a number of enemies in the magic community. That was, he'd told Bess, the price of being the best. His act had spawned imitators, and he'd crushed them, even going so far as to get his brother Dash to set himself up as a rival act so that he could draw out the copycats and use the publicity from discrediting them to promote his own show. They were all freeloaders, and they knew it. They'd stop at nothing to ruin him.

His mouth tingled. His tongue felt foreign, swollen. The cabinet seemed like it was moving. He fought to stay upright and realized he was about to lose consciousness. He leaned back so he wouldn't fall face-first onto the stage, and as he passed out he saw the face of his mother as clearly as if she were in the cabinet with him, smiling as though everything would be all right.

He floated in and out of consciousness. Sometimes he was aware of where he was, and sometimes he was transported elsewhere. The most vivid of these scenes took him back a year, to the bedroom of Milla Barry, an actress and singer who was sharing the bill with him in Munich. He was getting dressed, and Milla kept asking him why he didn't leave Bess for her.

"That's not how it's going to be," he said.

Milla sat up in bed. The sheets had ended up on the floor and she was naked. "Why do you want her when you can have this?"

"Don't talk like that." He turned to look at her. She was beautiful, but he never should have become involved with her.

She smiled that coy little smile that had started all this off. "Maybe I'll just have to tell her about us."

Before he knew what was happening, he'd crossed the ten feet between them and had his right hand wrapped around her throat. His left hand was raised, and only her flinch made him realize what he was about to do. He released her and stepped back, startled.

"You won't say a thing to Bess," he said in a voice he barely recognized.

Milla got off the bed and picked up a sheet to cover herself. "You won't say a thing to Bess," he repeated.

She swallowed. "No, of course not. I was only fooling."

He watched her for a moment longer, picked his coat up off the chair, and left.

In the cabinet, eventually he was able to regain consciousness. He concentrated on his breathing, taking one slow breath and then another and then another. His legs had pins and needles and he was unbearably hot. He had to get himself out of the cabinet. His tools were in his coat pocket, but without the real cuffs he'd be found out the moment they were examined. He had to do the switch.

With great effort he moved his body left and then right and then left again, swaying back and forth until he felt some sensation return to his legs. He had to try to stand or else risk passing out again. On the other side of his thin curtain four thousand pairs of eyes were focused on him.

He pulled back the curtain and stood up, shaky and weak. Some people gasped. Others cheered until they saw him, saw the sweat running down his face, saw the cuffs still fastened around his wrists.

Kelley came up to him, obviously concerned. He considered telling him he'd just been drugged, but he didn't know if Kelley could be trusted. Drugged or not, he still needed to complete this escape or the man he'd painstakingly created would become a footnote in history.

"Ladies and gentlemen, I apologize for the delay. These handcuffs are indeed a formidable opponent. I would like at this point to remove my coat. Mr. Kelley, would you be so kind as to unlock the cuffs so that I may make myself more comfortable."

For a second he thought Kelley was going to do it. The man looked terrified. "I'm sorry, Mr. Houdini," he said in his odd baritone. "But the terms of the challenge do not allow me to take the cuffs off unless you have conceded."

"I will do no such thing!" He looked over at Bess. She could see something was wrong with him. "Houdini does not admit defeat!" This was an old code phrase of theirs. He'd only used it once before, in Blackburn with the plugged cuffs. It meant: Get help. Quick.

Houdini reached into his pocket and pulled out his pocketknife. At the same time he palmed his tools and slipped them into the front pocket of his trousers as he opened the knife. He cut at his coat from the sleeve up, tearing at his lapel with his teeth, ripping the coat. The coat was rigged to come off easily, and in a matter of moments he had, to all appearances, cut his coat off. His head was foggy and he was having a hard time standing up, but he hoped that the audience would attribute his distress to the exertion of his escape.

In his peripheral vision he saw Bess leave, walking briskly and then running. He couldn't see the man who'd examined his water anywhere.

"Mr. Kelley, I appreciate the situation you're in and want you to know that I bear you no hard feelings." He said this facing the audience—it was for their benefit. "I wonder, though, if I might have a cushion for my knees. I've been in there a while and though I am in excellent physical condition they're quite sore."

Kelley motioned to one of the stagehands. Houdini took the cushion and bowed to the audience before returning to his cabinet. As he closed the curtain his vision faltered, and again he felt his head swim. There wasn't much time.

Grigoriev had been right. Where before there was only one lock on the door on the wagon, there were now several, each of them modern and complicated. Not necessarily unpickable but more of a challenge than he'd agreed to.

Inside the prison he was taken to a room with a bare table. Zubatov was waiting there with a man who appeared to be some sort of doctor and an assembly of guards. Grigoriev was there as well, which surprised Houdini, but he decided not to let on that he knew him.

"We had an agreement that there would be no additional locks used," he said to Zubatov.

"I wouldn't think that a few extra locks would pose any impediment to a man of your skill. Am I to assume that you wish to back out?"

"No," Houdini said, "it makes no difference to me."

"And I assume you are still willing to consent to being searched?"

"Yes, of course."

He removed his jacket and shirt. Two guards held his wrists and the doctor, a spectacled man with a sharp face and narrow eyes, ran his hands through his hair, then into his ears, and then over his neck. His mouth was forced open and the doctor's fingers, ripe with the taste of stale tobacco, explored so far down his throat that he gagged.

The examination continued downward, and then his hands were forcibly held out in front of him. The doctor peered at them intently, turning them at every conceivable angle, checking the webbed skin between his fingers, then moving up his arms, pressing his thumbs hard into the flesh of his armpits.

The guards let go of his wrists but did not move away from him. Houdini removed his shoes and socks, then unbuckled his trousers and stepped out of them. The doctor performed an equally thorough search on his feet, beginning with the soles and working up his legs.

The guards at his side seized his wrists and the doctor pulled his briefs down.

"I assure you this is unnecessary," Houdini said.

Zubatov remained immobile. "Standard procedure," he said.

Whether this was standard procedure or not Houdini couldn't say, but the ensuing search was both methodical and coarse. He had anticipated it, and the fact that they would immediately notice he was circumcised, a revelation that could prove far more dangerous than being locked in a wagon. To disguise this he'd constructed a fake penis of sorts—the tip was a prosthetic, convincing to the eye, but it would probably not hold up to a detailed examination. Fortunately the doctor did not seem interested in the tip of his penis.

His wrists were released and he pulled up his briefs. It was cold but he repressed the urge to shiver.

"I assume you're satisfied that I am in possession of nothing but my wits?"

They returned to the courtyard. As they approached the wagon Houdini looked again at the additional locks, shaking his head and whistling. An officer came up behind him with a set of British handcuffs.

"Really?" Houdini said. "You're changing the game, Chief Zubatov." He extended his wrists and allowed the cuffs to be fastened. He then clambered into the wagon. The door was shut behind him and the locks engaged. A series of chains was wound around the door and additional locks fastened to these chains.

Zubatov's face appeared in the window. "One more thing, Mr. Houdini. The lock for the door is a peculiar one. To prevent escape, and to discourage attempts to free the imprisoned, there is no key to the lock here at Butyrskaya. The only key is in the possession of the prison warder in Siberia. It will take about three weeks for you to get there."

He heard laughter from the guards, and then the scuffling of their footsteps as they retreated inside the main prison building. He waited until he was satisfied they were gone and then got to work.

Three quick slams and the handcuffs popped open. The locks on the wagon door were irrelevant—he had no intention of dealing with them. He felt he could probably pick them, but there was an easier way out. Despite their attempts to search him, he had managed to get his tools inside. He reached down to his right hand and pulled off one of his fingers.

He smiled. It was amazing how similar all searches of his person were. Some were rougher than others, some looked harder than others, but once an area had been searched it was assumed irrevocably clean. Searches never made allowances for the possibility of change.

When they checked his hands, they found four fingers and a

thumb on each one. They could look forever and all they'd see was an ordinary set of hands. After they'd searched his hands, however, they'd allowed him free use of them to remove his shoes and trousers, and he'd taken advantage of this to slip his hand into his waistband where a false finger was waiting. It was, as far as misdirection goes, a fairly easy maneuver. Once the finger was in place, all he had to do was contort his hand slightly and control the angle it was viewed at and no one would be the wiser. And they never searched his hands twice.

He'd identified the wagon's weakness the day before. A quick look at the underside showed the floor was made of one-inch-thick wood planks, braced in two places. The floor was lined with zinc sheeting, not one solid piece but several strips overlapping each other. The zinc was presumably intended to aid in cleaning out the remarkable filth that would accumulate during the trip to Siberia, during which, if Zubatov was correct, the prisoner would at no time leave the wagon. But the zinc floor was the key to his escape.

In a situation like this escaping from the wagon wasn't enough. He must also be able to conceal how he got out. From inside the false finger Houdini retrieved a small metal cutter, similar to a can opener, a Gigli saw, and a small hand drill. With the metal cutter he began to slice through the zinc, cutting a square just large enough for him to fit through, the cuts in a spot where the zinc sheets overlapped. He peeled back the first layer of zinc and then, leaving an inch of overlap, cut through the second layer.

Once he'd bent back the zinc and exposed the floorboards, he put down the cutter and picked up the Gigli saw, which was essentially a garrotte with teeth. He drilled a hole in one of the corners of his hatch, then another about ten inches away. It took some skill to thread the saw down one hole and up the next, but he was practiced and patient. The wood was relatively soft. He focused on the rhythm of pulling the Gigli back and forth, and soon enough he'd cut two lines about a foot and a half long. He then cut away the short sides of the hatch. When he was done he had created a trapdoor in the wagon about eighteen inches wide and ten inches long with two inches of zinc sheeting extending beyond the wood.

In drilling the holes and sawing, he'd been careful to make sure his cuts were at an angle, so the boards wouldn't fall straight down. From there it was a simple matter of pulling up the hatch, bending the zinc so the location of his cuts would be virtually invisible, and squeezing through the hole in the floor. Once outside he reached up and moved the hatch back into place, shaking the straw he'd piled on top so that it would fall naturally across the floor of the wagon. He used the metal cutter to dig a small hole, buried the false finger and his tools, concealed the hole, and scrambled out from underneath the wagon.

Now that he was free he considered undoing the locks—they were not complex locks by any standard—but decided against it. He had escaped, and while the courtyard was empty at present there was no guarantee it would stay that way. It would be a disaster if someone were to stumble upon him picking the locks outside the wagon. Now that he was free, even if his method was detected, Zubatov wouldn't be willing to reveal it; it would seem to everyone that he was making it up.

Houdini smiled as he thought of the reaction waiting for him inside. Zubatov had seemed so smug. They would never let him publicize what he'd just done, but word would leak out nevertheless. He'd make sure of that.

The air inside the cabinet was hot and hard to breathe. His vision wobbled and his hands felt dull. From his pocket he retrieved his tools, and in less than thirty seconds he'd unscrewed the fastening mechanism on the cuffs and freed his hands. He then took his knife and cut away four inches of the stitching on the cushion. Inside was a small vial containing a phosphorescent liquid, a needle and thread, and the real *Mirror* cuffs. One shake of the vial and the cabinet was illuminated. He took the fake cuffs, placed them inside the cushion, and began to sew the seam back up. This should have taken him less than five minutes, but he was having trouble seeing straight, and he still felt as though he might pass out. After about ten minutes he succeeded in repairing the cushion.

He didn't know what was going on outside. The escape was taking far longer than it should have. He'd been in the cabinet for almost an hour, he thought, and there was a fine line between tension and boredom. His escapes offered very little for the audience to witness—it was mostly done out of their sight—and he relied on their tension to sustain the show. This was a lot to sustain, even given the frenzy they were in.

But he wasn't ready to leave the cabinet. There was more going on than he could process in his drugged state, and he didn't know who he could trust.

All magicians had to be on guard for jealous rivals. But there was something different about this. This was not the normal way that a magician would go about destroying a rival, and it was too sophisticated for a regular Joe. The common man used far blunter instruments than poison.

The man who'd inspected the water. Houdini still couldn't place him, but he had no doubt that he knew him. He had to be the one. It would be easy for him to have spiked the water. Magician or not, it would be a simple sleight of hand.

He had to decide what to do. He couldn't stay in the cabinet forever, but there was someone onstage intent on malice. Either way he was in trouble.

In reaction to Houdini's escape, Zubatov had barely said a word, just stood in the corner and chewed his lip. Grigoriev gave no indication whether he was pleased. Houdini was escorted out of the prison without fanfare and told it would be unwise if he were to in any way advertise what had happened. Zubatov's grand spectacle of the American escapist being carted off to Siberia had been so unsuccessful that it might be wise for Houdini to leave Russia.

By the time his show started at the Yar restaurant that night, it was clear that even the Okhrana couldn't keep a secret. When Houdini stepped onstage, he knew that the story had spread. His presence was met with a mixture of whispering and applause, and he could see Bess growing more and more agitated as she became aware of the crowd's fevered interest. Houdini searched the room for Okhrana agents but couldn't detect any, which was in itself suspicious. There had always been at least a few, stern men whose modest dress stood out amid the opulence.

Afterward Houdini retreated to his dressing room with Bess. They were both unnerved.

"I want to go back to America, or at least England," Bess said.

"We can't," he said. "Not now."

"What are you trying to prove?" she asked. "Why is it you need to conquer the world? We have a good life. Or we could, if you would let yourself enjoy it."

"I enjoy our life."

She shook her head and began to fold a pile of discarded clothes, even though there were people who would do this for them. "Moments, maybe. But you're never truly content. You're always thinking about what's next, what awaits you. It's as though the present doesn't exist for you. Only the past and the future. Why can't you ever stay still?"

He tried to answer her. There was a restlessness he could not contain—that his ever-expanding act could not contain, that other women could not contain—but he didn't know how to describe it to her any more than he knew how to explain Wilkie's and Melville's holds on him. Facts and feelings were jumbled as they stood there, staring at each other.

When the knock at the door sounded, his first impulse was relief—he had once again escaped. One more look at Bess, though, and he knew it had robbed him of a chance to explain himself to her, or at least to try to assure her that things were going to get better, that he would not always be this way.

The knock repeated. He recognized it as Grigoriev's and opened the door. As before, Grigoriev entered the room without saying a word. He handed an envelope to Houdini and bowed to Bess.

"Mrs. Houdini. Such a pleasure to meet you," he said.

Houdini watched Bess blush as Grigoriev kissed her hand. He didn't seem at all Russian, or at least he didn't seem like the Russians Houdini had met thus far.

Grigoriev turned to Houdini. "That was quite a display you gave Zubatov today."

"I only did what could be expected of me as an escapist."

Grigoriev laughed. "Of course you did. There's no need to be worried. Zubatov would love to have you disappear permanently, but he is no longer in a position to achieve that."

"Is that why there weren't any Okhrana agents in the audience tonight?" Bess asked.

"Oh no," Grigoriev said, shaking his head. "There were at least ten that I counted. But they were of a superior grade. No, the crème de la crème of Okhrana were here tonight. They probably still are."

"I don't understand," Houdini said.

"The Okhrana have many jobs. One of them, the most important, is protecting the royal family."

"What does the royal family have to do with this?"

"If you look in your hands, Mr. Houdini, you will see that I have come bearing an invitation to perform for Grand Duke Sergei Alexandrovich and Grand Duchess Elizabeth at Klein-michel Palace tomorrow evening. There is as well an excellent chance that the czar will be in attendance, in addition to several other members of the royal family."

Houdini tried to appear nonchalant. He had performed for royalty before. But this was a triumph for him. He imagined it would be of some interest to Wilkie and Melville as well.

"Needless to say," Grigoriev continued, "the interest the royal family has shown has eliminated any chance of Zubatov punishing you for embarrassing him. I think his days as head of the Okhrana are numbered anyway."

"Would you like a drink to celebrate, Mr. Grigoriev?" Bess asked.

"Of course, that would be fine."

Bess brought two glasses of brandy and handed one to Grigoriev, who took note that Bess didn't bring Houdini one, and paused.

"Will you be joining us in a drink?"

"No, I'm afraid I don't drink," Houdini said. "As a magician I cannot afford to dull my senses."

Grigoriev chuckled. "Fair enough. As a member of the Romanov household, I can't afford not to." He raised his glass to Bess and took a large mouthful, swallowing it without any indication whether he enjoyed it or not.

"Tomorrow night, should the czar ask you to have a drink with him, I suggest you relax your policy. As well, should the czar attempt to give you money, you would do well to decline. If you accept, the royal family will see you as a commoner, which would greatly diminish you in their eyes."

Houdini was about to protest that he was a commoner, then thought better of it.

"I must ask one thing of you, Mr. Houdini. The czar and czarina are extremely susceptible to fraudulent holy men. We have just succeeded in ridding ourselves of a man known as Philippe de Lyon, who using hypnosis convinced them that he could predict the future. Only after several incorrect and very public predictions that the czarina was pregnant with a son did we convince them that he was a charlatan. As I understand it, you do not suppose that you have mystical powers?"

Houdini smiled. "No, I do not suppose so. Everything I do is by natural means."

"So any man could do what you do if he had access to your secrets?"

"No, I don't think so. I have cultivated and mastered abilities that few men would have either the patience or talent for."

He took off one shoe and sock and removed a length of rope from his pocket. He didn't look down, stared Grigoriev straight in the eye, while the toes on his left foot tied the rope into a series of knots and then untied them.

Grigoriev clapped his hands together, almost forgetting the glass of brandy he held. "Wonderful," he said, laughing. Bess smiled as well, and Houdini put his shoe and sock back on and returned the rope to his pocket. "Best of all, I think, is that you keep a rope in your pocket." Grigoriev threw back the remainder of his glass and stood. "I'm afraid I have other matters to attend to tonight. I look forward to seeing you tomorrow. I'm sure the royal family is in for a treat."

"What on earth are we going to do for them?" Bess demanded as soon as he was gone. "We can't pack in props or any large equipment."

"Don't worry," Houdini said. "I have some ideas." He went to the desk in the corner of the room, sat, and took out some paper and a pen. Bess crossed behind him, pouring herself another drink.

"Are you writing a letter?"

"I am," he replied, not looking up, writing quickly.

"To who?"

"Mother, of course." The coded message to Wilkie was indeed addressed to his mother. He hated lying to Bess, but even more he hated how easy it was becoming, how he was able to do it almost offhandedly.

"Oh." She sat down on the far side of the room.

He thought of his mother, far away at home. He missed her. "Ehrie," she would say, "you should not have become involved with such men. No good will come of it. Do your tricks, entertain people. Be a good husband. That's what you're best at."

He put his pen down. Perhaps the letter could wait. He turned to Bess. "I was thinking we'd do some close-up, and a couple of other things I've got worked out."

"That sounds fine," she said without enthusiasm.

He thought she wasn't upset at him so much as she was worn down by the seeming futility of his endeavors. He was beginning to think there might be a fundamental flaw in his approach to life, the way he set about attaining goals that never seemed to bring him any real peace or happiness. But he wasn't sure what to do about this other than simply redouble his efforts. When he did finally succeed in a manner that satisfied him, she would also be fulfilled. He was sure of it.

The next evening a carriage brought them to Kleinmichel Palace. Houdini had spent the day preparing, and whatever mood had overtaken Bess the night before had run its course. They soon found themselves in a high-ceilinged room, surrounded by various members of the Romanov family. Grigoriev chaperoned him around the room, speaking in French or English or Russian depending on the situation and translating for him when necessary. They paused in front of a painting that he was pretty sure was a Rembrandt.

When he returned home his mother would want the whole story, as would both Wilkie and Melville, though they'd be interested in entirely different details. He noted the marble floors, polished to a high sheen, the plush Persian rugs, the ornately carved furniture. He cataloged the elaborate dresses and the pomp of the uniforms and formal wear on the men. Nearly everyone in the room was wearing diamonds, rubies, sapphires, emeralds. He had recently, at great expense, purchased for his mother a dress made for Queen Victoria. What he saw now made him feel fraudulent.

"Are you ready to begin?" Grigoriev asked him. "The czar will arrive at any moment."

Houdini swallowed.

"The royal family is divided into those who believe in these so-called holy men and spiritualists, and those who do not. Your hosts tonight, Grand Duke Sergei Alexandrovich and Grand Duchess Elizabeth, do not, while Czar Nicholas and Czarina Alexandra do."

"And how are they all related?"

Grigoriev shook his head. "It's a spider's web. The grand duke is uncle to the czar, and the grand duchess and the czarina are sisters, German princesses from the House of Hesse and granddaughters of Queen Victoria."

Grigoriev motioned toward two young men standing in the far corner. "Those handsome gentlemen are Grand Duke Dimitri, the czar's cousin, and Prince Felix Yusupov, one of the wealthiest men in Russia. They're lovers. Prince Felix has been off at Oxford, and things have been going badly between them since his return."

Houdini observed the two men, who were each surveying the room as though looking for something interesting and not finding it. They seemed like everyone else, an odd mixture of casual power and arrogance combined with a naïveté, as though they were completely unaware of the true nature of the position they occupied on this earth.

Bess was speaking with Grand Duchess Elizabeth, an extremely attractive woman of about forty. The grand duchess seemed absorbed by whatever Bess was saying. He smiled. Back when they were living in that one-room tenement in New York, would she have believed that she'd be making small talk with ranking members of the House of Romanov?

At that moment all heads turned toward the entrance. It reminded Houdini of the way a flock of birds changed direction in flight, each individual moving exactly the same way. Conversations halted midsentence.

The czar and czarina had arrived. The czar appeared somewhat younger than Houdini had expected. He wore black evening clothes with a high white collar and no visible sign of his rank. His beard was trimmed longer than was the general fashion but it suited him. His eyes were lively, and unlike some of the other men in the room he didn't look to be a complete fool. The czarina did not share her sister's good looks. While she was not exactly ugly, Houdini found her somewhat equine, though she carried herself with all of the grace befitting her upbringing.

Grand Duke Sergei and Grand Duchess Elizabeth stepped forward and bowed, and the rest of the room followed suit. Houdini joined in, and after a moment everyone rose and the music resumed.

Bess returned to his side and he took her hand. She smiled at him, and he leaned in and kissed her cheek.

"Well, my dear, it looks like it's time for us to begin."

Before the assembled crowd he went through a series of sleight-of-hand moves, some close-up magic. Then he did the Needles, inviting Grand Duchess Elizabeth to pull the needles from his hand.

Both the czar and Grigoriev were watching him intently. There was a way that people often watched a magician, where their attention was focused on his actions, trying to divine the means with which he was able to perform his feats. While Czar Nicholas was looking at him like a man who already knew a secret, Grigoriev was looking at him as though he'd just discovered one.

He had one remaining trick, and it was a good one.

"I would like, if you may permit me, to ask a favor of you all," he said in his most commanding voice. Bess began to pass slips of paper out, and then pencils. "I would like to perform an impossible task. Please write, as briefly as you can, something you would like me to do, something impossible. My dear wife will gather your suggestions when you finish."

A murmur rose. Houdini saw the grand duchess whisper into her husband's ear and smile at him, and the czar was participating as well. After a few minutes he signaled Bess to collect the slips of paper from each person and drop them in a hat.

Houdini retrieved the hat from Bess and approached the czar and czarina. He bowed.

"Your Imperial Majesty, would you be so kind as to draw one of the suggestions, at your pleasure, from the hat and read it aloud?"

The czar reached into the hat and his hand emerged with a slip of paper. He slowly unfolded it, read it to himself, and smiled.

"Mr. Houdini," he said, in lightly accented English, "I fear you've done yourself in." He showed the paper to his wife, who also smiled, and turned to the room. "Ring the bells of the Kremlin."

Houdini kept his face blank as people laughed or gasped. He let it go for a moment, then said, "I'm afraid I don't understand. What's so difficult about ringing a couple of bells?"

Grand Duchess Elizabeth spoke. "My dear Houdini, the bells of the Kremlin haven't been rung in at least a hundred years."

The czar nodded. "I would think that the ropes have long since rotted away. I'm afraid it's quite impossible."

Houdini frowned, though he knew full well that twenty years earlier the clapper from one of the bells had fallen onto a crowd of worshippers, killing nearly a hundred people, after which it had been decreed that the bells not be repaired. "Oh dear. That's too bad. Well, let's have a look anyway." He smiled at Grand Duchess Elizabeth. "Which of these windows faces the Kremlin?"

Grand Duchess Elizabeth led him to a set of large double doors which gave onto a balcony. She opened them and stepped outside. Houdini followed her, with the czar, czarina, and others close behind. The Kremlin was visible, far in the distance, illuminated by moonlight. It had begun to snow. Houdini frowned.

"This will indeed be a difficult feat. But I must try." He bowed his head in concentration and removed a handkerchief from his pocket. He waved it back and forth in the air, slowly at first, arcing his arm until his hand was above his head. He held it there, motionless, until he was sure every eye was locked onto it. Then he let the handkerchief go and the entire assembly of Russia's most powerful family watched it fall to the ground.

It lay on the floor for a second, and it seemed as if this was all that would happen. Then, muffled by the falling snow, the sound of a bell ringing could be heard, followed by another, until the clamoring of bells punched into the room.

The czar's eyes widened, his mouth half open with shock or incredulity or both. Someone cheered and people began to clap. The czar grabbed Houdini's hand and raised it in the air in triumph. Bess beamed at him, and from the other end of the world Houdini could feel his mother's pride. The czar leaned toward him, his lips close to his ear.

"I have been waiting for you, magician. Welcome to Russia."

It snowed heavily throughout the night in Moscow. In the morning Houdini sneaked out of bed, leaving Bess asleep, and went down to the lobby of the hotel to get breakfast. There were a dozen or so people in the restaurant, and he tried to determine which if any of them were Okhrana. There was no way to tell. Everyone seemed suspicious but no one stood out as exceptional. He shook his head—he was becoming paranoid.

His food had not yet arrived when Grigoriev sat down at his table without acknowledging him or asking permission. As usual he was dressed in black and his pale hair was impeccably neat.

"Well, Houdini, you're extremely fortunate you're not in jail right now," he said.

Houdini smiled. "I'm afraid I don't understand. Was last night not to your liking?"

"I don't think you do understand. You were there last night as a guest of the Grand Duke Sergei Alexandrovich. The governor-general of Moscow, the man who directly controls Chief Zubatov. The purpose of your visit was to put on a show that made the point that you do not possess magical powers. Instead you managed to convince the czar that you are some sort of wizard."

"I never told the czar I had any occult powers."

"Don't be coy with me. You know what you did." Grigoriev hailed a waiter and ordered coffee.

"I'm sorry for any trouble."

"Sorry doesn't matter. I was up most of the night attempting to convince the grand duke not to have you sent to Siberia."

Houdini took a sip of his tea. "I've already escaped from your wagon."

The waiter returned and set down the coffee. Houdini could tell that he'd misplayed this situation.

"Should it be wished that you were to be contained," Grigoriev said, ignoring the coffee, "you would be placed in the Black Maria with only five digits on each hand to help you. You're a clever man, Houdini, I give you that. When your wife palmed everyone's slips of paper I wasn't sure what you were up to. I assume all of the papers in the hat read the same thing. You're lucky the snow didn't stop you from signaling your confederate with your handkerchief. The same confederate who fired a series of gunshots at the bells of the Kremlin."

Houdini said nothing. He didn't know how Grigoriev had ascertained his secrets, but it was remarkable and frightening.

"In the end, I was unsuccessful in convincing the grand duke. The grand duchess attempted to intervene as well, also without success. Fortunately for you, as the sun rose the czar demanded an audience with the grand duke, during which he made a request that rendered the grand duke's wishes inconsequential."

"A request?"

"His Imperial Majesty wishes you to become his spiritual adviser."

Though his initial impulse was to laugh, Houdini realized at once that Grigoriev wasn't joking. But what could he possibly have to offer the czar of Russia in the way of spiritual advice? And what would happen when the czar discovered that he was a Jew and that he did not possess magical powers?

"This request has, obviously, changed the grand duke's disposition. We have been hoping for a long time to have someone of your nature advising the czar. After a series of swindlers and imposters, it would be an advantage to have you guiding Nicholas."

There was no question in Houdini's mind that he did not want to accept this offer.

"I don't think this wise. I have no ability or interest in matters of state."

"You do not need these abilities. We will tell you all you need to know."

"I have ambitions that go beyond being a servant, even to a man such as the czar. In America and Europe I'm rated as a star."

"You would be well compensated. I'm not sure you understand the gravity of the situation, Houdini. Russia is on the brink. Anarchists and leftists threaten us at every moment. They assassinated the czar's own grandfather twenty years ago. We will soon be at war with Japan. Without stable leadership and wise counsel we could lose everything."

Houdini rubbed the back of his neck. "I understand the situation. Perhaps I can help you. I will need to discuss this with my wife, and of course I will have to play out my existing engagements on the Continent. But you seem to me to be a man who can be trusted, as is Grand Duke Sergei Alexandrovich. If I can do more here for the good of the world than I can do as an entertainer, then I must consider it."

Grigoriev did not react. It was hard to tell if he believed him, and after a long silence Houdini became nervous. The waiter arrived with his breakfast, and Grigoriev stood.

"Very well. I cannot ask you to do more than consider our offer. In a few days the czar and most of the other members of the royal family will return to St. Petersburg. The grand duke will remain to fulfill his duties as governor-general of Moscow, but I will travel with the court. Please let me know your decision at your earliest convenience. I will in the meantime promise you that neither the grand duke nor Chief Zubatov will hinder your movements."

Grigoriev bowed slightly, turned, and left. His coffee remained on the table, untouched. Houdini looked at his breakfast. He'd lost his appetite.

Staying in the cabinet was not an option. The band had begun yet another song, and he could hear that even their enthusiasm was waning. He knew he was on a precipice. If he remained in the cabinet, people's minds would turn suspicious. It was now or never.

He picked up the *Mirror* cuffs and pushed the cushion to the back of the cabinet. It would be discreetly retrieved later and the dummy cuffs destroyed. That was the plan, at least. He would have to make certain it happened. He no longer knew who could be trusted.

After one last deep breath he pulled open the curtain and stumbled out onto the stage. At first it was unclear to the audience whether or not he still was contained by the cuffs, until he thrust them at Kelley. Kelley, fumbling, took them and at once dropped them. The sound of them hitting the floor ruptured the crowd's incomprehension. Four thousand people leaped to their feet and bawled their delight.

The suddenness with which Houdini emerged from the cabinet left him light-headed, and he keeled forward. The hands of the onstage committee members reached out to him and stopped him from toppling. Bess rushed toward him and arrived just as he was about to lose consciousness. She cupped his face in her hands.

"Fight it," she shouted, her voice nearly lost in the din. "I will get you backstage, but you need to hold on a bit longer."

With her help he was able to make it across the Hippodrome's vast stage and into the wings, and from there to a small dressing room. He collapsed into a chair. The crowd in the theater had begun to chant his name.

Harmsworth and Kelley rushed into the room, obviously concerned, but Bess shooed them out and shut the door.

"Someone drugged the water," he said.

Bess nodded and held out a small box of smelling salts. Houdini took it and inhaled deeply. As the sharp scent of ammonia dissipated, his head cleared a bit.

"There was a man onstage who inspected the water," he said. "Did you see him?"

"I did. He left after that." He could see she was concerned, though she was trying to hide it. He had forgotten how she did this—when he was weak, she became strong. It was one of the things he loved most about her.

"Have you seen him before?"

"No, I don't think so."

Houdini took a slow breath, then another. He felt a little better.

"You need a doctor."

"I know. But first I have to go back out there. Just give me a second."

Bess stepped back. "You can't be serious."

"They need to see I'm okay. Otherwise this was all for nothing."

She crossed her arms and then she embraced him. He took one last breath and pushed himself to his feet. He kissed her.

"You ready?" he asked.

Houdini knew they couldn't summarily leave Russia, but he had no desire to stay a moment longer than necessary. He finished his engagement at the Yar and did a few shows in neighboring cities. He knew he was being watched, and he'd had to part with a significant amount of cash to secure the passage of his baggage across the border, but neither Grigoriev nor the grand duke made any visible attempt to prevent him from leaving the country. He supposed it wasn't in their interests. They required him to be an ally, and so it only made sense that he should be free to leave. In London he received several telegrams from Grigoriev, and finally he responded.

I AM VERY SORRY. I WOULD LIKE TO BE OF SERVICE
BUT CANNOT AT THIS TIME ABANDON MY CAREER.
YOUR FRIEND, HOUDINI.

Soon after, he awoke one day to a summons from Melville to come to Scotland Yard. Melville was particularly interested in his assessment of various members of the Russian royal family. When he asked about Grand Duke Dimitri and Prince Felix Yusupov, Houdini relayed the rumor that they were lovers. Melville snorted.

"Oh, don't worry, we know all about those two. We once caught Yusupov, dressed as a woman, flirting with King Edward. But he may yet have his uses."

Houdini then told him about Grigoriev's offer.

Melville's mouth dropped open. "Are you serious?"

"Yes. I turned him down, of course."

Houdini was entirely unprepared for the force of Melville's vitriol. He leaped to his feet, unleashing a profanity-laden harangue that Houdini could barely understand.

"An opportunity to control the Crown of Russia and you say no? I've sent men to their deaths for a fraction of the information you would have seen on a daily basis."

Houdini sat still until Melville's rant had run its course. "I agreed to send you what information I could," he said, his voice low and calm. "What you ask of me is beyond what I can do and beyond the scope of our arrangement. I'm sorry."

A muscle in Melville's neck pulsed. Houdini picked up a water glass, found it empty, and set it back down.

"You are dismissed," Melville said.

Houdini rose and went to the door.

"If I were you," Melville said, "I would be very careful how I inform Wilkie about this situation. I think you will not find him as forgiving."

Houdini had the day before sent a coded letter to Wilkie, briefing him on the entire Russia trip. In the coming weeks he waited for a reply. He began a series of engagements and life returned to normal, more or less. Eventually he received a telegram.

INFORMATION RECEIVED

Nothing more. These men were beyond him, beyond what he wanted to know. He was foolish to have ever become involved with them.

He linked arms with Bess and stood in the wings, determined not to faint. The theater manager saw them and hurried over, handing Bess a note.

You work for us. Always remember that, Mr. Weisz.

"Who is *us*?" she asked.

"I don't know," he said. He knew she didn't believe him.

He squeezed her arm, smoothed his hair down, and stepped back onstage. Though it seemed impossible, the ovation grew louder. The assembly of men and women onstage reached out eagerly to shake his hand. He looked into the seats and saw a woman crying, though her face gleamed with a broad smile.

Harmsworth came up beside him and shook his hand. Houdini

grinned at him, but he had not forgotten the man who'd spiked his water. Was Harmsworth involved? It seemed unlikely. A defeated Houdini would cease to sell future papers.

"They want you to speak!" Harmsworth shouted into his ear.

Houdini stepped forward and raised his arms. The crowd became marginally quieter.

"Ladies and gentlemen," he began. Where had he seen that man? He knew him. "I entered this room feeling like a doomed man. There were times when I did not believe I could get myself out of those handcuffs."

It came to him. Like a name that's been forgotten, or a word on the tip of his tongue, the face came rushing back.

"But your applause gave me courage. It gave me the strength to do or die. These handcuffs were the hardest I've ever seen, with locks inside locks."

San Francisco. The gamblers. Houdini had seen his eyes. It was Findlay. Wilkie, the head of the Secret Service, had sent him.

"I thought this was my Waterloo, after nineteen years of hard work. I haven't slept for nights. But I will sleep tonight."

He bowed to the crowd and left the stage, leaning on Bess. It was time to return to America.

MARTIN STRAUSS

~ 1927 ~

IT WAS A LIFETIME AGO. I WAS TRYING TO OUTRUN THE
consequences of a mistake made in a moment of weakness. My days
were long, my nights were long, and the weight of what I'd done
kept finding me no matter how much I tried to hide from it. Like
any burden, however, I was beginning to learn how to bear it. Then
one night, months after I killed Houdini, everything changed.

As I lay in my boardinghouse room, sleep did not come. In-
somnia made me a bit too philosophical, and there's almost nothing
more dangerous than the combination of metaphysics and the dark.

The night wasn't anywhere near as quiet as I'd have liked.
Darkness has a way of making everything louder. There's no way
to identify the sounds coming at you. You can imagine what they
are, but it's always a guess, based on what you remember about
the world before the light went out of it.

There was the perpetual hiss of the radiator. I pulled the

blankets tight to my chin and wondered how certain I could be that what I was hearing was in fact the radiator. It sounded like the radiator. Possibly my brain was misidentifying the hiss of, say, an inland taipan, the world's most venomous snake. The stairs—can snakes do stairs?—or the Canadian winter or the double-locked door or any one of a hundred factors made it improbable I was hearing an inland taipan. But if someone had managed to plant one in a corner of the room, I would have no way of knowing what to listen for. Such were the thoughts of a man who had recently acquired a great many enemies.

I tried to calm myself. There was no way someone had placed an inland taipan in my room. I had gone to great lengths to disappear, and anyone capable of having found me would have more sense than to employ a cold-blooded reptile in winter.

My departure from Montreal had been swift; I was gone less than an hour after receiving the note warning me that I was in danger. I was surprised by both the courtesy of my potential assailant and my own sense of calm. I had been so uncertain about what would happen next that finally having a direction was a strange relief.

A car drove past my window, its tires cautious on new snow. I'd chosen my lodgings with care, one street back from a main artery. I'd be able to recognize anything out of the ordinary, but the safety of crowds was close enough. I listened to the car disappear into the night. Had it slowed down as it passed my address?

I had taken all precautions possible. There was no way for me to disappear more fully than I had, or if there was, I didn't know how to do it. I rolled onto my side and reminded myself that there is a fine line between vigilance and insanity. What I needed most was sleep.

When I was a child I hated going to sleep. Most children do, I think. It would make more sense for adults to resist sleep. As life progresses it is less and less likely that you will wake up. The more sleeps you have behind you, the fewer you have in front of you. But children, who have no need to count out their days and nights, fight the end of each day as though their lives depend on it, while adults seem almost grateful to get into bed and fall off without effort.

My mother would come and sit beside my bed whenever I was against the idea of sleep. Our deal, she said, was that as long as I lay down and kept talking to her, she would stay. This always seemed a wonderful compromise to me, but it was a rare night where more than a few minutes passed before my eyelids dropped and sleep claimed me.

This night, alone in the dark in a strange room, the thought of my mother was enough to quiet my mind, and after a few false starts where the abrupt and terrifying sensation of falling jerked me away from the precipice of sleep, I was able to rest. The myriad whisperings and rattlings of the night no longer demanded parsing.

"And how, my dear Martin, are you? What did you do today?" my mother asked me. I couldn't see her clearly—my eyes were fogged in, and after a moment I gave up trying to open them.

"I can't remember," I said.

"Nonsense. You can always remember. It might not be true, but you can always remember."

I tried to recall what I had done that day. "I listened to the radiator."

"Ah, yes. Did you know that a single bite of a radiator contains enough venom to kill a hundred men?"

I did not. Wait, this wasn't right. "I think you mean the inland taipan."

"Of course. Despite this, though, there are no recorded fatalities as a result of its bite. It's very shy. Like you."

"I'm not shy, I'm cautious."

"You are cautious. Which is why you probably have taken note that your door has been opened."

I told myself that this was just a dream, but in an instant my mother was gone and I was awake. I lay still, keeping my breathing slow and deep, and listened. I heard nothing, and then, directly to my right, between my bed and the small desk, the floor creaked. Someone was in my room.

"I know you're awake." A young woman's voice, confident and angry, careened out of the darkness.

She flicked on the light and I was blinded.

"I only want to know why you did it." The voice belonged to a young woman, maybe sixteen or seventeen. She was on the small side but clearly strong. She wore a black coat that went down to her feet, and had tied her thin black hair back with a ribbon. She wasn't dressed like a typical assassin, I thought, and then reconsidered, accounting for the fact that I had no idea what an assassin wore, aside from what I'd read in detective novels, which I was beginning to suspect were not the most reliable sources of information.

I gave her the only answer I could. "It wasn't my fault. I didn't mean for it to happen like that."

This seemed to surprise her. She didn't say anything.

"How did you get in here?"

"I picked the lock." She smiled, proud of herself.

"What's your name?"

"Alice. Alice Weiss."

"That's an interesting name," I said. Weiss. Could it be?

"I'm sorry," she said. "This isn't at all what I thought it would be like."

She pulled forward the shabby wooden chair and sat. She relaxed a little, but I could feel her tension and uncertainty. Her eyes wandered the room, settling back on me as I gathered enough courage to sit up in bed.

"How did you think it would be?" I asked.

She shook her head. "Not like this. This is all so . . ."

Neither of us spoke. The night became loud again.

"What is it you want?" I asked.

This wasn't going to plan for her. I sympathized—nothing had gone according to plan for me either. She folded her hands in her lap. "I'd like to know what happened."

She was who I suspected she was. Alice Weiss. Harry Houdini's daughter. I knew he and Bess didn't have any children, so she must have a different mother. She had tracked me down because I had killed her father. She wanted answers. I wasn't sure I could give her any.

"I don't know how to tell you what happened. It was an accident."

"I know. Everyone knows you didn't mean it." She said this like it was an insult.

"Then why are you here?"

"Because you owe me answers. You made all this happen. You ruined everything. I want you to fix it." Her head drooped and she sat still, as though checking her hands to see if they still held something important.

I didn't answer her. I couldn't. There was no insight I could offer, having never known the man. I'd killed him, that's all. If it weren't for me, then maybe she could have come to know him.

"It is a hard thing to grow up without a father," I said. "I understand that your lack of a father is my fault. I had a father, though, and it's possible you were better off. Sometimes an absent father is better."

Alice seemed to be thinking about this. I remembered how Clara used to look when deep in thought. I missed her. Being alone with your thoughts can make you forget that the world is full of people with thoughts of their own. I should not have left the way I had.

"That's what my mother told me," she said. "That my father was a good man, but what he was great at was disappearing."

"That sounds about right to me," I answered.

"Maybe it is," she said. "But he was never there to begin with. You can't disappear if you never appeared."

"What is it you want, then?"

She got up from the chair. "You could start by helping me find him," she said. For a moment it seemed as though she was going to say something else. She took one last long look at me before walking out the door. It clicked shut behind her and left me alone again, listening to the sound of the dark.

Alice's words rattled around my room for months. What did she mean? We both knew where her father was. I was the one who had put him there.

By the spring my savings had run out and I was forced to find work. I got a job on a construction site using an alias. It was hard labor but I didn't have to talk to anyone. I showed up, did my work, and went home.

Every so often I'd open the small leather book I'd found in my pocket and leaf through it. It seemed to have come into my possession the night I punched Houdini. I knew I didn't have it before then. The pages made no sense, a bunch of jumbled words with confused letters. I'd also begun to have the feeling that someone was observing me, following my every move. It was an odd feeling.

I thought about Clara a lot. Constantly. For a while when I thought about her, it was in the present tense, still existent as part of my current reality. Soon, though, that began to fade. She became part of the past, a memory, and she ceased to live in my mind as anything other than a string of moments. But there was an ache there, a physical sorrow that increased the more she passed from substance into memory. For a while I could mitigate this by retreating to memory.

There was one particular moment that I kept going back to. We were at the park, sitting on a bench, talking and watching people walk by. There were some birds milling about, hoping that we were the sort of people who brought birdseed for them, but we weren't, and eventually they figured this out and left. Clara was wearing a white cardigan and a blue dress with flowers on it. The wind kept blowing her hair into her face, but was warm enough that she took off the cardigan and put it on the bench next to her. We talked in a roundabout way about nothing in particular: school, people we knew, things we liked and didn't like. It was the sort of conversation people who haven't known each other long but understand they will have many more conversations have, uncomplicated and almost lazy but also anticipatory. Eventually we got up and began to walk out of the park, and shortly Clara realized that she had left her cardigan on the bench. I jogged to get it, only a hundred yards back, and when I returned, hand outstretched with her prize, the look on her face was full of simple pleasure. My seemingly mundane gesture made her so happy. It was a strange math, how the size of an action corresponded to the outcome. At the time it didn't seem particularly significant, but afterward this became the one moment out of all of them that I kept returning to.

Whenever my mind went too far into this line of thinking, my mother would intrude into my consciousness.

"You're scared. You're afraid there's a darkness inside you that might escape. But the hiding you're doing isn't going to help, is it?"

It wasn't, but this was the price I had to pay for my actions. I had abandoned Clara, killed Houdini, disappeared without a trace. There must be some cost to this. "It's like you said. Not everything is reversible."

"That's true," she said. "But almost everything is forgivable."

"How do you know if it is?"

"You ask."

She was right. She was always right. But I couldn't ask for Clara's forgiveness, not now. Forgiveness is earned. What had I done to earn anything? And I couldn't ask Houdini's forgiveness either. Alice, though, that might be possible. She'd asked me to try to fix things. It seemed to me she needed a memory of her father that would help her better understand herself. If I could give that to her, that might at least start me on the way back to Clara and the life I'd left.

What could I give to Clara? The only firsthand knowledge I had of Houdini was the feel of his gut as my fist sank into it. But I could find someone who knew more. That person, I realized, was Bess Houdini. If there was one person alive who understood Houdini, it was her.

Bess Houdini wasn't hard to find. Her house in Harlem was a well-known landmark, its address in the papers. In a matter of days I had quit my job, emptied my room, and made the trip to New York. I rented an equally spare and desolate room on the Lower East Side of Manhattan, paying cash and using a false name. It felt better to be doing something active, but the feeling that I was being watched didn't abate.

MARTIN STRAUSS

✺ *Present Day* ✺

AND NOW I'M ANGRY AGAIN. THIS BENCH, DR. KORSA-koff, my own mind—it all boils up. I want to hit something or scream or pick up the trash can and throw it through the automatic doors, sending pebbles of glass skittering across the lobby. I haven't been this mad in years. Not since my father died, at least. No one could make me as angry as he did.

Do we ever really get over the things that our parents do to us? There was no grand cataclysm that marked my childhood, but the sum total of it left an echo that is still here. My mother was everything gentle. She made things better, she fixed what went wrong, and she remains what I conjure when I think of goodness.

My father was not a villain, though he did villainous things. He was cold, distant, and had no time for children. At his best, he was an actor playing a father. At his usual, he was a man who endured his children. At his worst, he resented us.

He often appeared as though he wished he were elsewhere. He'd stare out the window, look at his watch, complain that we needed to go no matter where we were or where we had to be next. We were perpetually arriving early and leaving early, trying to keep up with his restless feeling that something was about to happen elsewhere. I imagine it exhausted my mother. I know it exhausted me.

Until I started to become like him, at about the age of fourteen. I ceased being a mere hindrance to him and became an adversary. A young man has options in life an older man doesn't. I would get out of our town, see the world, and do things he knew he would never do. My ambition diminished him, but I couldn't see that. Every time he reacted to me with jealousy, I redoubled my efforts to become free of him.

I should be going. There are all sorts of minor tasks I need to accomplish. I have a half-dozen books due back at the library. One of them is a new Houdini biography. I read these books on Houdini with great interest. A lot of them come remarkably close to the truth, but no one knows the story quite like me. I imagine that by now I might be the only one left alive who knows the truth, though it's possible that there are details in some archive or government file that would lead a curious investigator to the correct conclusion. Either way, as far as I know I've read every single book ever published by Houdini or about Houdini, and no one's got the whole story yet.

Aside from the obvious reason, I've stayed interested in Houdini because of his escapes. He became the world's most famous man in an era when it was hard to be world famous, because he was able to get out of the most impossible setups. Nothing could trap him. But of course this isn't true—all of his escapes were manufactured. He never really escaped because he was never really confined. It only seemed like he was.

My interest in magic has been lifelong; as a boy I was fascinated by any trick, no matter how poorly executed. My father laughed at this. He thought I was a fool, easily manipulated, but he wasn't seeing what I saw. Even with the worst of magicians I saw wonder. It didn't matter that I knew how the trick was done, or how inexpert their methods were. That wasn't the point. They made me believe there was more to the world than I was able to see. Or better, that it was possible for multiple worlds to exist at once.

An orderly in a white shirt and pants comes out the door and stops. He turns to look at me. He unnerves me. I can't tell what he's looking for. It's possible he's deciding whether to sit and maybe smoke a cigarette or eat his lunch on the empty half of my bench. He stares at me as though trying to figure out if I belong where I am. I'm afraid I can't help him, as I no longer have any clear indication of my place in the world. My head begins to hum, like a mosquito has flown into my ear.

His uniform makes him look like an ice cream man—all he needs is the little paper hat. I'd probably buy a Fudgsicle from him if he asked, but he gives me an uncomfortable feeling. I find myself hoping he doesn't come over and sit. Thankfully he seems to have completed his scrutiny of me and goes back through the doors to whatever tasks await him.

The hand is quicker than the eye. Now you see it, now you don't. This is classic magician stage patter. It's a lovely bit of misdirection, set up as a logical and provable statement. But the hand isn't quicker than the eye at all. A magician knows this. And so does our own brain.

Most of us, when trying to catch a ball, will place our hand ahead of where the ball is when we saw it. Part of this is us reacting to where we think the ball's trajectory will best intersect our hand, but we overshoot even more than that, because it takes time, about two hundred milliseconds, for the information about the ball's whereabouts to travel from our eye to our brain and then to the muscles that control our hand. Our brain knows this. It knows that by the time it's told the hand to move to the correct location, it's dealing with out-of-date information. The ball has moved. The conditions have changed. The trick is afoot.

So the brain makes an unconscious logical assumption. If it didn't, we'd be incapable of functioning within the world. That's its job. But these unconscious rationales can also make us believe the impossible.

In 1918 Harry Houdini made an elephant disappear onstage at the New York Hippodrome in front of more than five thousand people. A box about eight feet wide and high and twelve feet long was wheeled onstage. An elephant named Jennie was then led out by a trainer. The box was up off the ground on wheels, with the long side facing the audience. Jennie and her trainer walked up a ramp into the box and the doors were closed. The stagehands rotated the box a quarter turn so that the entrance was facing the audience.

Houdini stared at the box and clapped his hands. A curtain was drawn back from a circular hole in the front of the box, and the back doors were opened, allowing the audience to see right through the box. Jennie was gone, Houdini said, "In an instant."

But it wasn't an instant. It only seemed like one. In reality it took Houdini over seven minutes to make an elephant disappear.

I made Alice's father disappear by an entirely different method, but it was the same effect. We both turned something enormous into thin air. That night she first found me, she was trying to find out what her father was like. She was trying to add substance to a ghost.

I know exactly what sort of man her father was. I've told her the barest details, I've told her facts, and I've told her mechanics. But I've never given her what she really wants to know. What he was like. Why he was absent.

I can't imagine what that's like, given the almost constant presence my own parents have in my consciousness, even now, years after they've died. I didn't see my father ever again after I left home, so when I finally found out he was dead, it wasn't a shock. His ghost had been haunting me for years before he died.

When I was about sixteen, we got in a fight. I don't remember what it was about, but there was a moment when his arm was cocked, ready to backhand me across the face, but it never swung. I realized that I hadn't flinched. I stood my ground, and then I understood that I could resist him. I might not win, but he would get as good as he gave. He seemed to come to the same conclusion.

"You're not worth it," he said as he dropped his hand and walked away.

My mother sat at the table, listening to the front door slam. She'd seen the entire exchange.

For the first time in my life I felt powerful. "What a fool," I said.

My mother shook her head and got up. "You're just like him," she said, as though that wasn't a bad thing.

I remember thinking that, no, I wasn't. I was the opposite of him. And to this day, I still think that. But I can't discount the fact that my mother loved him just as much as she loved me. And I can't discount that his genes make up half my being. I just don't feel like him. But then again, I never really knew how it felt to be him—I only saw it from the outside.

The urge to resist becoming my father has dominated my adult life. When in doubt I ask myself what he would have done and I do the opposite. It's not even something I do consciously. He has infiltrated me to the core.

Once, years ago, I asked Alice what her mother had told her about her father. "One moment he was there," she said, "the kindest and gentlest man she'd ever met, and then he just disappeared. It was an illusion. He was someone else completely."

My rage is beginning to dissipate. Anger is a hard machine to maintain. It comes at the speed of light, and when it hits, it seems as though it will never leave you, but then it fades in a few exhales, and while it's never completely gone it loses its power.

I should have been more honest with Dr. Korsakoff. I have been having these false memories for a while, I know. What I don't know is what to do about them.

There are a few that keep coming, unbidden, and they seem so real. It's frightening. There is one in particular. It's early morning and I'm in bed. The room is cold, but I've kicked off the blankets. As I wake I feel the weight of someone else's arm on my chest. I turn and look, see the arm is Clara's. She's asleep and there are lines in her face from the pillow. I can smell her, a mix of laundry soap and toothpaste. She's not young anymore, but she's still beautiful. I lie there, listening to her breathe, and I am overcome with the knowledge that one day either she or I will die; only one of us will be left, alone without the other. All the air is sucked out of the room and I feel like I've been shot into the vacuum of space though I haven't moved from the bed. My sorrow is so enveloping that it's physically painful. All I can think is that this can't be right—the world could never be so cruel. Then Clara's eyes open and she smiles at me, rubs my chest, and I feel myself warm like a child in front of a woodstove. I grow calm and content. Happy.

I know this memory isn't real; I know this didn't happen. But I wish it did. If only this were how my life had turned out instead of the utter waste it has ended up being. If Dr. Korsakoff were a better doctor, if he could cure me, then maybe this false memory and the pain that comes with it would be taken away. He could even leave me with the memory if he could blunt the pain.

I don't really want to go back inside and yell at Dr. Korsakoff anymore. That feeling is gone. The sun on this bench has had some sort of effect on me. It's made me remember things that give me comfort. Real or not, they're still my memories. I would like very much to recapture the feeling I had on that picnic with my parents. If I could go into the hospital and buy a roast beef sandwich, if I could stretch out on the ground and feel the breeze and look at the clouds as I ate, feel that serene unbridled elation I remember so well, open my eyes and be next to Clara, I'd trade that for any disappearing elephant.

HOUDINI

⤙ *1918* ⤚

"THE MOST IMPORTANT THING IS NOT TO PANIC. NO MAT-
ter what happens, you must keep your wits."

Houdini paused to make sure that his point was understood.
For the last year he'd been giving American soldiers and sailors
lessons on underwater survival and general escape techniques.
It was hard to tell how much they learned—it had taken him a
lifetime to master skills he attempted to pass on to them over the
course of an afternoon. Still, he liked to think that his efforts were
saving lives.

"People drown in a sinking ship because they lose their sense
of direction. If you become disoriented you're done for. Watch
the air bubbles. They're your best clue to which way is up. Obviously, that's the way you want to swim."

The soldiers laughed nervously. There were about twenty of
them, fresh-faced and fidgeting in their crisp new uniforms.

"I did a bridge jump some years ago," he began, trying to sound as casual as possible. "I think it was in Detroit. The plan was for me to be manacled by the police, jump into the river, and escape. I've done dozens, if not hundreds, of such feats. The night before the jump was unusually cold, however, and in the morning we discovered the river had frozen over."

Some of the soldiers nodded, as though they'd been there or done something similar.

"My wife wanted me to cancel. She said it was too dangerous, and she was probably right, but I knew that if I didn't do it, they'd say I was a coward. So I had a hole chopped in the ice, which was about three inches thick, and in I jumped.

"The first part of the plan went okay. It was unbelievably cold, but I'd trained for the cold by submerging myself in baths of ice water. I got myself free of the handcuffs and leg irons easily enough, but I hadn't counted on the speed of the current. The water was dark. I had been carried past the hole and couldn't see where it was. As I ran out of air I made my way upward, where I discovered that between the ice and the surface of the water was a gap of about two inches that contained air. I was able to get myself a few breaths that way, but things were getting pretty grim.

"But I didn't panic, boys. I stayed calm. My assistants had orders to leave me submerged for five minutes, and after that they should send a diver down on a rope to look for me so that my body could be returned to my wife. After eight minutes—I gave them hell for that extra three minutes, I can tell you that—they dropped a rope into the water. The diver was in a boat above getting ready to go into the water. He probably didn't want to, cold as it was. I was still down there, breathing the air underneath the ice, looking for the hole to get out. And I saw that rope fall into the water, about twenty feet away from me. I don't know if I've ever seen a more welcome sight. I pulled myself up it just as the diver was coming down.

"So don't panic. You never know what's about to happen, and your job is to stay alive so that when an opportunity presents itself, you can take advantage of it."

He had their full attention. They'd listen to him now, and with any luck they'd remember what he told them when they needed it. He thought about the advice he was giving them. It was good advice, he knew. Maybe he should take it.

"Let's move on and look at some techniques for getting out of ropes."

Chung Ling Soo was dead. Houdini read the news in a telegram from London sent by Soo's wife, Dot. When he told Bess, she'd given him a look that could fry an egg and walked out of the room. Her reaction didn't surprise him. Despite the official explanation, he knew Chung Ling Soo's death was no accident.

Chung Ling Soo had been one of the top-drawing magicians of the last fifteen years. His show was a spectacle of what a Western audience imagined Chinese magic to be. He was billed as far away as Australia as "the Original Chinese Conjurer." Chung Ling Soo performed a dazzling array of illusions, including a bullet catch. It was a terrific trick, one that few magicians would dare risk. Even Houdini was hesitant to perform a bullet catch.

Chung Ling Soo's bullet catch was the best one around. Two audience members, preferably soldiers, would be chosen. They would each select a bullet from a box of bullets, which were then taken by Soo's assistant to two different audience members. Using a knife, these audience members scratched a mark into the bullets that they would later be able to recognize. Then two assistants dressed as Boxer soldiers would bring out the rifles. They were old-fashioned muzzle-loaders, ornately decorated and well polished. The volunteers would inspect the rifles, stare into the barrels, pull the triggers. When they were ready to pronounce the guns as real, an assistant would bring out a tin of gunpowder, pour some of it onto a tin plate, and hold a match to it. It would explode with a cloud of smoke, and all would agree that it was real gunpowder. The gunpowder was poured into the rifles. Each rifle had a ramrod housed in a tube underneath the gun's main barrel. The ramrod was removed and used to tamp the powder down with a cotton wad. The bullets were brought to the volunteers, who looked at the marks closely so that they could verify them later, and each dropped a bullet down the rifle barrel. The bullets were tamped down with another cotton wad and the ramrods placed on a table for inspection. Percussion caps were placed into the breeches and the guns were handed to the Boxer soldiers.

"Silence! Quiet for Chung Ling Soo," the assistant, a man named Kametaro, would call. He pointed to the volunteers. "You have seen the marked bullets. You have loaded them into the rifles. Now watch closely." He turned and waved a hand at the audience. "Everyone must watch very closely."

The Boxer soldiers took up a position on the left of the stage. Chung Ling Soo stood on the right of the stage. He was presented with a porcelain plate, which he gripped in his hands. Kametaro stood between them, a sword held high above his head, and addressed the crowd.

"During the Boxer Rebellion, Chung Ling Soo was sentenced to death for defying his cruel and brutal oppressors. He faced a firing squad that day many years ago in Peking, but he triumphed over their bullets. We will now see if he can do so again."

Chung Ling Soo braced himself as if against a coming train and raised the plate until it was in front of his heart. He waited until the tension in the room was almost unbearable. Then he nodded at Kametaro. Kametaro lowered his sword and the harsh crack of gunfire ricocheted through the theater. Chung Ling Soo stepped back and in one fluid motion rotated his plate down and away from him. As the echo of the gunshots faded away, the sound of the bullets rolling around the rim of the plate could be heard all the way to the back of the room.

The volunteers would be brought up to verify that the bullets in the plate bore the same marks as the ones they dropped into the rifles, and were invited to keep them as souvenirs. Chung Ling Soo would bow gracefully and the show would be over.

It was a remarkable exploit. What made it even more remarkable was that Chung Ling Soo had no more escaped the Boxer Rebellion than Houdini had been born in Appleton, Wisconsin; Chung Ling Soo wasn't even Chinese.

William Robinson had come up through vaudeville at the same time as Houdini and Bess, and they had become fast friends with Will and Dot. Both Bess and Dot were small, built like pixies, and the four of them spent many fond times together. Robinson was never able to achieve success as a magician, but as a stage assistant and builder he was possibly the best man around.

For a while, Robinson worked as an assistant for Alexander Herrmann and Harry Kellar, two of the world's finest magicians, rivals who would each periodically hire Robinson away from the other in an attempt to learn the other's secrets.

Then he vanished. It was as if he'd simply disappeared from the face of the earth. Houdini knew that William had done this before, in a way. He had been married to another woman before Dot, and they had had a daughter. William had more or less abandoned her to be raised by her grandfather when he met Dot.

Houdini told Bess about this almost offhandedly. The color drained from her face and she stared at him.

"I don't know how anyone could do that," she said. "How could you walk away from your child?" She raised her head to look at him. "But I suppose it's no surprise. He's a magician. They disappear. Isn't that right?"

He smiled, hoping she was making a joke, but she wasn't. "Not all of them," he said.

"Enough of them," she answered. "It's what happens when you believe in a mystery."

Houdini didn't know what to make of Robinson's disappearance until one day, a year later, he stumbled upon a pamphlet titled *Spirit Slate Writing and Kindred Phenomena*, written by Robinson. It was published a few months before he disappeared and contained different techniques for secret writings using invisible inks. Houdini knew immediately that it was just the sort of thing John Wilkie and William Melville would be interested in. About six months later he was walking down a street in London and passed a lithograph advertising a Chinese conjurer. He stopped, backed up, and took a closer look at the man in the picture. His old friend William Robinson had become known to the world as Chung Ling Soo.

And now he was dead. When the guns fired, Chung Ling Soo dropped the plate, fell backward, and clutched his chest in agony. His assistants stood dumbfounded. And then the man who most people had been told did not speak a word of English shouted, without a trace of an accent, "Oh my God, something's happened. Lower the curtain." The band played "God Save the King" and the crowd left, wondering what they had just witnessed. When they awoke the next morning, it was to the news that Chung Ling Soo, aka William Robinson, was dead.

Robinson had known full well how dangerous the bullet catch was. When working for Harry Kellar, there had been an incident that Kellar had been extremely fortunate to escape from without serious injury. But Robinson had, he believed, designed a nearly foolproof version of it. The marked bullets were palmed, taken backstage, and their markings duplicated. The original bullets were given to Robinson and the duplicates taken to be loaded into the muzzle of the rifle. The gunpowder was real, and the bullets did indeed enter the barrel of the gun.

When a muzzle-loading rifle is fired, the trigger causes a hammer to hit a percussion cap, directing a small explosion down a narrow hole and into the barrel of the rifle, where it ignites the gunpowder and propels the bullet out of the gun.

The conventional method for performing a bullet catch was to somehow ensure that no bullets were loaded into the gun. Robinson, however, used guns that had been modified so the percussion cap's charge was instead directed into the ramrod tube, a smaller cylinder of metal underneath the main barrel. In

Robinson's modified guns, the ramrod tube contained a second charge of gunpowder only, which when ignited would create the illusion that the gun had fired, but the tube was not large enough in diameter to accommodate a bullet. There was, as far as he knew, no way for the bullet that sat inside the gun to leave it, because there was no way for the spark from the percussion charge to reach it.

Yet Robinson was dead, shot by his own guns. Houdini did not know how it had happened, but he didn't believe it was an accident. And remembering how Wilkie had treated him after his refusal to work for the czar, he wondered whether Robinson had been working for Wilkie too.

"Tie it as tight as you can," he said. The soldier grinned and wrapped the rope around him again and tied another knot. Houdini was seated in a chair with his hands tied behind his back and his feet tied at the ankles. His students were gathered around him in a circle.

The soldier tying Houdini wrapped the long rope around his torso and secured a final knot at the back of the chair. The rest of them looked at the knots.

"So you'd agree that I'm tied up pretty well, then?" Houdini said. "Terrific. Now I want you to observe a few things. The first is how I positioned my body when the ropes were being secured. If possible, cross your hands behind your back. Flex your muscles as much as possible, but try not to have it look like that's what you're doing. You want to appear casual, but the entire time you should be doing an undetectable dance, a half inch this way, an inch that way, thinking what space you will be able to use later. Arch your back. Roll your shoulders forward. Breathe in as deeply as you can—a deep breath will increase the size of your chest. Then breathe short, shallow breaths, even while speaking, making sure you never let out all your air. When you finally empty your lungs you will be able to gain enough slack to work with."

The soldiers watched as the rope loosened around his chest.

"All you need is a little room to work with. If you are able, release your hands first. If this isn't possible, try your feet next. Always wear your shoes or boots loosely so that they can be slipped off if needed."

He wriggled his feet until his shoes came off, which allowed him to pull his ankles and feet free.

"If you're tied to a chair, that will be of some help. Usually you can break the chair, but this particular chair is US Army property, the destruction of which is a crime. So I won't do that."

He leaned forward, stood, and then tipped the chair to the side, toppling to the floor.

"Work the rope from side to side, up and down, until you have enough slack to slip out. It is particularly helpful if the rope's been tied to the chair, as that will give you a force to oppose."

The soldiers watched as Houdini slipped out of the ropes that held him to the chair. He rolled over, got his feet under him, and stood, his hands still bound behind his back.

"Now for the tricky bit. If you have crossed your arms at the wrists and the person tying you has allowed you a little slack, it's no problem to get out. Just raise your hands up toward your shoulder blades, push your chest forward, tuck in your thumbs, and slide your hands away from each other."

He turned around and the soldiers watched as his hands slithered free.

"Sometimes, though, they won't let you cross your wrists. If this is the case it will be necessary to get your hands to the front of your body."

He had the soldiers line up and one by one he tied their hands behind their backs.

"This takes some practice. You will need to lean your body forward and then, inch by inch, work your arms down and over your hips until they are behind your knees. Sit on the floor, cross your legs, and work your left arm down over the knee and withdraw your left foot, and then your right. You should then be able to untie the knot with your teeth."

He could see from their faces that they didn't think they could do it. It would be difficult for them, and painful at first. But it could save their lives.

"Before we begin, are there any questions? Just raise your hand. No? Good. Let's see who can get free first."

After the *Mirror* challenge he had phased handcuff challenges out of his act. He still used handcuffs but not as a challenge, and they weren't the focus anymore. Audiences had grown tired of them, and so had he. He'd also begun doing bridge jumps as an alternative to breaking out of jail cells. The bridge jumps could be unpleasant but the publicity was magnificent, and he didn't need Wilkie or anyone else to pave the way for him with the police anymore.

Wilkie had officially left the Treasury Department in 1908,

but was more active than ever. The US government believed that war was only a matter of time, but Wilkie's espionage activities ran counter to the country's official position of neutrality, so Wilkie had taken his operations underground. In the lead-up to the war, Houdini willingly provided intelligence to both Wilkie and Melville—he knew the insides of nearly all the prisons in Germany and Austria and provided detailed drawings of these for his masters. Since the war began he'd stayed in America, focusing on selling war bonds, entertaining the troops, and giving training sessions. He hadn't had any communication with Melville for nearly three years, and even Wilkie had left him alone the last while. He was now quite likely the most famous man on earth, and his career was beyond their reach.

Houdini added more exciting and potentially dangerous acts to his show. His first successful stage escape was the Milk Can escape. In it he would be submerged in a large milk can filled to the top with milk, or whatever else would get him some free advertising. Sometimes it was beer, though that left him stinking for days to come. A committee of audience members would be given an opportunity to inspect the can before he entered it. He'd then lower himself inside and the lid would be placed on top. The committee would then be allowed to lock the lid on, each person given a padlock to secure and the key to open it. A curtain would be lowered so that the committee and the audience couldn't see the can, and Houdini would emerge a few minutes later, dripping but unharmed. The locks securing the lid would still be fastened.

The trick wasn't as dangerous as it appeared. The locks were for show—the entire top third of the can came off. It was held in place with false rivets, which were easy enough to undo from inside. There was a bit of air available at the top of the can—the lid was slightly rounded, allowing enough air for a couple of breaths if necessary.

In 1912 he added the Water Torture Cell. In it he was hung upside down in what amounted to an oversized coffin with a see-through front. As with the Milk Can, a curtain concealed the apparatus from the audience at the key moment. An assistant would stand at the side of the stage with a fire ax as a safety feature. The key to the trick was for him to take long enough that people wondered if something had gone wrong but not too long that it was obvious in hindsight he'd been drawing it out.

One night in the fall of 1912 he was reading at home. He'd bought a four-story brownstone in Harlem, a truly magnificent house, for him and Bess and his mother. On the third floor was his study and library, with what he imagined was the world's most comprehensive collection of literature relating to magic and spiritualism. He'd had to hire a librarian to catalog it all.

For weeks after they'd first moved in, his mother would wander from room to room, not touching anything for fear it might break. "Such a house," she whispered. "I never could have imagined it."

It was late that night, just after eleven, and everyone else had gone to bed. A stack of letters on his desk awaited his reply, and numerous other tasks required his attention. He was just about to put down his book when he heard a knock at the door.

It was unusual for anyone to call this late, but his life was an unusual one. As he descended the stairs, however, whoever was outside knocked again, and he froze with four steps to go. He knew that knock.

It had been nine years since he'd seen Grigoriev. Sure enough, there he was, dressed in black, his hair and mustache impeccably trimmed.

He nodded to Houdini and looked inside. Houdini hesitated—they weren't in Russia anymore. He should shut the door and send him packing. But instead he stepped aside and motioned for him to enter.

"What an interesting door," Grigoriev said as Houdini bolted the lock.

Houdini had altered the door so that it opened on what appeared to be the hinged side. It was one of many small but intriguing modifications he'd made since moving in.

"This is a magician's house."

They exchanged cursory pleasantries, Houdini took Grigoriev's coat, and they went into the sitting room. Houdini brought Grigoriev a glass of wine, and water for himself. Grigoriev sipped his wine and took in his surroundings.

"My wife decorated this room," Houdini said.

"She has excellent taste." Grigoriev picked at a speck of lint on his sleeve and placed his glass on the side table. He looked directly at Houdini.

"I need your help."

Houdini stared back at him. "I cannot come to Russia. I cannot advise the czar on matters of the spirit."

Grigoriev shook his head. "I'm afraid that even if you wished to do so it is no longer possible. The swindler who has taken that position will be the ruin of us all."

Houdini sat back. He'd heard the man's name mentioned by a few magicians. Their opinion was that he was of questionable ability.

"Grigory Rasputin poses as a holy man and a healer, but I believe, as do others, that he is interested only in power."

In 1905 Grand Duke Sergei Alexandrovich Romanov had been assassinated on his way to the Kremlin. His head was blown off his body. Grand Duchess Elizabeth had renounced her titles and worldly possessions and entered a convent.

"And who are you working for now?" Houdini asked.

"I am under the employ of Grand Duke Alexander. His daughter, Irina, is married to Prince Felix Yusupov. Perhaps you remember him. But there are others in the Romanov family who feel the same as Grand Duke Sergei did. I represent them all."

Houdini smiled. He remembered Felix Yusupov and Grand Duke Dimitri at Kleinmichel Palace. His smile faded when he realized that he was on the verge of being drawn back into a sphere of intrigue he had no desire to inhabit.

"I'm afraid I can't help you," he said.

Grigoriev said nothing. He retrieved his wineglass, then set it back down. When he spoke again, his voice was quiet. "I give you my word that nothing you tell me will make its way to either Wilkie or Melville."

Houdini was unable to prevent a look of surprise.

"You must remember that we are all technically allies," Grigoriev said. "Melville has long-standing ties in Russia with the Okhrana. No one likes Wilkie, but the anarchists who killed President McKinley also killed Czar Alexander II and tried to kill Queen Victoria. It behooves them to work together on occasion."

"How did you know I was working for them?"

"How is it you think a Jew got into Russia undetected? My meeting you was no coincidence, Mr. Houdini. It was my job."

Houdini took a long sip of his water. Grigoriev was risking much with what he had just revealed. Wilkie wouldn't be pleased with this conversation.

"What do you want from me?"

"I need to expose Rasputin. Many people do not give him enough credit. He has been exceptionally difficult to trap in deceit."

Houdini considered Grigoriev's proposal. Rasputin was trading on the czarina's worry for her son, using her fear and desire to gain power. This was far worse than what he had done to Harold Osbourne that night in Garnett, Kansas.

"I'll help you as best I can. Tell me everything you can about him."

By the end of the day Houdini had managed to teach the recruits enough that they at least stood a chance if they ended up in the water or were captured. That night he sat in his study and read a letter from Harry Kellar, Robinson's former employer.

Please, Houdini, listen to your old friend Kellar who loves you as his own son and don't do it.

These were the final words of his letter. Houdini set the paper down and picked up a gun. It was a percussion lock muzzle-loader, an ornate but outdated firearm with an ivory-inlaid stock. He turned it over in his hands, running his fingers along the polished wood of the stock and the cold smooth steel of the barrel.

The gun had been modified for the bullet catch in the exact manner as William Robinson had altered his rifles. Houdini had tested the gun dozens of times in the past week and could detect no flaw in the system. It should have been foolproof.

A great many magicians had begun to work for the government beginning in 1916. As Wilkie had known all along, the skills of a magician and the skills of a spy were nearly identical. Through the Society of American Magicians, Houdini had, against his better judgment, actively recruited a number of magicians into service at the command of Wilkie. Most of them were involved in training troops, code breaking, and rather mundane deceptions, but some of them did the sort of work he had done for men like Wilkie and Melville. Harry Kellar wasn't one of them, but very little happened without Kellar's knowing about it.

And now this letter from Kellar. Houdini set down the gun and picked the letter back up. It read as a warning and it was, but not exactly as it appeared. It was a coded answer to his coded message. And its message was clear. William Robinson, aka Chung Ling Soo, had been murdered.

Grigoriev and Houdini talked all night. At dawn Houdini went upstairs and retrieved an armload of books. They contained all the information Grigoriev would require. Almost every trick, illusion, technique, and principle had been exhaustively described in some book or other, dating back nearly a hundred years. If a person was willing to go to the effort and expense, there were very few actual secrets out there. Grigoriev was willing to do the work, and he was obviously clever.

When morning came and Grigoriev left, Houdini went upstairs and slept for four hours, waking at ten. When he went downstairs his mother, Cecilia, was still not out of bed.

"She's not well," Bess said to him.

Houdini smiled. "She's fine. She's getting a little older, and she's learned to rest more. It's a good thing."

But it was not a good thing, and over the coming months her health deteriorated even more. Bess tried to look after her, but Cecilia wouldn't hear of it. "It is I who should be looking after you, dear girl. You and Ehrie have given me so much." She eventually allowed Houdini to hire a girl to help her, and he consulted every doctor he could find, but they all told him the same thing. She was seventy-two and had persistent stomach problems. Her hard life was catching up with her. "Pfft," she would say to them. "My life has not been hard."

Houdini had accepted a booking in Europe, during which he would perform a show for the king of Sweden and the Danish royal family. He delayed it as much as possible but eventually couldn't put it off any longer.

The morning of his departure his mother was uncharacteristically somber.

"My feet are cold. They're always cold," she said.

Houdini took her feet in his hands and rubbed as much warmth into them as he could. "I'll buy you a pair of the finest slippers in Europe."

"You're a good boy. You've always been a good boy. Even when you weren't."

Houdini hired an extra car to take Cecilia and other assorted family members to the pier from where his ship was departing.

He repeatedly boarded and then left the boat so as to give her one more kiss, until she finally told him to stay on the ship.

"You hear that, everyone? My own mother tells me to go!"

Those nearby laughed, and his mother blushed. "Ehrie! What did you tell them?" Despite being in America for more than thirty-five years, she had never learned English.

Houdini ran back up the gangplank, and then tossed his mother one of the streamers that were flying from the ship. "Hold on, Mother," he cried, and for the first time in years felt almost like a child.

His brother Dash caught the other end of the streamer and handed it to her. "Size six. Don't forget!" They both held on until the ship pulled away and the streamer broke in two.

He arrived in Hamburg eight days later and took a train to Copenhagen. He barely had time to check into his hotel and then rush to the theater. Bess stayed behind, tired from the journey. Before he went onstage, an assistant handed him a telegram but he was too busy to deal with it and put it in his pocket.

At the reception following the show he began to feel feverish and light-headed. He excused himself and went to the wash-room to splash some cold water on his face; he decided it was best if he left as soon as possible. He had just returned to the reception when he remembered the telegram. He opened it and read the contents. The world went black.

When he awoke he was on the floor with people crowded around him. His head throbbed and his throat felt like he'd ac-tually swallowed needles. For a brief instant he forgot the con-tents of the telegram. Then he remembered.

"My dear mother. Poor Mama." Tears coursed down his cheeks, and he resisted all attempts to help him up.

The telegram was from his brother Dash. He could not believe it. It seemed impossible. She was not a young woman, he knew that, but the idea of a world that did not have his mother in it was unfathomable. How could this be?

He didn't say another word, just lay on the floor crying. One by one people left the room, and still he didn't move. He saw his mother baking pies in their house in Appleton when he was a boy. He saw her in the house in Harlem, smiling as he showed it to her for the first time. And he saw her holding one end of a paper streamer, connected to him by the thinnest of strands, disappearing into the distance.

Bess sat down on the floor beside him. Someone must have sent for her. She didn't say anything for a while. He stared at the ceiling and she smoothed his hair off his forehead.

"What am I going to do now?" he asked her.

She stood up and reached down to take his hand. "Let's go home."

"I can't get up."

Bess tried to pull him to his feet but couldn't. She rushed out of the room and returned with help, and it took two men to help him up. With their assistance he made it to a waiting car, and then to his hotel. He collapsed into bed and a doctor was sent for. Houdini passed in and out of consciousness, waking to fits of wracking pain. He couldn't tell how much was grief and how much was physical. Maybe they were the same thing.

"Wire Dash," he called to Bess, his voice weak and rasping. "Tell him not to bury Mama until I can come home."

At some point the doctor arrived and examined him. "He needs to be hospitalized," he heard the doctor say from the other room. He had passed out again during the examination.

"Absolutely not. I need to return home at once."

Bess closed the door. He couldn't make out their words, but he could tell that the conversation was heated. There was a tone to Bess's voice that he recognized. She was strong when she needed to be, stronger than he. He wondered when he had forgotten that.

The door opened and Bess came in. She sat on the edge of the bed and took his hand. "He says you have chronic kidney disease."

Houdini smirked. "If I had a nickel for every doctor who has told me I was sick or injured we could've retired years ago."

"Get out of bed."

He knew he couldn't do it, and so did she.

"We're going home. A doctor will accompany us, and you will do exactly as he says. I've taken care of everything."

Bess lay down beside him and he listened to her breathing. He thought about his mother, whom he would never see or talk to again.

"I wish I were someone's mother," Bess said.

They had not spoken of this in a long time.

"You'd have been a terrific mother," he said. But was this true? He loved her, but she could be difficult, she could be irrational. Bess would not have been a bad mother, he thought, but maybe she would not have been a good one either.

And what of him as a father? He was no better than Bess. He knew he was arrogant, quick to anger, impulsive, and selfish. That didn't necessarily mean he was a bad person or would be a bad father. But there was something deeper. At times he didn't know what parts of him were real and what parts of him had been made up in order to become Harry Houdini.

"Maybe it's not too late," Bess said. "Maybe we could still adopt a child."

He barely heard her. The one person who fully understood him was dead. He closed his eyes and hoped he would not dream that night.

The next day he was well enough to stand, and he had Bess take him to the finest shop in Copenhagen before their ship left. He bought a pair of lamb's-wool slippers, size six. Back in New York, ten days later, he went straight home where his mother lay in the parlor, dressed for burial, looking more peaceful than he'd ever seen her. He removed her shoes and placed the slippers on her feet. He then sat in a chair at the foot of her coffin and did not budge until the next day when they buried her next to his father.

"Go ahead, shoot me."

Bess stood fifteen feet from him with the gun pointed at his chest. Houdini had his hands cuffed in front of him and a blindfold on.

"I don't want to." Bess stepped forward and lowered the gun.

"Don't worry. It'll be fine."

"No, it won't. Don't talk to me like I don't understand why you're doing this. Don't treat me like I'm falling for your act."

A little light shone through his blindfold, but he couldn't see much. They were on the stage of the New York Hippodrome, rehearsing for that night's show. He'd had the house cleared, demanding secrecy, and it was strange to be alone with Bess in this cavernous room that was usually humming with activity. She was right. It was all an act. William Robinson was a great actor playing a great magician. When he had performed as himself, he was wooden. But as Chung Ling Soo he was graceful, funny, magnificent, without ever speaking a word.

"I've checked and double-checked everything," he said to Bess. "You know how the trick works. It's safe. It's safer than most of the other things I do."

"I don't care."

"Pull the trigger."

"No."

"Please, Bess. I can get one of the assistants to do it, but you're the only one I trust completely."

"Do you? That's great. Lucky me. Here's the thing, though— I don't trust you completely."

Houdini pulled off the blindfold and slammed the handcuffs against his leg, where a piece of lead was sewn into the fabric of his trousers. They clattered to the floor. He took the gun from Bess, pointed it at the footlights, and fired. Bess yelped, flinching, and he dropped the gun onto the ground.

"I'm sorry," he said. He had resolved to control his temper better, especially around Bess, and once again he'd failed.

"You're always sorry, and I don't care."

Bess turned around and slowly walked off the stage. Houdini picked up the gun and turned it over in his hands. The bullet was still loaded, just as he knew it would be.

. . .

In the weeks following his mother's death he could barely function. He stayed home and didn't receive visitors. Some days he read in his library, and more and more he found himself drawn to the volumes on spiritualism. He felt his mother's absence as a clutching yearning. He began to wonder if it was possible he had been wrong. He knew that everything the so-called mediums did could be replicated by an even half-competent magician, but that didn't necessarily invalidate their claims. Was it possible he could speak to his mother again?

He resolved to make an appointment with a reputed medium named Kenneth Gaston. He dyed his hair gray and put on glasses and a false mustache. It was a disguise he'd used before, and he was certain he wouldn't be recognized.

Kenneth Gaston held his séances in a well-appointed house in New Jersey. Houdini waited in a drawing room with six other people, two men and four women. He caught each of them sizing him up when they thought he wasn't looking. Two of them once attempted to engage him in conversation, but he refused to say much beyond giving them a name, Erik, and saying he had come from New York.

A servant let them into a room with eight chairs set around a table. Thick black velvet curtains hung over the windows and a heavy rug covered the floor. Once they were seated Gaston entered the room from a different doorway. He was overweight, sweating profusely, and held a handkerchief that he used to mop his forehead. He had a pencil-thin mustache and a glowing bald spot on the top of his head that he had tried to disguise with an unfortunate hairstyle.

He waddled to the round table, his maw contorted into a wide smile, and pulled out a chair. It had a pillow that he had to grip to stop it from sliding to the floor.

"Good afternoon, my friends. Let us hope that the spirits are feeling talkative today." Gaston smelled of smoked fish and cheap perfume.

Houdini stood up.

"Sir! Please take a seat."

He shook his head. "You're a goddamned maggot," he said, and walked out.

It was the cushion. None of the other chairs had one. The others had steered him away from it because it was Gaston's chair—the cushion was for his fat ass. And they knew it. So it was a simple confederate scheme. They'd have gone around the room, starting with others who'd have amazing and enlightening experiences, which would make the rube feel comfortable about giving up information that would allow the medium to give a false reading.

He was enraged, and this rage stayed with him for weeks, alongside his grief. After a while the two felt similar to him, twin encumbrances he could not shake.

He returned to a semblance of his life. He began a tour of Germany and Europe, but that had to be cut short when the war began. On the ship back to America he performed a mock séance for Theodore Roosevelt, who came to Houdini privately the next day.

"Tell me, man to man, was what you did last night genuine?"

Houdini was shocked that a man of Roosevelt's stature, a

man of science, a man who had risen to be president of the United States, had been fooled by parlor tricks.

"It was pure hocus-pocus. If there is such a thing as genuine spiritualism, I have never seen it."

In the summer of 1916 he received a visit from a pair of plainclothes policemen who showed him a card with John Wilkie's name on it and requested he accompany them. They drove in silence to a restaurant in midtown, where he was taken into a back room. Wilkie was already there, looking older but still more like an unfriendly librarian than a spymaster. Seated beside him was a clean-shaven man, muscular and balding, with a sour look on his face.

"Hello, Ehrich. Have a seat." Wilkie pushed out the chair opposite him with his foot. "This is John Scale. He's one of Melville's."

Scale didn't extend his hand, merely nodded at Houdini. He nodded back, and was aware that Scale was studying him.

"I would have thought that our neutrality in the war had ended your association with Melville," Houdini said.

Wilkie smiled. "Glad to see you haven't lost your sense of humor. Mr. Scale is about to be assigned to St. Petersburg. We're having a bit of a problem with your friend Rasputin."

"I've never met the man. We're not friends."

"That's good news for you," Scale said. He had an upper-class accent, which was out of place with his working-class appearance. "What about Viktor Grigoriev?"

"You know we're acquainted. It was you and Melville who arranged it."

Wilkie held up a hand. "I'm not interested in squabbling,

Mr. Scale. Ehrich, we suspect that Rasputin is working on behalf of German interests. His influence on the czar and czarina is undermining Russia's involvement in the war. If it keeps up there will be revolution, and without Russia it will be very difficult for us to stay out of the war."

Houdini said nothing. Grigoriev had clearly failed to expose Rasputin as a fraud. But Houdini could not be held accountable for Russia's involvement in a world war. That simply was not in his control.

Wilkie continued. "We know that Grigoriev visited you four years ago. He asked you to help him and you refused."

"I did no such thing. He asked me for information and I gave it to him."

Scale and Wilkie exchanged a look of surprise. "You mean he didn't ask you to come to Russia and debunk Rasputin?" Scale spit when he said this, spraying the table. Wilkie pretended not to notice.

"No. Nor would I have accepted."

"When you were in Russia, did you make the acquaintance of a Prince Felix Yusupov?" Wilkie asked.

"Very briefly."

"And what did you make of him?"

"I didn't make much of him. He was a bit of a dandy."

"Could he pull off a murder?"

"Maybe. I doubt it. Who's he killed?"

"No one." He waited. "We have an operation about to be put into place. Should it be successful, I anticipate Grigoriev will again offer you a post advising the czar. This time, refusal is not an option."

"Are you threatening me?"

"No, of course not. I am surprised at your lack of gratitude for all the help I gave you, but perhaps I shouldn't be. Your ego has become the stuff of legend. Either way, this is the sort of request that one does not turn down, not if you consider yourself a patriot. I will remind you that I am an extremely powerful man. It would not be prudent to make an enemy of me."

"Sounds like a threat to me," Houdini said.

Wilkie smiled. "I suppose it is. But we would not be in this position were it not for you." Both men stood up. "We'll be in touch, Ehrich. Stay close."

A few weeks later he opened his morning paper and read of Rasputin's murder. They'd pinned it on Yusupov and Grand Duke Dimitri, but Houdini felt sure those two hadn't killed anyone. Grigoriev sent a cable two weeks later. Houdini waited as long as he could before he wired back his acceptance. He would embark immediately for Russia.

Bess did not want to go. He couldn't blame her. He told her that the czar had requested him, that they would be paid better than ever in their lives. For a week she barely spoke to him and he desperately wished he could tell her the truth. It was for her own good that he refrained: to keep her innocent was to keep her safe. If the price for that was her anger and disapproval, then so be it.

On the morning his ship was scheduled to depart he said good-bye to Dash and drove to the docks with Bess. They loaded their luggage and went aboard an alarmingly small ship. After three hours the ship hadn't left. Then he saw the crew unloading their baggage. The captain came up to him, a grim look on his face.

"Problems with the ship?" Houdini asked, trying to hide his glee.

The captain shook his head. "No. Trip's canceled."

"Canceled?"

"The czar's abdicated. I just got the word. We're not going anywhere."

As Houdini and Bess drove back to Harlem, New York seemed to him about the greatest place on earth. He may not have believed in luck, but fortune had favored him that day. A month later America declared war on Germany.

Houdini followed Bess backstage through the winding halls of the Hippodrome. When he got to their dressing room, the door was closed. He paused for a moment. Perhaps doing a bullet catch was a bad idea. Part of him wanted to do it as a tribute to his friend Robinson, and part of him was hoping to draw out his murderer. But Kellar might be right. Bess might be right.

He threw his hat into the room and waited. Nothing happened. When he entered, Bess wasn't there. Seated in the corner, looking so disheveled that it took Houdini a moment to recognize him, was Grigoriev. He hadn't seen him in more than four years. His hair was long and dirty, and his beard had not been trimmed.

"Hello, old friend." He tossed Houdini his hat.

"Where's Bess?"

"I advised her to take a taxi home. She is fine."

Houdini closed the door and sat, keeping the gun on his lap.

"You won't need that, not with me at any rate."

"It's a prop."

"Well, you might want to consider getting a real one." Grigoriev lit a cigarette. "Do you remember when we first met? In a dressing room not very different from this one at the Yar."

Houdini didn't answer. It seemed to him that it was a rhetorical question.

"They're all gone now. All that's gone."

"What do you mean?"

"The czar, the czarina, their children, Grand Duchess Elizabeth, most of the rest of the Romanov family, they're all dead. Shot, thrown down a mine shaft, they're all dead."

"I'm sorry."

"And we're next."

"What do you mean?" His fingers tightened around the gun, even if it was incapable of firing a live round.

"I've come with a warning. They're cleaning up after the Rasputin affair. Everyone who knew about it is in danger. Your friend Robinson knew about it. He might have even had a hand in planning it. That's why he was killed. There are others who've been eliminated as well. We're not safe."

"Wilkie's having people killed?"

Grigoriev shook his head. "Not Wilkie. Melville. It was his man Scale and another named Raynor who shot Rasputin. Yusupov met them while at Oxford. But Melville didn't have approval from his superiors. If they find out it was him, he's sunk."

Houdini thought about this. If Melville had indeed assassinated the czar's adviser without clearance from his masters, there would be a heavy price to pay.

"You were involved?"

"Of course. I'd have preferred to have done it without violence, but I had no choice. We should have acted earlier. It was too late to make any difference."

"What will you do now?"

"I don't know. I am in exile. I have lost everything."

Houdini crossed the room and opened a trunk that belonged to Bess. It had a false bottom, inside of which was a bottle of gin. She didn't know he knew about it. He poured Grigoriev a glass and gave it to him.

"Why have you come here?"

Grigoriev drank the gin in one gulp and coughed. "Because the last time I asked you for help, you gave it. I felt obliged to warn you about Melville."

"Surely he can't touch us here without Wilkie's permission."

"He can. It wouldn't surprise me if Wilkie's on the same list we are."

Houdini leaned back in his chair. He needed to get Bess out of danger. He couldn't cancel that night's show. It would arouse too much suspicion and ruin him with the Hippodrome as well. But this was his last scheduled engagement for a week. He had time to get out of town.

"What will you do?" Grigoriev asked him.

"I don't know. I'll figure something out."

. . .

A few hours later, when he took to the stage, he was nervous. If Melville could get to Robinson, then he could get to him too. And if Melville was using magicians' acts as an instrument of death, there was no magician on earth whose act contained as much danger as Houdini's.

The first part of the program went without incident. After he was finished with the close-up magic, he did the Milk Can and then a straitjacket escape. The elephant vanish was last on the bill. Before that was the Water Torture Cell. If tampered with it could easily be fatal. To tamper with it, however, a man would have to know how it was done, and fewer than a half-dozen people alive knew the secret.

His team of assistants brought the cabinet onstage as he invited a committee to inspect the apparatus. A dozen men climbed onto the stage and examined the cabinet. He watched each of them closely, but saw nothing unusual. He launched into his usual patter and the cabinet was filled with water. The stocks were lowered and his ankles were locked into them. As his assistants pulled the ropes that would hoist him aloft, he noticed one of the committee men touching his mustache, as though he was pushing it back onto his face. He lost sight of the man as he was hoisted upside down.

Should he stop the trick? He hadn't really seen anything that he could justify to the audience. But his gut told him something was wrong.

They lowered him into the water, and the locks were fastened. The lid of the cabinet had two holes that secured his ankles, and was split through the middle of each hole and hinged on one side to open, forming a set of stocks. On the side opposite the hinge was a legitimate lock.

The lock that fastened the lid to the cabinet, however, was a gimmicked lock. When a normal lock's key is turned it does one thing—engage the bolt. This lock did that, but it also simultaneously disengaged a second bolt that allowed the rear half of the stocks to slide backward, giving him enough room to free his feet and push himself up and out of the cabinet. It was simple and foolproof; if the lid was locked on, then the stocks had to be unlocked.

As the curtains were drawn around the cabinet, he caught another glimpse of the man who had been fiddling with his mustache. The man turned to him, his mustache gone, and looked into his eyes. He hadn't seen him in over a decade, but there was no doubt: it was Wilkie's man Findlay, who had poisoned him during the *Mirror* cuff escape and who had kidnapped him all those years ago in San Francisco.

Houdini did what he'd told his recruits never to do. He panicked. The air went out of him and he nearly swallowed a lungful of water. The blood in his head pounded like an executioner's drum, and his arms flailed.

Without thinking—he had lost his reason at this point—his legs kicked the stocks back. He'd done the upside down so many times that possibly it was muscle memory at work, or maybe he was just lucky. The moment he felt the stocks release his feet a sense of calm flowed through him. Even if Findlay was there, he could still escape.

As he'd done a thousand times before, Houdini placed his

hands on the side of the cell and pushed himself up, one hand and then the other, until his waist rested on the roof of the cabinet. He wriggled out of the cabinet and slid the stocks back into place. In his bathing costume was a small pocket from which he removed a key, unlocking the lid and thus securing the stocks in their original and undetectable position. As he did this he noticed, on the floor in front of the cabinet, a newspaper. There was not normally anything inside the curtained area other than the cell.

He climbed down off the roof of the cell and picked up the paper, a copy of the *Daily Mirror*. It was folded to highlight an article several pages in. Houdini read the headline.

WILLIAM MELVILLE, FORMER SUPERINTENDENT OF SCOTLAND YARD, DEAD AT 67.

The article said he died of liver failure. When Houdini looked at the paper's date he knew better. The paper was for the next day. He smiled as he thought of his old friend Harmsworth.

He tucked the paper under the cabinet and opened the curtain. The audience cheered, and he went through his spiel, searching the committee for Findlay. He wasn't there.

As he donned his robe he retrieved the newspaper. He went backstage to change for the elephant vanish. Grigoriev was there, and Houdini handed him the paper. He only had a few moments and was pulling his tuxedo on as quickly as possible.

Grigoriev looked at him. "How did you get this?"

"Someone put it behind my curtain. One of Wilkie's men."

Houdini wriggled into his shirt and began to fasten his tie. "I think this means we're in the clear," he said. If they had intended to harm him, he would have been harmed. They had given him the newspaper to show him that, to demonstrate their power. Wilkie had always had a flair for the theatrical.

"Not necessarily. Maybe you are. I'm not so sure I am."

"Why?"

"You're still useful to Wilkie. But I know too much."

The band was nearly at the end of its interlude.

"Everything will be fine." He pulled on his coat and smoothed down his hair.

"I doubt that."

"You Russians have no imagination," he said, turning back toward the stage. "Once I've made this elephant disappear, I'll do the same for you."

MARTIN STRAUSS

~ *1927* ~

I emerged from the 116th Street subway station to a gray and cloudy day. I walked south and turned left onto West 113th Street. Halfway down the block was Houdini's house. I paused outside, stared up at the narrow, brown, four-story building that had been his home. The house was grand, but at the same time there was something commonplace about it that surprised me. I knew he was mortal—no one knew this better than I—but seeing where he lived, ate, and slept nearly made me lose my nerve.

My plan was imperfect. For all I knew, the person who had warned me to go underground, who may have been threatening me, could be in that house. Who would have more cause to do me harm than Houdini's widow? Yet it was my intent to knock on the door and explain to her who I was.

Each of the eleven steps up to the small landing outside the front door was an obstacle of its own. When I reached the top, I took from my pocket the piece of paper on which I'd written what I intended to say, and clutched it in front of me.

A young woman in a black dress and white apron answered the door. I glanced down at my paper, about to start reading from it, then realized that this could not be Bess Houdini.

"Yes?" she said.

I folded the paper over. "I'm here to see Mrs. Houdini," I said, aware of how nervous I sounded.

The maid looked surprised, which I thought odd. Did I have the wrong house?

"Come in," she said, opening the door and leading me down a small hall decorated with photos of Houdini and a large bust of the man himself. Despite his death his presence was everywhere, and I had to resist the urge to run away.

At the end of the hall was a sitting room, and the maid motioned for me to take a seat. There was already a woman there, her eyes on the floor, hands folded in her lap. She looked up, startled, then relieved. She was not Bess Houdini either.

I sat at the opposite end of the room from the woman. When the maid had left, she looked at me. "Did you get a letter too?" she asked in a quiet voice.

"No," I said.

"Why are you here?"

I didn't want to say why. "I have business with Mrs. Houdini."

"I got a letter saying she had something for me."

The maid entered again with two more women, each appearing somewhat uneasy, and I stood up as they came in, but no one spoke. We sat there in uncomfortable silence, and then the maid came back with another woman and another and another until there was myself and ten women in the room. It seemed that each of them had received a letter or telegram from Bess telling them she had something for them from Houdini, instructing them to come at an appointed time to collect it.

I became aware that each of these women was both young and beautiful. I doubted if I'd ever been in the company of ten more attractive women in my life. None of them could hold a candle to Clara, though. I missed her like you miss the dead, with a terrible finality that made me panic every time I looked directly at it. If I only took it in sideways, it was almost bearable. The hint of a hem of a dress might invoke a pleasant memory, a specific smell might take me to a moment with her that buoyed me, and if I was careful to take that instant snapshot and not dwell, then it was like Clara was still with me. But if my mind lingered, it would remember that she was not. Then the loss of her would sink me.

We all sat there for some time. It seemed that we were being made to wait on purpose, that the tension created by our uncomfortable coexistence was intentional. I reminded myself that whatever was happening I was not technically a part of it.

The maid returned carrying a box. One of the women, with a blond bob, leaned forward. The maid shielded the box from her view and stood next to me in the corner of the room.

Bess Houdini walked through the door. She was a tiny woman, barely five feet tall, and despite being over fifty looked at first glance like a child's doll. She was dressed all in black, and her dark hair was styled with care. Her movements were precise, as if they required great effort, and I saw her left hand shake slightly before she steadied it.

A shapely brunette who looked to me like I'd seen her in a movie at some point stood up and stepped forward as if to embrace her. "Oh, Bess, I'm so sorry for your loss. He was a great man."

Bess waved her hand through the air like a knife, warding her off. The woman stopped herself, arms outstretched, then retreated. Bess stared at her, her face hard and unmoving. The woman's mouth hung open, dumbstruck, and then she closed it.

No one was spared Bess's gaze. She went from one woman to the next, forcing them to look at her directly, not stopping until they looked away again. They all knew what was happening, it seemed. I didn't, but I could tell that whatever was taking place was a serious matter.

Eventually Bess turned to look at me. A flicker of uncertainty crossed her face. Then she reached into the box the maid held and removed a bundle of letters tied together with string. She read the label and crossed the room toward one of the women. She held out the bundle and the woman took it, blushing when she realized what had been given to her. Then Bess stepped aside and the woman stood and walked toward the door, her footsteps accelerating once she was out of our sight and down the hallway.

Bess returned to the box and retrieved another bundle of letters and calmly presented them to the tall brunette, whom I was now positive I'd seen in a film. The woman grasped the letters, and Bess hung on to them an instant longer than she needed to. The woman pulled them away and rose to her feet, towering over Bess. Conscious of the previous woman's footsteps, she walked with measured steps across the room and down the hall, shutting the front door quietly behind her.

One by one each woman was given a package of letters, and

each of them left the room in silence. As the last woman departed, Bess's shoulders dropped, and the echo of the door closing seemed to knock her over. She collapsed to her knees and let out a sob. The maid didn't move, and gave me a look that made it clear I shouldn't either.

The three of us stayed where we were. It was as if we were each in our own separate rooms, trapped by an unseen force. Then Bess pulled herself to her feet and shuffled over to a chair. She waved a hand at the maid, who left the room.

"Who are you?"

For her to absolve me she needed to know the truth. "Martin Strauss."

Bess bit her lip. Then it hit her. "Martin Strauss?"

"I'm the man who punched your husband in the stomach in Montreal."

"Why are you here?" She sat up straight.

"To tell you I'm sorry," I said. "I didn't mean to kill him. I don't even know why I hit him."

She relaxed a little. Perhaps she had thought I was here to do her harm. I still wasn't sure what I had just intruded upon, but the situation was more complicated than I'd anticipated.

The maid returned with a bottle of white wine and two glasses. She placed the tray next to Bess and exited the room.

Bess poured herself a glass but didn't offer me one.

"You didn't kill him," she said.

"But the papers said—"

"My husband had several substantial life insurance policies," she said. "One of which paid double indemnity for accidental death."

"I don't understand."

"Mr. Strauss, he died as the result of a burst appendix. No matter how hard you may have hit him, it wouldn't have caused his appendix to burst. But a burst appendix is not considered an accident by the insurer, unless caused by something unnatural."

I couldn't think of any words. How was it possible that I hadn't killed him? If I hadn't killed him, who had warned me to go into hiding?

I thought about Alice Weiss and her odd request. I knew that Bess was not her mother. Did Bess know of her existence? Should I tell her?

"Is there anything else I can do for you, Mr. Strauss?"

I reached into my pocket and took out the leather-bound book. I walked across the room and handed it to Bess.

"Do you know what this is?"

She set the book on her lap without opening it.

"I don't know how, but somehow it ended up in my pocket."

Bess picked up her wineglass and held it for a moment, turning it around in her fingers, then drained it. She opened the book, flipped through the pages, and handed it back to me.

"This is my husband's book. If it's in your possession I imagine it's because he wanted you to have it."

"Why?" I took a seat in the chair next to her.

Bess poured herself another glass of wine, and one for me without asking if I wanted it.

"He was involved in a great many things. I don't know the full scope of his life. Every day I learn of something new. Most of what I learn I would wish not to know."

She turned to look at me, and her eyes were teary. "Those women just now. I returned their correspondence with Harry. It was not the sort of correspondence a wife would ever wish to read."

Could any of the women have been Alice's mother? It seemed unlikely—they were all too young.

"That book," she continued, "is written in code. It's not a code I recognize. But he didn't write in code unless he felt it was necessary. If I were you I would be careful who I showed that book to."

The maid returned to the room, though I had not heard her footsteps come down the hall. "Is everything all right, ma'am?"

Bess smiled at her. "It's fine, dear."

The maid glanced at me and left.

"Harry could never rest, never let anything go. He was a marvel of a man. Many people wished him harm, and he took pains to protect me from that. When he first took ill, I suspected that he'd been poisoned."

"By whom?"

"It could have been any one of a thousand spiritualists. A jealous husband somewhere, maybe. A jilted woman. I don't know."

"Someone sent me a note," I said, feeling like I could trust her. "It told me I needed to leave town and hide."

Her face dropped. "I don't know who sent that," she said, "but if I were you, I'd take it seriously." Her voice fell to a whisper. "There is a man who may be able to help you. He has known my husband for a long time, and has worked with him in secret. His name is Grigoriev. He may know the code for this book. It's possible Harry intended for you to give it to him."

"How do I find him?"

"I don't know. I haven't seen him in years. No one is supposed to know he exists."

How was I supposed to find a man who didn't exist? Nothing made any sense.

"His daughter came to see me."

Bess sat up straight. "I didn't know Grigoriev had a daughter."

"Not Grigoriev. Houdini."

She stood up, almost knocking over her chair. "You need to go."

"I'm sorry," I said.

"I do not wish to discuss him any further with you." I could see she was trying to appear firm, but she seemed tiny and afraid.

"Her name is Alice."

Bess said nothing.

"She wants to know about her father. What he was like. She asked me to find him for her."

"I don't care!" Bess shouted. "I don't care about any of that!"

The maid came running. I rose and retreated down the hall past all of the tributes to the great man and out the door.

On the subway back downtown I once again examined Houdini's book, but it all remained as cryptic as ever. Pressing Bess about Alice had been a tactical mistake. Bess Houdini would never see me again now.

And what did I have to tell Alice? I had learned nothing about her father, except that he was a relentless womanizer and that he had not been a good husband. This was not what I wished to be able to tell her. I needed more, for her, if I wanted to return to Clara.

But I hadn't killed him. At least that's what Bess thought. I wasn't convinced. Would doctors lie just to get her some life insurance money? Could they do that? The newspapers said I did it, and history would say I did it. Did it matter what Bess Houdini privately thought? I had punched him and he had died. I'd hoped Bess's forgiveness would mean something, but how could she forgive me for something she denied I'd done? Thwarted, I was unsure of what to do next.

The next day I went out in search of work. New York was humming, a city under construction, and it didn't take me long to find a job as a laborer on a construction site. The job started immediately and I spent the next ten hours alongside thirty other men, digging out what would become the basement and foundations of a modest skyscraper. It was exhausting labor, but the job site was about fifteen blocks from my rooming house, and I opted to walk back instead of taking the subway.

After a few blocks I noticed my bootlace was untied, and I moved out of the sidewalk's flow to tie it. As I bent down I caught a glimpse of someone behind me, maybe twenty feet away, darting into a doorway.

I tied the lace and continued onward. After half a block I stopped suddenly, feigning interest in a pair of shoes displayed in a shop window. Sure enough, behind me a tall, clean-shaven man in a long brown coat changed his course and loitered outside an apartment building. I continued on, and after another block I bought a newspaper and the same man again veered down an alley.

I needed a plan. Whoever he was, leading this man back to where I was staying wasn't a good idea. I turned right, away from my room, and headed uptown. After three blocks I could tell as I crossed the street that the oncoming traffic would make crossing behind me difficult. As I reached the curb I broke into a run, sprinting for the next five blocks, turning right, running for another long block. I looked back, but there was no sign of the man.

Up ahead of me was the Bowery. I'd overheard a couple of men on the job site talking about a blind pig around here. I couldn't find it for a while, but eventually I saw a group of men enter an unmarked door. After a few minutes someone emerged from inside, and though he wasn't outright drunk, he wobbled down the street in a way that made it clear he'd had at least one or two.

Before going inside I took one last look up and down the street. I pushed open the door. There was a narrow flight of stairs, and at the bottom a short hallway led to a large open room with low ceilings and floors covered in sawdust. I found myself a stool at the far end of the bar up against the wall and ordered a whiskey and what passed for beer.

I put back the whiskey and started in on the beer. Could I return to my room? I had Houdini's book and my money in my pockets. Whoever was following me must know where I was staying. But how had they found me?

Tucked inside Houdini's book was a letter I'd written to Clara. I'd addressed the envelope and even put a stamp on it. I told her I was sorry for everything that had happened that night, sorry I hadn't spoken to her afterward, and sorry I'd left town. I told her I couldn't come back, not now, and that I did love her but it didn't matter because everything was ruined. I wasn't the person she'd thought I was and I was sorry for that too. It was a poor attempt to explain myself, I knew, but the best I could offer. I didn't have the courage to mail it. What do you do when the best you have is not very good? I had always been paralyzed by my own inadequacy.

A man sat down beside me, and I shuffled over a bit to accommodate him. I didn't make eye contact—this place looked like it could get rough and I wasn't looking to make any friends. He sat for a moment but didn't wave the bartender over, which seemed odd, so I risked a glance sideways. It was the man who had been following me.

He seemed larger up close. He was nondescript, with short brown hair, dressed to blend in with a crowd. Despite this there was a composed force about him. He kept his right hand under his coat, the significance of which I realized too late.

"I'll be taking that book you have in your pocket, Martin," he said, his left hand pulling his coat aside a few inches, revealing a revolver pointed at my chest.

I didn't move. Perhaps I was panicking. It seemed like the thing to do was pretend he wasn't there. This probably wasn't the best plan I've ever come up with.

"Now Martin," he said, leaning in close to me, "I know you're not deaf." His breath was surprisingly pleasant.

"How did you find me?"

He laughed. "Oh, I'm a regular Sherlock Holmes. I'm not here for chitchat. Give me the book and that will be that."

"You'll leave me alone?"

"If it were desired that you be harmed," he said, "you would be. All we're interested in is the book. Let's not make this messy."

I'd never had a gun pointed at me before. Really, how many people experience such a thing? I was frightened, there's no doubt about it, but we were in a crowded room, surrounded by more or less law-abiding people, excepting the fact that they were all presently violating the Eighteenth Amendment.

"I'll have to think about it," I said, taking a sip of my beer.

This seemed to confuse him. "Think about it?"

"Well," I said, feeling a lot more confident all of a sudden, "it's not like you're going to shoot me here in front of all these people. And I'm certainly not going anywhere alone with you. So it seems that as long as this place is open we're at something of an impasse. I'm going to use this time to consider your proposal."

He sat there, stunned.

"You may as well have a drink," I said, and waved the bartender over. I ordered two whiskeys and two mugs of beer, sliding one of each over to him when they came. "My treat," I said.

"All right," he said, not at all pleased. "You realize this ends one way, though."

He took a sip of his whiskey and I took a sip of mine. It began to sink in that he was right. All I'd done was buy myself a little time. Why didn't I just give him Houdini's book? I couldn't make sense of it anyway. But that felt wrong. My fate was connected with the book, and it was quite possibly the only link I had that would ever help me understand what had happened. Houdini had given it to me for a reason, and until I knew, I couldn't part with it. Whatever was in that book would determine whether I would get my life back or not. If I wanted to return to Clara, I couldn't give it up. Plus I didn't appreciate being followed or bullied. I'd had more than enough of that.

"But Martin," my mother's voice said to me, unbidden, "what does it matter? What's in the past is in the past. Right now you're in a strange illegal drinking establishment with an odd man pointing a gun at you. I think you really need to be more concerned with that fact and less concerned with the intentions of a dead magician."

If I could have answered without arousing suspicion, I would have said that fortune favors the bold and patience is a virtue. I was awaiting an opportunity.

"Of course you are. And I'm sure one will present itself at any moment, dear."

My would-be assassin never once took his eyes off me. "How is it you see this ending?" he asked.

"I can't read the future."

"Let me read it for you. At some point, you're going to have to get up off that stool, and I'll be with you when you do. I will get the book from you. And the harder you make me work to do that, the more I'm going to hurt you."

"But I bought you a drink." I raised my mug of beer to him, holding it aloft in a sort of toast, and that's when my opportunity presented itself.

There was a commotion at the stairway leading up to the door. A crash and some shouting, and everyone turned to see what had caused it. The man didn't turn, but glanced involuntarily in that direction. In that instant I changed the direction of my mug and smashed it into his temple.

"It's a raid!" someone shouted, and as the man slid to the floor, blood running down his face, glass protruding from his forehead like an extra eyebrow, the bar broke into pandemonium.

I bent down and searched through his pockets, removing a few crumpled banknotes, two envelopes, and some assorted papers. There was no time to do a more thorough search—I could see police at the far end of the room. I looked behind me and saw a well-dressed man disappear behind a curtain that had appeared to hang in front of a solid wall. I followed him, finding myself in a dark passageway. After about thirty steps there was a stairway that led upward. A small door opened into an alley. A single policeman stood at one end of the alley but seemed unconcerned with either my presence or the gentleman's who had exited before me. To be safe I walked away from the cop.

I could feel my pulse in every part of my body and my mouth was dry. I couldn't go back to my rooming house. I'd have to leave New York. It didn't matter. I had disappeared before, and I could do it again. As I made my way north toward Grand Central Terminal I kept my head down, not stopping except for traffic and to drop my letter to Clara in a mailbox.

MARTIN STRAUSS

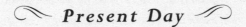 *Present Day*

ONE PLUS ONE DOES NOT EQUAL TWO, AND I CAN prove it.

Another confabulation has come to me, unbidden. I'm sitting at a kitchen table. I'm tired. My face is hot and my mouth is dry. In another room I can hear a child crying, but I'm trying to ignore it. I want a drink. What I would really like to do is get up, cross the room, and leave. I can feel the door pull me toward it. Just as I am about to succumb, Clara sits beside me. She is tired too, exhausted. Her shoulders slump and she rubs the back of her neck.

"This," she says, "is hard."

I agree with her, though now I'm not entirely sure what we were talking about.

"It will get better."

"Will it?" she asks, and I don't know that it will. I feel powerless. I want to say something that will reassure her, perform some action that will fix everything, but if such a thing is possible it is beyond my ability. Again I feel the pull of the door, and I know that when Clara leaves the room I will succumb to its call. I will go out that door and I will not come back.

I wonder about this false memory. If I had somehow had a life with Clara, if I hadn't run away when we were barely beginning, would this be how it was? Would I always want to be escaping? I want to believe that I would have been steadfast, but maybe not. It is entirely possible that I am capable of simultaneously loving someone and not treating them well.

A couple walks past me and toward the street. They're arguing about something, but soon they're too far away for me to hear their voices. The woman is poking at the air with her finger and the man is shaking his head. They stop walking, apparently unable to continue their discussion while in motion, and the man throws his hands up in the air as if in surrender. The woman doesn't seem placated, though, and she keeps on. I wonder what he did. Or is going to do.

Most argument, and in fact most conflict, has nothing to do with the present. It's always about the past or the future. People can't agree on the details of what has happened or is going to happen. But we rarely know what has happened, and we never know what is going to happen. What is really at dispute is how we will deal with not knowing.

Even though I can't hear them, these two aren't any different from the rest of us. They're walking down a street, and instead of enjoying the sun and each other's company they're fighting. But maybe it has to be this way. Maybe you can't go through your life trying to make the best of the present. I certainly haven't.

One plus one does not equal two. Well, yes, it does. Sometimes. But not always. I realize the impossibility of this. Much of the world is binary. You're alive, you're dead. But what if it was uncertain whether the number one existed?

Imagine I have a cookie. I'm allowed to eat this cookie, but before I eat it I must first eat half of it. So on the first bite I eat half the cookie. On the second bite I eat half of that half, am left with a quarter, and so on.

I keep eating, and the cookie gets smaller. It won't take long until the piece I'm left with is too small for me to physically divide. But if I could shrink myself down to scale I could continue, on and on, forever. There would always be a tiny piece of cookie left; it would never completely disappear.

Which makes getting to zero impossible. And if one and zero exist as opposites in a binary world, that makes one impossible too.

So one and one cannot be two. There is always that tiny piece remaining, that tiny fraction that makes infinity and illusion possible.

Then there is the Indian rope trick. It goes like this: a rope and a basket are brought to a field. One end of the rope ascends until it disappears into the sky, too high to see. The magician's assistant, a boy, climbs it. The magician calls after him, but he doesn't come down. Enraged, the magician seizes his sword and climbs the rope. A terrible argument is heard, and then limbs begin to rain down from the sky as the boy is hacked to pieces. The magician descends and the rope falls to the ground. He gathers up all the limbs and places them in the basket, says a few magic words, and the boy emerges unharmed.

It's a good illusion. So good, in fact, that it has never been done. It began as a story, a false description of mystic Eastern magic, and then it was repeated so many times and with such fervor that people believed it was true—some even would swear they had seen it with their own eyes.

I worked as a draftsman of architectural plans after I came out of hiding, disappearing in plain sight. I'd wanted to be a doctor, but that didn't work out. By the time everything settled down after Houdini's death I was too old to go to medical school. I'd more or less lost my enthusiasm for doctoring anyway. What I liked about my job was its certainty—I'd draw up plans for something and it would be made accordingly. There was a concrete outcome that I could control.

I'm not sure how to characterize my life. Missing? It's like there's a big chunk of time missing, except there isn't. The time is there. Nothing happened other than it filled. A minute turned into an hour turned into a day, a week, a year. Years became decades. And here I am. Old and alone.

Except for Alice. She's the only real person I know. We don't see each other often, maybe once or twice a year, but I have a hard time keeping her at bay when I do see her. She's the one person who knows what I've done, all the gory details. Almost all of them. It's time for me to reappear.

The ice cream orderly is back and staring at me again. He checks his watch as if he's waiting for a bus. He's about forty, tall, and I imagine women find him handsome. Maybe they like the uniform. Maybe they think he will give them free ice cream.

He turns and a woman comes out of the hospital. She stops to talk to him, and I'm momentarily jealous. I can see only a bit of her—the great lug blocks my view—but I catch a glimpse of a

blue cardigan and light brown hair, and I get a feeling that whoever he's talking to is worth his time.

He steps aside and points at me. For a moment I'm surprised,
but then I get a look at the woman he was talking to. It's Alice,
and I remember now that we were supposed to meet today. She
must have come looking for me here—I likely mentioned on the
telephone I had an appointment—and of course this guy knew
where I was. This is probably a tactic he uses to meet women. That
and the ice cream.

For a second I panic. I don't like surprises. I turn away,
hoping she didn't see me looking at her.

She sits next to me. "Hello, Martin."

I turn back to her and smile. "Hello. I forgot about our plans."

In truth, I can't exactly remember what it is we were going to do
today. I normally have a book that I write things down in, to help
me remember, but I don't seem to have it with me today. In the past
we have been to movies, gone for walks, eaten at restaurants. Our
relationship is comfortable and strained at the same time.

"It's okay," she says, and I can tell by the way she looks at me
that it is. She's a pretty girl. Scratch that, she's well into her
forties, and there are lines around her eyes—she is no longer a
girl. She was married once but isn't anymore, and doesn't have
any children, which is a shame because I think she'd make a
good mother. There's something about her, an ineffable gener-
osity and kindness, that reminds me a bit of my own mother.
But we've both grown old.

I swallow. My mouth is dry. "I have some news I need to tell
you."

Her hand picks at the hem of her skirt, and she looks at me.

"I have some news as well." Her voice is soft and cracks slightly. "I think you already know, or maybe you don't. But I have to tell you."

She sees that I'm watching her closely and composes herself. I do the same, and neither of us speaks. The orderly comes back out through the automatic doors. I wave at him. "I'll have two scoops of vanilla, and the lady will have a Popsicle."

He scowls at me and goes back inside. Alice laughs, a singsong of a laugh that makes me feel like I've just done the greatest thing ever. It's a sound I haven't heard for a long time.

HOUDINI

~ *1926* ~

THE SUN HAD SET SOME TIME AGO. SUMMER WAS COMING
to a close, and there was a coolness to the breeze. Soon it would
be time to dig sweaters and shawls out of storage, and not long
after that heavy coats and gloves. The trees would shed their
leaves and snow would swathe the city. But not yet. None of that
had happened yet.

Houdini peered out the window. Rose Mackenberg was on her
way in her car, and it was critical that their dealings this evening
go undetected. He studied the street for any sign of the unordi-
nary. The floor above him creaked, and he glanced upward. Bess
was asleep, or at least she had been a few minutes ago when he'd
checked on her, and the housekeeper was in her room at the rear
of the house. He turned his attention back to the street.

He had always had enemies. For the most part they'd been
harmless; even at their most malevolent they had been courted

and destroyed. In a way they'd been useful. They kept him sharp, kept him on his game. And the free publicity he gained when he destroyed them, revealing them to the world as the imposters they were, was priceless.

This time was different. Not only were these enemies dangerous, they were persistent and skilled. They'd gained the upper hand for the moment, and he had no choice but to retreat from them, though it was completely against his nature. He had misjudged them and now he was paying for it.

He'd spent much of the day in his lawyer Bernard's office. The lawsuits lodged against him by spiritualists totaled well over a million dollars, but most of them were spurious and a nuisance at worst. Defending himself against them was a matter of money and time. He had plenty of money but not much time.

Throughout the meeting he'd been distracted, and now couldn't remember much of what had been discussed. That morning he'd telephoned Rose and told her to come get him as the sun went down. It wasn't like her to be late.

Tonight's work would need to be completed whether Rose showed or not. There was no time left—if not tonight, then never. He thought of Bess, somewhere in this house that had once held their whole happy family, of his mother, rest her soul, of his brothers and sister and his father. They seemed so far away now, and he could feel his memory of them fade each day.

He was sore. He could not deny that his body was letting him down. Fifty-two years of strain and tension, of unbreakable bonds broken and leaps into icy waters, of little sleep and much travel; it had all caught up with him. Fifty-two years. It

was hard to believe that it had gone by so fast and yet there he
was, exhausted by it. He wished Rose would hurry up.

Six years earlier he'd gone to lunch with Sir Arthur Conan
Doyle. He'd been excited about it—Sherlock Holmes, cham-
pion of rational thought and logical conclusions, was possibly
his favorite literary character. He'd been good friends with Jack
London, but Jack had died in 1916, and afterward Houdini had
made the awful mistake of carrying on an affair with his widow.
It had become messy—he was sure Bess knew all about it—and
he'd been lucky to end it without lasting damage.

Doyle was by reputation a perfect gentleman, though tem-
peramentally at odds with his famous creation. Not only did he
despise Sherlock Holmes, he had become a devotee of spiritualism, the very antithesis of rational thought. Houdini wondered
whether Doyle was merely humoring his second wife, Jean, who
was said to fancy herself something of a medium.

The invitation to lunch at the Doyle estate, Windlesham Manor,
had come after Doyle had witnessed one of Houdini's underwater
crate escapes in Bristol. Doyle had been completely enthralled. "I
don't care what you say," he said, clapping Houdini on the back,
"that's as clear an instance of dematerialization as I've ever seen."

There was a gleam in his eye as he said this, and Houdini
couldn't tell if he was being serious or not. It was puzzling, but
there was nothing he liked more than a good puzzle, so he'd
accepted Doyle's invitation.

As his hired car negotiated the narrow country road that led to the Doyle estate, Houdini wondered what to expect. Doyle's first wife, Louisa, had died in 1906 of tuberculosis. For the last nine years of her life, Doyle had an apparently platonic relationship with Jean Leckie, whom he'd married a year after Louisa's death. Houdini was skeptical. His curiosity was not based on moral qualms about infidelity. He was in no position to judge anyone on that account. What interested him was the deception. In his estimation, there could be only three types of spiritualists: the charlatans, the dupes, and those who actually communicated with the dead. Given that he knew the last to be impossible, there remained only the fakes and the believers. So if Doyle did not possess actual mediumistic powers, he must either be a fool or a liar. It seemed unlikely that the creator of Sherlock Holmes was a fool, but by reputation Sir Arthur Conan Doyle was a meticulously honest man. These two conditions could not mutually exist.

Ahead of him Windlesham Manor came into view. It was a large, rambling house set back on a lawn. An impeccably dressed servant met the car, opening the rear door for Houdini. He stepped out onto the gravel driveway and followed the servant down a path to the rear of the house, where he found Doyle waiting at a table set outside on a paved patio. He was a large man, over six feet tall, with a mustache that struck Houdini as extremely commanding, and wore a three-piece suit despite the heat of the day. An Irish wolfhound lay at his feet, perking up when Houdini approached.

Doyle looked up from his newspaper and smiled. He sprang out of his chair, startling the enormous dog. Doyle paid no attention to the dog's scrambling attempts to get out of his way as he crossed the distance between himself and Houdini, extending his hand eagerly.

"Harry Houdini! I'm glad you made it all the way out here to our little spot in the country."

Doyle's handshake was firm, almost aggressive, but Houdini smiled back all the same, returning Doyle's force.

"I'm a small-town boy myself," he said. "Always glad for a chance to get out of the city."

"Good man, good man. Come, sit. Lady Doyle will be with us in a moment." He looked around as if to confirm the obvious fact that Houdini had come alone.

"I must apologize. My wife, Bess, is under the weather today and was unable to come." This was more or less true—Bess had been unwell lately, but she hadn't come because she didn't want to.

"Please send her our best wishes." Doyle smiled again.

Houdini sat at the table and a different but equally gallant servant poured him a cup of tea.

"I hope tea is sufficient," Doyle said. "I can provide you with something stronger if you like, but I don't touch the stuff myself."

Houdini shook his head. "I don't either. I've never understood the point of ingesting a substance that is known to dull your senses."

Doyle gazed at him, inscrutable, then laughed. "A great many men wish for nothing more than to be relieved of their senses. You and I, we are not such men."

The wolfhound nuzzled Doyle's hand, and he gave it a cursory pat on the head before sending it off.

"When the war was on, I could hear the guns in France from this spot, if conditions were right. I used to imagine that my son Kingsley heard those same guns, and I suppose that sometimes he did."

Houdini nodded. He knew that Kingsley Doyle had died in the war, along with several other members of Doyle's family.

"Don't be so glum, Houdini. I still speak to him often. But of course you know that." He stood up. "Lady Doyle. You look as wonderful as ever."

Sir Arthur's wife had arrived. She wore a simple but elegant blue dress and white gloves. Her hair was pinned up and she moved stiffly, as though her joints gave her trouble. There was something severe about her—she seemed to disapprove of the condition of being alive but was trying to make the best of it. Houdini stood and kissed her extended hand, then they all sat. Jean said little. Where her husband was jovial, she remained withdrawn and almost hostile.

If he was aware of this contrast Doyle didn't show it. "Let me say again how much I enjoyed seeing your escape the other day in Bristol. A remarkable feat. One of the best I've ever seen."

"Thank you. Years of practice."

"I don't think so. I think you do a disservice to your abilities to pretend that you use trickery."

"I'm afraid it's the truth. I do not dispute that I have extraordinary abilities, but they're achieved by human means. Of that I am sure."

Doyle smiled. "Ah, well, perhaps we are in agreement. I, for one, dislike this arbitrary distinction between the natural and the supernatural. They are two sides of a coin, that is all."

Houdini was about to protest, but thought better of it. The three of them sat and ate cucumber sandwiches, and for a while the conversation was the sort of small talk that could be found at the table in any club in London. Houdini was growing bored, and he could tell that Doyle was as well. The question was which one of them would break first.

After a discussion about the weather in which Doyle delineated four distinct types of rainfall that could be found in this area of Sussex during the spring, Houdini wanted to stand up and shout at this ridiculous man, this giant of literature who bore a striking resemblancc to an oversized Yorkshire terrier.

To his surprise, Doyle broke first. "Let me ask you, Houdini, are you a believer?"

At first he didn't understand the question. "My father was a religious man," he said.

"No, that's not what I mean. We both know that we share an interest in life beyond the veil. Are you a believer or a skeptic?"

Houdini knew the answer that would be of most benefit, and he knew the answer that was the truth. He chose the middle ground.

"I've never seen any phenomenon or act that I can say without reservation is the work of anything otherworldly. I remain willing to be convinced of life after death, even eager, but thus far I remain uncertain."

Doyle nodded to his wife. She stood and left the table, heading back inside the house. "I suspected as much. There was a time when I felt as you did. Of course wanting to believe does not make something true. Every day the postman brings me at least one sack of mail from people who are writing to Sherlock Holmes or Watson. They offer to help with their investigations. They offer to be their housekeeper. They simply cannot fathom that these people are inventions. They believe them to be real."

Houdini understood this impulse; he had created a fiction that pcople believed was real. There was even a part of him that believed in the myth that was Houdini. "How is that different from talking to the dead?"

"Evidence. I've seen things with my own eyes, eyes trained by years of medical and scientific study, that have convinced me beyond a doubt that there is life after death."

Houdini listened. Was it possible that Doyle had secured proof of life after death? His fervor was convincing.

"Of course there will always be those who distort the truth for financial gain. I'm sure we agree that these people are the lowest of the low. There is nothing more despicable than trading on a man's sincere beliefs and heartache for financial gain. But the fact that some people are liars does not invalidate the existence of the proof. And I have witnessed many instances of this proof. I have spoken to those who have gone over to the other side, and they have told me things of which only they could speak."

Houdini leaned forward to give Doyle the impression that his words were affecting him. "They are still with us?"

Doyle nodded. "It was in the time of the war, when all these splendid young fellows were disappearing from our view, when the whole world was saying, 'What's become of them, where are they, what are they doing now? Have they dissipated into nothing, or are they still the grand fellows we used to know?' It was then that I realized the overpowering importance of knowing more about this matter. I felt the highest purpose to which I could devote the remainder of my life would be to bring across to other people the knowledge and assurance that I have acquired. To tell them I have heard the sound of a vanished voice and felt the touch of a vanished hand."

Lady Doyle returned and handed a bundle wrapped in black

cloth to her husband. He set it on the table and pointed to Houdini.

"You are a remarkable man. I believe the extent to which you are remarkable is unknown even to you. You are a man of rational thought, like myself. You require proof, you require tangible evidence of a thing's existence, before you will allow yourself to believe in it." Doyle pushed the bundle across the table. "Here is the proof you've been looking for."

Houdini pulled it closer and moved aside the cloth. Inside was a photograph of a young girl, maybe ten years old, seated behind a thicket of shrubs. She was a pretty girl, and her eyes stared straight at the viewer. In the foreground were four fairies, each about eight inches tall. One of the fairies held a flute to her mouth and the others appeared to be dancing to the tunes.

Houdini was surprised. Spirit photography had been around for over sixty years, and the techniques by which a photograph like this could be faked were numerous. He couldn't believe that Doyle was being serious.

"Have you ever before seen such a thing?" Lady Doyle asked, her voice a reverent whisper.

Houdini didn't know what to say. He had no wish to insult his hosts.

"Lady Doyle, if this is a genuine photograph it is indeed amazing. That said, there are a number of means by which a photograph like this can be faked."

Doyle shook his head. "The glass-plate negative has been examined by experts, and they have said that the photograph is genuine. It was taken by two girls in Cottingley, aged sixteen and ten, who would not have the expertise necessary to produce a fake. They maintain that these fairies are real and show themselves to them regularly, and the photograph is proof."

Houdini said nothing. It seemed impossible to him that a man of Doyle's intellectual heft had been so easily fooled.

"I will think on this," he said. "It's a compelling photograph."

Doyle glanced at his wife, who smiled slightly. Evidently they were happy with this response.

In the car back to London, he wondered whether he was the one who was being deceived, if he had become such a slave to logic and reason that he was blind to the possibilities of the world. He remembered the yearning that he had felt after his mother's death. He could see how this might lead a man to suspend his reason. But was there another possibility?

A few months later he received a letter from Sir Arthur. They began corresponding, and Houdini eventually expressed his disbelief in the Cottingley photograph. Doyle said nothing of this, but suggested that Houdini visit a medium who had been proven genuine. Houdini agreed to do as Doyle suggested.

The medium in question was named Joseph Davidson. He'd been holding séances for some of New York's wealthiest citizens, and it took some doing for Houdini to arrange a sitting under the name of Harry White.

The séance was held in the drawing room of a magnificent home on the Upper West Side. There were about fifteen people in attendance, all instructed to sit at a large, carved oak table. One woman in particular caught his eye. He couldn't say exactly what it was—she was about thirty, dressed well but modestly, and while not unattractive was not particularly beautiful. Houdini could see that she was examining him as closely as he had her; for a moment he feared his disguise had been detected. If Davidson had a plant in the room, it was her.

Joseph Davidson finally entered the room. He was a fine-boned, almost feminine man, a little over five feet tall, with shoulder-length hair that had a glossy sheen that reminded Houdini of an Irish setter. His voice was soft but authoritative, a slight stutter occasionally breaking through.

"Good evening, my friends. I'm so glad you're here to join me in our attempt to speak with those who have passed."

Davidson sat, and they were instructed to join hands as he recited the Lord's Prayer. A lone lit candle remained in the center of the table.

"We all must keep each other honest," Davidson said. "Please keep your hand firmly grasping your neighbor's. If the circle is broken, it is your duty to make that known."

Davidson nodded and the candle went out. Houdini smiled. That was a good trick. For a while no one spoke, and then Davidson began what Houdini felt was an unnecessarily long speech during which he repeatedly thanked the spirits for their guidance and wisdom, finally inviting them to make their presence known.

For a minute or so nothing happened. He could hear people breathing and shifting in their seats. Then he felt a breeze behind him, faint at first and then stronger.

"Someone is here," Davidson said. "A man, about thirty years old. He wears a military uniform and holds a bouquet of flowers."

The woman he'd been observing earlier spoke. "Is that you, dear?"

There was a pause. "He says it is him. He wants you to know he's happy, that you have no reason to worry anymore."

"Ask him if he's seen our son."

There was another pause. "He's standing right beside him."

The woman gasped. "May I speak to him? May I hear his voice?"

Houdini shook his head. Davidson was timing his responses perfectly. In the dark anything could be happening.

"Spirit, make yourself known," he said.

A voice, small and reedy, spoke. It seemed to Houdini that it was coming from the middle of the table, slightly above their heads. "I am here, Mother."

A few people murmured, and the woman next to him said, "Oh my."

"My son! I've missed you."

"I've missed you too, Mother. But I'm happy here with Papa. Thank you, Reverend Davidson, for letting me speak again to my beloved mother."

A light pierced the room, shining directly on Davidson. He froze, his mouth wrapped around a long metallic tube Houdini immediately recognized as a spirit trumpet. This device enabled him to make his voice sound as though it was coming from the center of the table and above them. His left hand held the hand of both the person on his left and his right, so the circle was unbroken, and his right hand held the spirit trumpet. It was with this device that he'd projected his voice to the center of the room. It was likely handed to him once the lights were out.

It took Davidson a moment to recover from the shock. He threw the spirit trumpet across the room and soared to his feet. Houdini looked left, toward the source of the light. The young woman whom Houdini had scrutinized held a small flashlight in her hand. She had maneuvered the hands of the people beside her in the same way Davidson had, so that one of her hands contained both of theirs. Then her light went out and people began to move. The room was dark for a moment before the lights were turned on.

"Nobody move," a voice called out. Houdini turned to look, and a middle-aged man who had been seated at the far end of the table held out a police badge. "Joseph Davidson, you're under arrest."

Davidson shrieked, moving back as the policeman advanced toward him. Houdini saw the woman who had shone the light on him quietly make her way to the door. He followed her out into the street.

"Miss!" he called to her after a block. She was walking quickly, not looking back. When she heard him she walked faster, and he had to break into a run to catch up to her.

"I have a gun," she said, turning to face him.

"That's great," he said. "If you did what I think you did tonight, you're going to need one."

In all the years since his first encounter with Rose Mackenberg the evening that Joseph Davidson was exposed she had never once been late or forgotten anything. If she was late there was a good reason.

She had not been carrying a gun that night, after all, and despite his subsequent attempts to convince her, she still refused to arm herself. Houdini felt comforted by the slight but significant weight of the derringer in his inside jacket pocket. He didn't like guns—they were crude and artless—but that's what the world had become.

A car slowed in front of his house but didn't stop, instead

continuing down the street and turning south down Eighth Avenue toward the park.

He heard footsteps behind him. Bess, in her nightgown, stood in the doorway. She rubbed her eyes, trying to wake herself.

"What are you doing?" she asked.

"I have some business to attend to." His tone was harsher than he'd intended it.

She was awake now. "What kind of business?" Her voice was equally curt.

"It doesn't matter. There are some files in the basement that I need to move."

"In the middle of the night?"

"There's a bit of a situation." He tried to sound conciliatory.

"We're supposed to be at the train station at seven, and you've promised you'll rest more."

He had indeed promised her this, but circumstances had seemed to prevent rest at every opportunity. And now he had no choice. Everything had been set in motion and there was nothing to do but follow through.

"I'm sorry. This won't take long," he said. "Rose will be here with her car any moment."

"Something's happened."

Houdini paused. He didn't want her to know how much danger she was in. "It will be fine."

Bess shook her head. "No, I don't think it will. You tell me very little about what you're doing with these spiritualists, and you think that will protect me. But what you've done can't be taken back."

She crossed the room, shuffling her feet on the floor like a child. She raised herself to her tiptoes and kissed his cheek. "Be careful," she said, and he could hear fear in her voice. She turned and padded out. Her footsteps receded up the stairs and he turned back to the street.

After the Davidson séance Houdini had sent Sir Arthur a long letter detailing what had happened. Doyle was not deterred—that one medium had been exposed didn't alter the fundamental truth. Houdini then sent Doyle a photograph of him posed with Abraham Lincoln, along with an explanation of how the photograph was produced. Again Doyle was undeterred. He almost seemed annoyed at Houdini's insistence on pointing out the facts.

In 1922 Doyle came to America for a speaking tour. Crowds showed up to hear about Sherlock Holmes, but Doyle was more eager to talk about spiritualism. Houdini continued to portray himself as ready to be convinced.

Houdini invited Sir Arthur and Lady Doyle over for lunch and demonstrated the usual tricks that mediums employed, but none of it convinced Doyle. Even when Houdini pretended to pull his thumb from his hand, Doyle was mystified like a child.

Houdini continued his efforts. If he could make Doyle see the truth, then the whole house of cards would come fluttering down. With this in mind he accepted Doyle's invitation for himself and Bess to join the Doyles in Atlantic City for the weekend.

The first night was pleasant enough. The four of them had dinner, after which Bess and Lady Doyle went to a casino while Houdini and Doyle strolled the boardwalk. Doyle was preoccupied with talk of spirit hands, which Houdini knew was a cheap trick using paraffin wax, but he said nothing. This was not the issue on which to confront him.

When they returned from the walk and met up with their wives, Lady Doyle gave a slight, almost undetectable nod, and Doyle smiled faintly. Houdini had seen that look before, either between two cardsharps or between a magician and his assistant.

Back in their room, Houdini asked Bess what she and Lady Doyle had spoken about.

"Nothing much. We talked about your mother and Sir Arthur's mother."

"What did you tell her? Specifically?"

Bess put down her hairbrush. "Why do you want to know? They're a bit wacky, but they're entirely nice people. Not everything has to be about your crusades."

"Something's not right. They're up to something."

"I told them you loved your mother. That you bought her expensive clothes and when you were upset she would hold your head to her chest so you could hear her heartbeat. If that's nefarious, then you're a better Sherlock than his character."

He smiled. Bess had no idea how right she was.

The next evening after dinner, Houdini and Bess were sitting on the beach enjoying the dying light when he saw the lumbering figure of Doyle approaching, being led by a young boy. Doyle tipped the boy once he saw Houdini, and then walked up to them. He was hesitant in a way Houdini had never observed in him before.

"Good evening, Harry, Bess."

"Indeed it is," Bess replied, shielding her eyes as though there were a bright light shining into them, though there was not.

"I apologize for the intrusion, but my wife is most insistent.

She would like to invite you, Houdini, to our room for a reading. She feels that the conditions are most excellent."

He was surprised that the invitation had come so soon. "Are you sure?" he said, doing his best to sound excited.

Bess looked at him. "I'm afraid I'm tired this evening," she said, knowing he was pretending. "Could we possibly do this another evening?"

Doyle dug his shoe into the sand and stared down at it as though it contained some great secret. "I'm sorry, Mrs. Houdini, but my wife's invitation extends only to your husband. Were there to be two people there of such similar mind as yourself and your husband it would affect the energy of the room and possibly the reading. I hope you'll forgive us for this."

It was all Houdini could do to stifle a laugh, but Bess managed to hide her irritation. "Of course. It will be hours before my husband goes to sleep—he rarely sleeps at all, it seems."

The three of them walked back to the hotel, parting outside the Houdinis' suite. "Good night, gentlemen," Bess said, kissing him on the cheek.

When they arrived at the Doyles' suite, Lady Doyle was waiting, seated in a chair. Her eyes were closed, and it was only after they were inside and the door was shut that she opened them.

The room was lit by a half-dozen candles, and the curtains were drawn. Doyle motioned to a chair at her left, and Houdini sat in it. Doyle remained standing, directly behind his wife.

She looked at Houdini, her eyes wide. He stared back at her, careful to betray nothing. She placed a small writing tablet and sheaf of paper in her lap.

Doyle bowed his head. "Almighty, we are grateful to you for

this new revelation, this breaking down of the walls between two worlds. We thirst for another undeniable message from the beyond, another call of hope and guidance to the human race at this, the time of its greatest affliction. Can we receive another sign from our friends?" There was a seriousness, a piety about him, that Houdini could not help but admire.

Doyle reached down and placed his hands on Lady Doyle's, as though translating a sacrament onto her. She remained completely still. Houdini felt a tension building in him, even as he chastised himself for succumbing to her showmanship.

Lady Doyle's head snapped downward, and she grabbed hold of a pencil and slammed the heel of her hand against her leg.

"This is the most profound energy I've ever been presented with," she said, her voice strained as though she were lifting a heavy object. "Do you believe in God?"

Houdini understood that she was inquiring this of the spirit so as to discern whether or not it was malevolent. Lady Doyle struck her hand on her leg three times, as if to answer the question.

"Then I will make the sign of the cross." She drew a large cross on the top of the paper, and then, as though seized by a force outside of herself, began to write page after page of frenzied transcription.

"Who is standing here, alongside Houdini?" Doyle asked. "Is it his mother?"

Lady Doyle again hit her hand three times against her leg. Houdini was at once filled with both rage and joy. He knew they were playing him, but what if he was wrong? What if his mother was really there, about to speak to him? He felt a sliver of hope wedge its way into him.

Doyle placed his hands on Lady Doyle's shoulders, gently

rubbing them, as though trying to mollify the spirit that was controlling her. He then reached down and began handing Houdini the papers on which his wife had been scrawling.

> *You have answered the cry of my heart—and of his. God bless him a thousandfold for all his life and for me. Never has a mother had such a son. Tell him not to grieve, soon he'll get all the evidence he is so anxious for. Tell him I want him to try to write at his own home. He is so, so dear to me. I am preparing so sweet a home for him which one day in God's good time he will come to.*

> *I am so happy in this life. My only shadow has been that my beloved one hasn't known how often I have been with him. He gave me so much in my life, beyond the fine clothes and an apron full of gold. He may no longer be able to hear the beating of my heart but I am still with him.*

> *It is so different over here, so much larger and bigger and more beautiful. So lofty. Sweetness all around one. Nothing that hurts and we see our beloved ones on earth. Tell him I love him more than ever. His goodness fills my soul with gladness and thankfulness. I want him to know only that, that I have bridged the gulf. Now I can rest in peace.*

Lady Doyle collapsed. Sir Arthur helped her up, prying the pencil from her hand. Houdini still held the papers in his hands. He didn't know what to do. It was not real. He knew this. But he was stunned. These words were the words he longed to hear. There was nothing he wanted more in the world, even if they were false.

"She wants a grandchild." Lady Doyle's voice was weak, but he heard her with absolute clarity.

"I beg your pardon?"

"Your mother. She said to tell you to consider Bess's request, that there is no shame in adoption."

Doyle and his wife exchanged a brief look. He knew this look, because he had exchanged it with Bess many times during his act. The look said, "You are going too far."

He wanted to smash every last thing in the room into splinters. He wanted to squeeze the life out of Doyle and his wife. He stood, shook Doyle's hand, and walked out of the room.

"Houdini! Wait!" Doyle called. He went downstairs and through the lobby of the hotel, out onto the boardwalk, where he looked at the lights of the hotels and casinos, watched the people walking by. For a long time he stared, not caring when the occasional person recognized him.

His mother would never have been pacified by the sign of the cross. She was a Jew, devout until the moment of her death. She spoke no English whatsoever, and none of her patterns of speech were present in the words. She said nothing of her husband and failed to mention that today was her birthday.

He could not believe that Bess had told Lady Doyle that she had asked him to consider adoption. It had never occurred to him that Bess would discuss their marriage with anyone else. If he couldn't trust Bess, he was finished.

His stupor began to break. Doyle had tried to deceive him. He had played on his deepest hopes and desires. For what purpose he didn't yet know, but it didn't matter. Sir Arthur was no Sherlock Holmes. If anything he was a Moriarty.

He turned back to the hotel. A plan was forming. Only now did he fully understand what he himself had done to Harold Osbourne

THE CONFABULIST   231

all those years ago. There was nothing genuine to be found with these people. They were magicians without consent. They were grave robbers, but they weren't interested in the corpse. They took what was true and real in life, and put something of their own in its place. They stole from the dead their memory in the living. He could not imagine a more horrible thing.

He had been wrong to give Doyle, or anyone else, the benefit of the doubt. He knew how they did every cheap trick, every graft, every lie. He would expose them all for the frauds they were. He would become their strongest enemy.

When he returned to New York, he tracked down Rose Mackenberg. He met her in a diner, in disguise, and made his proposition.

"Why do you want to do this?" she asked.

"For the same reason you do it," he said. "They're lying to people."

"That's not why I do it."

"Then why?"

She took a drink of her coffee, thick as mud. "I believed in them once, like others. My sister died, and medium after medium promised me a chance to speak to her again. But it was never right. Eventually I saw what was happening, how they were using my grief against me."

"They did the same thing to me with my mother."

"All right, I'll work with you. I have conditions."

"Name them."

"My methods are my own. I am not a magician, but I have ways of accomplishing what needs to be done. I don't need anyone telling me how to operate."

"That's fine."

"There will be expenses. I'll try to keep them down as much as possible, but to do what you suggest is beyond my means. I trust that you will cover these expenses?"

"Spare no cost, Rose."

She folded her napkin and placed it on the table. "This last one is a deal breaker. You will, at no time, make any romantic advances toward me. If you do, I will immediately leave your employ."

Houdini feigned surprise. She was shrewd, he thought. He'd been admiring the smoothness of her neck, wondering if she would be as businesslike and matter-of-fact in bed. "I can assure you I would do nothing of the kind."

The waitress interrupted them to take their plates away, and when she was gone Rose put her elbow on the table and rested her chin in her palm. "I'd like it if we were honest with each other. I'm not a fool, Houdini. I know you. I've known you since the night we met. And I'm still here about to go to work for you. But let's not pretend that the world is other than how it is. That's what we're fighting against."

Houdini felt like a schoolboy caught in a lie. A part of him wanted to get up and walk away from this woman who had pegged him, seeing through all his misdirection and showmanship. But he knew that if she could see through him, she could see through almost anyone.

"I agree to all your conditions."

He had decided Rose wasn't going to show, when her car raced around the corner and pulled up out front. Houdini went to the basement to unlock the door leading up to the street.

"Sorry, boss," she said as she met him. "They were watching me. It took me a while to lose them."

Of course they were watching her. His organization was unraveling. He pointed to a stack of file boxes. "We need to move these to the safe house."

Rose picked up a box. She had been good to her word, and he had been good to his. They'd exposed several prominent mediums, but the two of them could only do so much. They needed to expand.

As any magician knew, it's one thing to make something disappear. If you really want to wow people, make it reappear. So he contacted his old friend Grigoriev. The spiritualists were now watching him as closely as he was watching them, but they were no match for him when it came to deception.

Grigoriev had been in hiding ever since Melville had been removed. The communists who ran Russia now were intent on eliminating anyone connected to the Romanovs. He'd been in Appleton for the past five years, living off the jewels he'd sewn into his clothes when he fled Russia. Houdini had bought him a small house there, and when called to do more, Grigoriev had agreed without hesitation.

Houdini put him through barber school and rented a small shop in the Bronx. From there Grigoriev managed a team of thirty investigators, all of whom had been secretly trained by either Rose or himself. Most were magicians who had fallen on hard times, and some had been hurt by the frauds they now pursued.

Every so often Houdini would go for a haircut and while he sat in the chair Grigoriev would update him on their progress. He'd slip him coded information if possible. They never met outside the barber shop. Houdini thought that his old friend Chung Ling Soo would be proud of the lengths he'd undertaken to maintain this deception.

Houdini, Rose, and Grigoriev began to realize how ingrained into the halls of power the spiritualist movement had become. Rose and other operatives had observed congressmen, senators, judges, mayors, and their wives at séances, where they were advised on matters of state, and had seen the wonder in their eyes as they listened intently to the advice they later acted upon. Margery Crandon, the witch of Beacon Hill, managed to capture the ear of some of the leading power brokers of Boston society as well as more than one former skeptic. Through Walter, her deceased brother and erstwhile guide to the afterlife, she became a central figure in the overall movement.

Grigoriev had argued that she was of more value to them unexposed, that the files they were amassing in investigation of her held information that was of greater importance than the exposure of any one medium. Now, Houdini wished he'd listened to the cagey Russian.

As Houdini sat in Margery Crandon's downstairs sitting room waiting for the rest of the *Scientific American* committee on the existence of psychic phenomena to join him, he considered what to do next. These five men, assembled because of their scientific backgrounds and ability to distinguish fact from falsehood, had one by one fallen under her spell. They all clearly believed they had just been visited by the spirit of Margery's dead brother, Walter. They had forgotten they were there to test the veracity of her claims.

He could see how it had happened. Margery Crandon was much more ingenious than most mediums, and definitely talented. Though not conventionally beautiful, she was alluring in a way that was hard to resist. When she looked you in the eye, you could not look away, and there was a hint of salaciousness in the way the corner of her mouth turned up when she smiled. She was small and strong, and unusually athletic.

Her husband, Dr. Le Roi Crandon, was in almost every way her opposite. Dour, ugly, and devoid of charm, his presence propelled people toward her. They were making a fortune, and while Margery didn't seem to care about money, the same could not be said of Dr. Crandon. Houdini wondered how certain women manage to get entangled with men who are in every way their inferior.

Rose had been to several of Crandon's séances, and believed she was engaged sexually with members of the committee, particularly Malcolm Bird, the secretary. Houdini assumed that her husband put her up to it.

He heard footsteps approaching. He had not yet decided whether to announce his conclusion here at the house or if it might be wise to wait until he got back to New York. Boston was not his town, and there were people here who wished him harm.

Malcolm Bird appeared in the doorway, paused as though surprised to see Houdini there, and then continued into the room. Never had a man been so incorrectly named. Malcolm Bird resembled a bespectacled ferret. He was tall, lean, and awkward, and his suit did not quite fit. It was possible, Houdini decided, that the fault lay not in the garment but in what was holding it up.

Behind him followed Orson Munn, the editor in chief of *Scientific American*. He was a marked contrast to Bird: sharply

dressed; his silver hair receding with dignity; a smooth, confident stride that identified him as a man of intelligence. He seemed
unusually flustered.

Houdini waited for the two other members of the committee,
Hereward Carrington and Daniel Comstock, to join them. Munn
sat down in the chair beside him, while Bird loomed like the oversized weasel he was.

"Where are the others?" Houdini asked.

"They've gone back to the hotel to begin preparing our report," Bird said in an excited tone.

"Shouldn't we at least discuss what we saw?"

Orson Munn looked at him, incredulous. "What is there to
discuss?"

Houdini didn't want to cause a scene, not here in the Crandons' home, but he could under no circumstances allow them to
include him in any report that verified Margery's claims as true.

"I saw no evidence of psychic ability," he said in his most
measured tone.

Munn's jaw hung farther open, reminding him of a dead fish.
"But you saw it the same as I did," he said.

"He doesn't care about the truth," Bird said. "There's too much
money at stake for him."

Houdini ignored this obvious attempt to bait him. He turned
to Munn. "What did you see?"

Munn closed his mouth enough to wet his lips. "Walter rang
the bell box. He threw the megaphone across the room, and he
tipped over the table. We were there, and Margery was under
our control at all times. There is no other explanation."

"There is another rational explanation for each of these things, and indeed I can reproduce these phenomena right now, if you like."

"Preposterous!" Bird was almost in flight. Houdini would have laughed if there wasn't so much at stake. "This is slander, nothing more. He's had it out for her since the very beginning."

"Enough, Bird," Munn said, warning him away with a dismissive wave. "Tell me, Houdini, if this is a ruse, what her method was."

The séance had begun with them sitting in a circle of chairs. Houdini controlled one side of Margery, his hand holding hers, and their legs touching. Bird did the same on the other side, and Munn sat between Bird and Houdini in similar fashion. Once each person had a hand and leg in physical contact the lights were extinguished. The bell box, a small wooden box with an electric bell inside that rang when the box's lid was pressed down, had been placed under Houdini's seat. The idea was that the ringing of the bell would announce Walter's presence.

"Through a series of small movements," Houdini said, "Mrs. Crandon moved herself toward me, shifting her leg against mine enough so that she could ring the bell with her foot. It's a simple trick, hard to detect, but one that is easily replicated."

Bird snorted. "How was it, then, that you were able to detect it?"

Houdini leaned down and rolled up his pant leg. His leg was red and swollen. "I have, since this morning, been wearing a rubber bandage around my leg. I removed it immediately before the séance, but it has left my leg raw and extremely sensitive to movement. Even the subtlest shift from Mrs. Crandon's leg was immensely painful and easy to detect."

"Says you."

"Yes, says I. Do you suppose I am not on this committee for a reason?"

"Fine," Munn said. "It is possible she rang the bell in this way. What about throwing the megaphone?"

The megaphone, a large wooden cone, amplified spirit voices when required. At one point Walter, speaking through Margery, had asked for an illuminated plaque to be placed on top of the bell box. Then Walter had said that the megaphone was floating in the air, and Houdini should tell him in what direction he wanted it thrown. Houdini asked that it be thrown at his feet, and it was. They then reconvened in the dark around a table. With her hands and feet still under control, and sitting well back of the table, Margery/Walter caused the table to lurch violently up in the air and land again with a frightening crash.

"The megaphone was the cleverest of her deceptions. As a magician I cannot help but admire it. Mr. Bird, do you admit that when, on Walter's request, you left to retrieve the illuminated plaque for the bell box you released control of Margery for a moment?"

"I did," Bird huffed. "But the megaphone didn't fly through the air until well after I had regained control."

"I agree," Houdini said. "The plaque gave off just enough light for us to see the floor, but not much else. So we were unable to see that Mrs. Crandon had, while her hand was free of yours, placed the megaphone on her head. It was a simple matter for her to tip her head in whatever direction I selected and let the megaphone fall to the ground."

Bird glared at him. He was in on the whole thing. Houdini

knew that Rose had been correct—Bird was sleeping with Margery Crandon.

"And the table?" Munn asked.

"An old trick. We assume because she sat back from the table that this decreased her ability to move it. All she had to do was lean forward, place the back of her head underneath the edge of the table, and then sit up sharply. I felt her do exactly this, as plain as day."

"You're a liar, Houdini, and you know it." Bird's voice reminded him of a petulant child denied a sweet.

"I think we all know what's gone on here," he said. "My reputation will remain intact, sir."

"Enough." Munn stood up. "The committee can meet tomorrow in full to discuss the matter."

Houdini stood, and with Munn he moved toward the door. Bird stayed still.

"Will you be joining us?" Munn asked.

Bird shook his head. "I am lodging here as a guest of the Crandons."

Houdini snorted, though only for show. He had known Bird was a houseguest of the Crandons. "And you have the nerve to question my credibility."

Outside, in the hall, Dr. Le Roi Crandon stood motionless. Houdini met his gaze as he passed him. He could feel Crandon's eyes on him as he made his way to the door.

"Have a safe trip back to New York, Houdini."

The committee met late the next morning, and they bickered through lunch. Houdini let them shout it out. He planned to resign the moment he'd written letters to the *Times* and a half dozen other papers explaining the Crandons' subterfuge.

When he returned to his room there was a note waiting, slipped under his door.

Lennox Hotel, room 314, 4 p.m. Please come alone. MC

A few hours later, at precisely 4 p.m., Houdini knocked on the door. There was a light shuffling from inside and then silence. The lock clicked and the door opened inward.

Margery Crandon, seeming smaller than she had in her séance room, stood, feet bare, dressed in a simple cotton dress with mother-of-pearl buttons running down the front. She stepped aside but he didn't enter the room.

"I didn't think you'd come," she said, her voice low.

"Are you alone?"

"Yes." She smiled a little. "Do you think I intend to do you harm?"

"There are a finite number of reasons a married woman would invite a married man to a hotel room in a city that she has a house in. I cannot dismiss anything at this point."

Her smile broadened. "We are not ordinary people, Houdini. The usual reasons do not apply to us."

He walked past Margery. It was a sparse room, weakly lit, with a bed on one side and a small sitting area on the other. He chose a high-backed chair that was pushed up against the wall and sat. From here no one would be able to sneak up behind him—he could see the whole room, including both the main door and the door to the bathroom.

Margery closed the door and did not address his rudeness. She sat opposite him, hands folded in her lap. She stared at him, her eyes light brown with flecks of yellow. She seemed to Houdini to be very different from the previous evening, when she remained in control but slightly vacant, as though but a cog in a larger machine. She was playing the part of a medium. Now she was playing another role. Or she was herself. He didn't know. She seemed apprehensive, even vulnerable.

"Well," he said. "Why are we here?"

"I know your opinion of me. I heard everything you said to Malcolm Bird last night."

"I realize that. Do you dispute my assessment of your methods?"

She looked away toward the window, and he wondered if she was about to signal a confederate, but she simply gazed at the empty space. After a time she looked back at him.

"It's more complicated than you think. I don't think you realize who you're dealing with, how completely they believe in what they're doing, or what they will do to those who make themselves their enemies."

"Are you threatening me, Mrs. Crandon?"

"No," she said. "But you know as well as I do what kind of a man my husband is. And he's not the only one. They will not hesitate to kill you. They have already begun to plan."

"But if I don't expose you, they will reconsider?"

She tilted her head. "Yes, they will."

"You know I can't do that."

"Can't you?"

He leaned back in his chair. He knew he should leave, that every moment he spent in this room with Margery Crandon risked his reputation. But there was something about this woman that he was drawn to, and it was more than simple charisma.

"Why do you do it?" he asked. "Why do you lie to these people?"

She scratched her forehead, a gesture that Houdini recognized as anything but casual or offhand—it was a stage gesture. This woman was a magician.

"When I met my husband, I was a widow with two children. We had no money and I had no prospects. In the beginning things were fine with Le Roi, but soon I could feel him tiring of me. I knew what would happen if he abandoned me. But then one night, for fun, we took part in a séance with a Ouija board. In an instant I realized I knew how to manipulate it. I did it for fun, out of boredom, but Le Roi believed it, and everyone else did. That night at home he looked at me differently, like he needed me. Like I could be useful in his world."

Houdini thought about this. He'd heard this story from more than one debunked medium. Many had expressed relief at having been revealed. But she didn't seem to be expressing relief.

"He can't believe what you're doing is real."

"He knows there are tricks and gimmicks, but at its essence he believes there is truth to my abilities and all we do is enhance people's experience of that truth."

"And you do not dissuade him of that?"

She snorted, the first lapse in her performance. "What do you think would become of me if I did? He would kill you in a heartbeat if he could, and I do not doubt that eventually he will if you persist. That pales in comparison to what he would do to me. What they would do to me."

"Who are 'they' exactly?" he asked.

She looked at him and he saw her fear. Whatever facade she had been maintaining had dropped away. "If you think I'm going to tell you that, you're a fool. I'm not here to help you make things worse, Houdini. We have common interests."

"And what are our common interests?"

"Survival."

"I don't follow."

"I am beginning to doubt the considerable intelligence you have loudly and publicly credited yourself with. Do you not understand that if you successfully discredit me, then we will each of us likely end up dead?"

"These risks," he said, "are risks we accept. You've gone down this road, as have I. It's hard to imagine turning back now."

"There is a way you could discredit me without destroying me." She unbuttoned the top button of her dress. "You could give away a few things, the odd trick. The true believers would brush it off. You would maintain your credibility." Her hands continued undoing buttons with a deftness that confirmed his belief that she was a skilled magician. She paused when she reached her waist. "Neither of us would lose our reputations."

"Or," he said, "you could simply stop lying."

"Is it lying? I suppose it is. But there's no force on earth or beyond it that can make a man believe in something he doesn't want to." She stood up, and with a subtle roll of her shoulders her dress collapsed to the floor. She wore nothing underneath. He rose from his chair. She did not seem nervous or apprehensive. She was offering herself to him in the way one might offer a houseguest a drink. She was a striking woman, with flawless skin and a combination of softness and muscle that he wanted to reach out and touch.

"Mrs. Crandon, I'm a married man."

She stepped slightly closer to him. "I know that," she said, and he could smell lavender bath soap. "And I also know that you do not take those vows very seriously."

He stepped away from her. "How is it that you know this?"

"We know everything about you." He wondered how it was that she was naked and he was fully clothed yet somehow she was exposing him. "Remember, we can talk to the dead."

She laughed at this, and he backed away. He knew the thing to do was to escape. He desired her even though he knew he was being manipulated. Every time he had been unfaithful to Bess, he knew that it was dangerous and wrong, but there was a part of him that spoke louder. Was it simple lust? There was no earthly reason he should still be here in this room with this woman who was his enemy. And there was no reason he should be stepping forward and pulling her to him, his hands on the small of her back, then her buttocks.

Just before he kissed her, though, he stopped and pushed her away. She stumbled back, almost losing her balance, and in that moment he saw an ugliness in her, pathetic and desperate, and felt that same ugliness in himself.

"Please, I'm begging you." She folded her arms to cover her breasts.

"The lies you've told are yours," he said. "You'll have to live with what they bring you."

"Everybody lies," she said. "Even the great Houdini."

"Yes," he said. "No doubt I will get what's coming to me."

He moved past her, and she shuddered as their shoulders brushed. When he reached the door, he opened it without hesitation, not caring if someone passing in the hallway should look in and see her, or him leaving her like this. He closed the door behind him and made his way out of the hotel.

As he passed Rose on the street, he touched the brim of his hat, a signal that instructed her to stay put and monitor the hotel. She walked on as though she hadn't seen him, but when they met up hours later back at his hotel his suspicions were confirmed.

"Dr. Crandon arrived about ten minutes after you left, to pick her up. They looked grim when they came out of the Lennox." Rose sat in the leather armchair by the desk while Houdini stood beside the window, watching the street below.

"So it was a setup all along."

"Did you ever think otherwise?"

The image of Margery, naked before him, came into his mind. "No."

"So what now?" He couldn't tell if Rose was tired or excited. His ability to read her hadn't improved.

He crossed the room to the desk and retrieved an envelope. "Mail this to the *Times*."

Rose took the envelope but didn't move. "So you expose this séance. They'll just change their methods, change their effects."

He said nothing. Rose was right. They were fighting a losing battle. "What would you have us do, then?"

"Go to one of your politician friends. What they do is fraud, the same as writing bad checks or rigging the stock market. It should be against the law."

"No politician will bring in a law like that."

She smiled. "What if they had no choice?"

He understood her immediately. In the course of their

investigations, they'd become privy to all sorts of information about various leaders of society. The sort of information those men would want to protect. He smiled back at Rose. "You're worth every penny I've ever paid you."

"I'm worth triple what you pay me." She held up the envelope. "What do you want me to do with this?"

"Mail it."

When he told Grigoriev of his plan, the wily Russian wiped his scissors on the towel that hung over his shoulder and studied the back of Houdini's head.

"There are fourteen million spiritualists now," Grigoriev said to him, "maybe more. And that's just in America."

"I know," Houdini said.

Grigoriev snipped off a bit of hair and considered his handiwork. "You'll find in today's files a very interesting letter our man in London intercepted from Doyle to Le Roi Crandon."

"Really?"

"It seems Doyle's talking spirit has predicted your death."

Houdini snorted. "That's no surprise."

Grigoriev put down the scissors. "I don't think it's a prediction. I think it's an order."

Houdini stared at himself in the mirror. It was strange for him to see himself now, middle-aged and tired. In his core he felt like the same boy who'd rapped off handcuffs in Appleton. "You give the slowest haircuts of any barber in America."

"I like to do a good job."

He held the scissors above Houdini's head. "Are you sure you want to do this?"

"The haircut?"

"No."

He didn't answer. Whether he wanted to or not was immaterial. He was a man who finished what he started.

A few weeks later Houdini was backstage after a show at the Hippodrome when three men came into his dressing room. They were serious men, and he could immediately tell they were carrying guns. For a second he thought that Doyle was about to make good on his threat, but as he got to his feet John Wilkie walked in. One of his men closed the door behind him and the other two stood off to the side.

Wilkie observed him for a moment. Houdini couldn't tell what he saw—his face betrayed nothing. He hadn't worked for Wilkie for years, and the man had no hold over him now. There was no reason he should be afraid, and he wasn't.

After examining the room, Wilkie nodded to his men and sat down. The men left, closing the door behind them. It was the first time since the day they'd met that the two of them had been alone.

"Hello, Ehrich." He looked old. Houdini wondered if he could still palm cards like he used to.

"Hello, John."

"I saw the show. It was good." He leaned forward and put his hands on his knees. "I'm coming here as a courtesy, a sort of thanks for all you've done for your country over the years."

Houdini said nothing. It surprised him that Wilkie saw it this way. From his vantage point, it had seemed like Wilkie always wanted more of him, that whatever he had done was insufficient and by not doing more he had put himself in danger. Was that not the point of Findlay's ominous appearances?

"It would be a bad thing for you if you testified against the spiritualists at the congressional hearings next month."

"It would put them all out of business. How is that a bad thing?" Wilkie seemed bemused.

"Don't tell me you're one of them. Have you been talking to the dead? What did our old friend Melville have to say?"

Wilkie sat back. "I'm surprised at you. I thought you were a much smarter man. I'm not a spiritualist, Ehrich. But if you've learned as much as I think you have, you know how far up this goes."

He was fishing for information. "The truth is as it is," Houdini said. "A man of principle can't ignore it or pretend it to be otherwise."

"You don't understand these people. It's a religion to them. They base their lives on what the medium tells them. They listen to the dead. That's a powerful thing, and you and I both know that power is never relinquished voluntarily."

"I have no illusions that they will do so. I intend to take their power from them."

"You don't want to go in front of Congress."

Houdini stood up. "You've intimidated me plenty, John. I remember all those times your man Findlay hovered around, worse than any ghost, and still I'm here. I appreciate the warning, if that's what this really is, but you and I have no further business to discuss."

"Do you ever wonder," Wilkie said, his voice low and commanding, "how it is you came to be where you are? Do you remember yourself, before there was a Houdini, a magician, a crusader? There was a person there, once, I suspect. And to survive, as we all must, you invented a persona, a shell to show the world. But at some point that shell took over. I don't think you know which parts of you are real and what parts are made up, and I think this frightens you."

Houdini felt the blood rush to his face. Wilkie had rattled him, and he couldn't hide it.

"Maybe you're right," he said. "Is it different for any of us? Can you honestly say you're not the same?"

Wilkie shook his head. "I may be just as caught up in my own illusions as you. But I am not an invention. And whatever I am, it does not frighten me."

"You're not going to change my mind."

Wilkie rose, and Houdini thought he looked genuinely disappointed. "I'm sorry we're here," he said. "I'd hoped it would be different."

Wilkie held out his hand and he shook it. When he released Wilkie's hand, a quarter was in Houdini's palm.

Houdini stood in the basement. There were only two boxes left in the pile he'd set out for removal, but the rest of the space was cluttered with hundreds more boxes, all of them full of the files he'd amassed on the followers of spiritualism. Every time his agents visited a séance they took meticulous notes.

Rose returned and placed her hand on his shoulder. "We should get going."

"Is all this worth it?"

She removed her hand. "Of course it is. You know that too."

"Do I?"

"Yes, you do. The truth is the most important thing of all."

Rose was right. But the truth wasn't easily identifiable. You could spot a lie, but the opposite of a lie wasn't always the truth. He was against the liars, and those who capitalized on the pain of loss, but was what he was pursuing the truth?

"Is it possible that the truth is what you believe?" he said, startling himself.

"No," Rose said.

But still he wondered. If something was not known to be true, was it therefore *un*true? Was truth the absence of a lie? And what was it exactly that people had been getting from him all these years? The magic, the escapes, the challenges. He'd been careful ever since Harold Osbourne to make it clear that what he did was amazing and marvelous but not occult. But had people listened to him? Had they believed him? Maybe they had decided to believe that there was such a thing as magic in the world. He had made them believe in magic because they had wanted to. He knew it wasn't real, but they didn't. For them, none of it was a lie.

He had refused Bess's request to adopt a child. They argued, they fought, and he kept refusing. She hadn't forgotten about it. And she was right. There was no reason not to adopt. But he'd lost the ability to tell which parts of him were real and which were tricks. If there was a center to him, he didn't know what it was. All he knew how to be was Houdini.

"If Houdini isn't real," Bess had said, "it's because you made him that way. You are hiding from yourself inside a fiction."

"Why do we need a child?"

"Why would we not? It is a part of life, a part of being a human. We can't have our own, but why should that matter?"

"That's not the issue."

"No, it isn't. The issue is you are unwilling to be anything other than the focus of attention. You must maintain your illusion at all costs, because without it you fade away."

She was right. How could he be a father to a child, then? How could he teach anyone anything about how the world worked, about how to be a person, about what could be trusted and what could not, if he was nothing more than an artifice?

Rose reached for one of the two remaining boxes. "We have to go," she said. "It's late, and we have only a few hours before the train leaves."

He bent down and picked up the last box of files. It felt heavier than the others, and as he carried it out of the basement its weight increased. When he heaved it into the car his arms ached and a drop of sweat rolled down his brow and off the tip of his nose. He couldn't remember ever having been so tired.

The day of the congressional hearings Houdini woke up before the sun, having barely slept. He dressed in silence and left the hotel early, careful not to wake Bess. He walked the streets of Washington, deserted except for those few whose work necessitated forsaking their beds. He walked past the White House, where he knew President Coolidge held regular séances. He walked past the homes of members of Congress, where he knew matters of state were being regularly discussed with false mediums. He had irrefutable proof.

He reached into his pocket and unfolded the letter he'd received from Doyle the day before.

> *I write to you because we were once friends, though I now admit I may have been mistaken, that you may have been performing one of your ruses on me for our entire association. But your treatment of Margery Crandon and her good husband has left me no choice but to issue this dire warning to you, in the hopes that you will exercise your better judgment. If you do not desist in your slander, there are forces at work who shall see to it that you desist. I have been so told from beyond the veil. The enclosed list should convince you of his veracity. Out of respect for your wife, who I believe to be a good and dear woman who has likely suffered much on your account, I pledge that I will not betray the Spirits' confidence. But there are others who have access to beyond the veil who may not be so inclined, unless you were to amend your ways. Be warned.*

> *ACD*

The list, which he had already burned, contained the names of every woman he had ever slept with while married to Bess. Names even he had forgotten. They were all there except Evatima Tardo.

He put the letter back in his pocket, watched the sun rise,

and then returned to his hotel. Bess had awoken and dressed, and he read the paper as he waited for breakfast to be sent up.

"I'm nervous," Bess said.

He put the paper down. "There's no need," he said. "All we have to do is tell the truth. This law will make it illegal for them to charge money for their séances. Take away the money and you take away the motivation."

When their food arrived, neither of them ate much. Houdini slipped a piece of toast wrapped in a napkin into the pocket of his coat in case he was hungry later.

The House Judiciary Subcommittee met in one of the larger rooms in the Capitol. He'd expected the room to feel like a courtroom, but it seemed to him more like a large meeting room. There was a table set up on one end where ten or so congressmen sat, and then they called on various people to address them.

His plan was simple. Houdini would show Congress how the cheats operated. He'd reveal how each of them had been duped. The two most strident spiritualists on the subcommittee were McLeod and Hammer. Houdini had files three inches thick on each of them. By the end of the hearings it would be illegal for spiritualists to collect so much as a dime.

Finally, after a morning listening to mediums and policemen, they called on him to speak. He was sworn in, and he wiggled his eyebrows at Bess as he took the oath. She raised a hand to her mouth to cover a smile.

One of his few allies, a congressman named Bloom, addressed the room.

"I would like Mr. Houdini to make a short statement about the bill."

Hammer leaned back in his chair. "May I inquire who he is and if he is not an astrologer?"

The gallery laughed at this, and Hammer scowled at the room. Even the spiritualists laughed. It was ridiculous that Hammer didn't know who Houdini was. Houdini was one of the few who didn't laugh. He knew this was gamesmanship, nothing more.

Bloom looked at Hammer over his glasses. "Mr. Houdini is generally regarded as the world's preeminent magician."

Houdini reached into his pocket, produced an envelope, and tossed it onto the table in front of him. "Congressmen, I have here ten thousand dollars, and I will happily forfeit it to any medium present who can produce an effect I cannot replicate."

The gallery erupted. Every medium in the place was screaming at him. He stood motionless, surveying the crowd dispassionately. Bloom and Hammer were shouting at each other, though he couldn't make out their words over the din.

McLeod waved his hands for silence, and the room gradually regained some semblance of order. McLeod waited for a few seconds before speaking.

"Mr. Houdini, you are here to answer the questions of this committee, not engage in publicity challenges. I will remind you this is the United States Congress, not some vaudeville house."

Houdini smiled, undeterred, and returned the money to his pocket.

"Have you any religious views?" Hammer asked, barely able to contain his anger.

"Yes, sir. I am the son of a rabbi. For hundreds of years my forebears were rabbis."

Hammer sneered. "I am surprised that a man of such faith so easily attacks another man's religion."

"Spiritualism is not a religion. It only operates under the cloak of religion. Its real purpose is less noble than any religion, and that is what I quarrel with."

"But your work is sleight of hand? You do not yourself claim any divine power?" Hammer spoke not to Houdini but to the assembled room.

"No. I call what I do mystification."

"Do you claim you have psychic power?"

"No one has. We are all born alike. I am an ordinary mortal. Like you."

McLeod laughed, but it was clear that he found nothing funny about what Houdini had said.

"I think you've admitted you are a fraud!"

"What I do is not real."

"But people believe it is."

"Some do. But I tell them it is trickery."

Hammer leaned in and spoke to an aide. Houdini tried to read his lips but couldn't. The aide nodded to Hammer and left his side, making his way to the gallery. McLeod kept on.

"Do they not pay an admission fee?"

"Yes."

"Then it is a fact that you do practically the same thing as those you denounce, only you call it trickery."

The spiritualists in the gallery bayed with delight. Houdini had to shout to be heard. "I do not call it religion, and I do not charge them for telling their fortunes. I entertain people."

The gallery again erupted into howls.

He looked behind him to where Rose Mackenberg was sitting. She had a box containing the transcripts of séances attended by both Hammer and McLeod. Hammer had asked a medium about a crucial vote, and had voted as the medium had suggested, as well as admitted to having accepted significant bribes. McLeod had repeatedly sought advice on the crafting of law and had revealed sensitive information that could compromise national security. In a few moments Houdini would present these files to the committee.

But something was wrong. Rose was gone. She had been there when he'd gone up, but had since vanished. He had nothing.

Grigoriev should have been in the audience as well, but Houdini didn't know what his disguise was, and there was no way he'd be able to pick him out of the chaos. He sank back in his chair. He'd been thwarted.

The committee asked him a few more questions, but the proceedings were going nowhere. In the end they voted against the creation of a law banning charging money for the telling of fortunes.

Houdini and Bess fought their way through the throngs of reporters and spiritualists to the street. Rose was nowhere to be found. Houdini dropped Bess back at the hotel and went to the meeting place he'd arranged in advance with Rose and Grigoriev— should anything go wrong, they were to meet on a bench in a park overlooking the Potomac. He waited until well after midnight, his hand on his derringer the whole time. But neither of them showed.

The next morning he took the train with Bess to New York. When he got home there was a small clump of hair inside the newspaper on the front step. He smiled and went inside, put on a hat and changed his coat, kissed Bess, and went straight out the back door.

It took him longer than usual to get to Grigoriev's barber shop. He took a circuitous route, in case anyone was following him. At one point he was sure someone was, but he ducked into a restaurant where he knew the owner and went out the rear exit. Satisfied that no one was shadowing him, he headed to the barber shop.

Grigoriev was sweeping a floor that was already clean. Houdini climbed into the chair.

"You don't need a haircut."

"Then I'm not paying you."

"A small trim wouldn't hurt."

"Where's Rose?"

"Safe."

"What happened?"

Grigoriev had been watching from the opposite side of the gallery when a man came up to Rose and grabbed her by the arm, his other hand inside his coat holding what Grigoriev knew was a gun. Rose had looked around for help and, finding none, had gone outside with him. They were about to get into a car when Grigoriev caught up with them. He was able to knock the man over and get away with Rose, but had judged it too dangerous to remain in Washington.

"The files?"

"They have them."

"Who has them?"

"Wilkie. The guy was one of his men."

It didn't make sense for Wilkie to steal his files. Whatever Houdini knew, Wilkie knew too.

"I think it's time to admit we've lost," Grigoriev said.

"What? You're out of your mind."

"I don't think you understand what's happened. You've become caught up in a game, in an idea of right and wrong. But this is no longer about crooks and liars. This is about power. They have it all, and we have none. We've been lucky up to this point. Do you think they would have just let Rose go? If she had gone in that car we never would have seen her again."

Houdini was about to argue but stopped. Like the final pin in a lock it all came together. Wilkie had all but told him, but he hadn't listened.

Wilkie wasn't protecting these men of power. He was controlling them. Most if not all of the mediums who held sittings for the elite set were former magicians. Vaudeville had taken a nosedive, and those hit hardest were the performers on the low end of the scale. But Wilkie knew the value of magicians. He'd known it when he'd approached Houdini all those years ago. When Houdini had turned out to be less than compliant, he'd simply found other magicians. He'd turned them into mediums and was using them to control the reins of power.

He knew about the women because he'd been watching Houdini all along. Evatima Tardo hadn't been on the list because she happened before Wilkie.

"We're in real danger," Grigoriev said. "You, me, Rose, the whole organization."

"We knew this would be dangerous."

"We did. Did Bess?"

Bess. If Grigoriev was right, she was a target.

Grigoriev put his hand on Houdini's shoulder. "They intend to kill you. Doyle actually thinks that once you're on the other side, you'll thank him for showing you the error of your ways."

Houdini snorted. "Doesn't he know that ghosts haunt you, not thank you?"

"The man has lost all sense, but that's beside the point. Wilkie controls this game. Or worse, there are men who control Wilkie that we don't even know about. You forget, I think, that I have significant experience in the machinations of powerful men. It is about to cost you your life. It's about to cost you Bess's life. It's time to end it. You know what we have to do."

Houdini sank farther into the chair. Grigoriev was right. He had no other choice. He could not allow them to hurt Bess. He'd already done that enough himself. "Okay," he said. "Shut it down. Shut down the whole operation."

Grigoriev shook his head. "That's not enough. They're still going to come for you."

Houdini nodded. "I know."

The car was loaded. The boxes containing the files of all high-ranking members of the American, British, and Canadian governments who were under the sway of Wilkie's mediums were inside. Houdini sat in the passenger seat while Rose closed the doors and got behind the wheel. The car roared to life and she put it in gear.

He handed her the address. The files would be secure there for now. They'd meet Bess and the rest of his crew at the train station in a few hours, go north on one final tour, and after that all of this would be done.

"Ready, boss?" Rose asked. She let off on the clutch and began to pull away.

"Wait. Stop," he said.

Rose brought the car to a halt. Houdini looked out the window. He remembered the theater in Garnett, Kansas, the look on Harold Osbourne's face as he stormed toward him, on Bess's face when the doctor told them she couldn't have children, the way she had cried when he said he wouldn't go along with any plan of adoption. He saw his father's skin, thin as paper, the slippers he'd bought for his mother and placed in her casket. All the escapes, the crowds cheering and carrying him on their shoulders. He remembered the day he bought this house, of telling his mother and Bess that this house was theirs, that from here on everything would be a dream. Had he lied to them? No, he'd just been wrong. He hadn't understood himself. He hadn't understood anything at all.

He buried his face in his hands. All the things that had never happened, that now would never happen.

"Go," he said to Rose, and the car pulled away from Bess, sleeping upstairs or maybe lying awake wondering where he was going. He looked out the window at the empty streets and murmured, "I'll never see my house again."

MARTIN STRAUSS

1927

I STOOD IN THE DARK ON LIME STREET IN BOSTON. A clouded sky obscured the moon, and the glow of the streetlight barely penetrated the night. I was glad for the shadows. Whatever was happening inside the large well-kept house that loomed in front of me was connected with my predicament. I wanted to know how, and I didn't want anybody to know I was there.

In the haste of my departure from New York I'd nearly forgotten the papers I'd removed from my attacker's pockets during the police raid. I didn't look at them until I was safely on a train out of Manhattan. There were a few loose bills and two envelopes. One of the envelopes was full of cash—when I counted it later, out of view of anyone who might like to deprive me of it, I discovered almost a thousand dollars. It appeared that my financial worries were over for some time. When I examined the contents of the other envelope, however, any relief this windfall had offered dissipated.

Our contact in the house of the disbeliever has located the whereabouts of his journal. She followed the pigeon to a flophouse at Hudson and Vestry. One Martin Strauss. Walter advises that it would be of great benefit if the hand of John G. Nemesis would retrieve the book and if necessary remove him from consideration. Expenses and remuneration enclosed.

The letter was on the stationery of a Dr. Le Roi Crandon, 10 Lime Street, Boston, his signature scrawled on the bottom of the letter. I didn't know who Walter was, but there was nothing comforting about either the tone of this letter or the rather massive sum of money he was willing to pay to gain possession of Houdini's book. I assumed that Nemesis was the man who had come after me.

I thought of Clara. The last time I had seen her was on a night like this one. I remembered the way she had looked at me, right before I punched Houdini.

A light came on inside the Crandon house, and then the porch light as well. A few moments later all of the lights on the second floor began to glow. There was a hedge in front of the next house over in which I found an excellent hiding spot.

For a time there was no further activity inside the house. Hiding in bushes made me feel I was doing something wrong. It would have been difficult to explain my situation to the police.

"Oh, Martin," my mother said, "you worry about the oddest things."

"They don't seem odd to me," I whispered.

"You don't need to worry about what things look like. You only need to worry about what they are."

Coming up the sidewalk was an older couple, possibly in

their late fifties or early sixties. Their clothes and the way they carried themselves revealed their wealth. These were the sort of people Clara's father associated with. People of stature, of substance, of reputation.

"My goodness," my mother said, "those are some well-dressed people."

When they reached the Crandon house, they turned and went up the short path leading to the door. The woman paused to adjust her coat and her husband knocked on the door. After a few seconds it opened, but I couldn't see past them to whoever was there.

Not long after, a taxi pulled up and four people got out, three men and a woman. Another car arrived close behind with another quartet. Together the eight of them walked up to the door. They had a jovial air.

The door opened, but once again I was unable to catch a glimpse of the person inside. No one else arrived. From where I was hiding I couldn't see much of what was happening, only a shadow of someone at a window, a silhouette imprinted on the drapes. I would have to get closer.

I stood and crept nearer to the house. There was possibly a good vantage point on the far side of the property, and if I were to climb the large tree in the front yard I might be able to see into the second-floor window.

"I wouldn't do that if I were you," said a voice behind me. I turned and saw a man dressed in black standing in the shadows.

"I wasn't doing anything."

"Of course not, Mr. Strauss."

"How do you know my name?"

He stepped forward into the light. He was in his early sixties, with white hair, but appeared to be in good physical condition. He was dressed modestly but wore his clothes with precision. It was easy to imagine him springing from bed in the morning with not a hair out of place.

"I've been watching you for a long time. You've done well. But you don't want to get any closer to the Crandons. You shouldn't be here."

Just then the lights upstairs went off.

"They're starting now. We should go."

"Who are you?"

"My name is Grigoriev. I'm a friend."

Grigoriev. This was the man Bess Houdini had told me about. He might know about the book, why Houdini had planted it on me, and why Dr. Crandon and Walter wanted it.

I followed him down the street to a car. It had a scrape on the side. I got in the passenger side and he drove us away from Beacon Hill. He kept his eyes on the road while he spoke.

"There is much I cannot and will not tell you," he said. "Some of it is for your own safety, and some information I am not at liberty to divulge. I work on behalf of Houdini. I know that you are in possession of his notebook, and I have been keeping track of you for some time. Unfortunately, when you went to visit Bess, the maid alerted those faithful to the spiritualists. Since then you have been in danger."

"You've been following me?"

"Yes."

"Were you there in New York when John G. Nemesis attacked me?"

"The way I saw it, you attacked him. John G. Nemesis is a

spiritualist catchall name for the hand of fate. He has many guises
and can be anyone. In this case, he is a man we know very well."

"Who is Dr. Le Roi Crandon? Who is Walter?"

"Dr. Crandon is the husband of Margery Crandon, the witch
of Beacon Hill. She's possibly the most prominent medium in
America. Walter is her dead brother, with whom she claims to
communicate from beyond the grave."

I remembered Houdini talking about the witch of Beacon
Hill at the Princess Theater in Montreal. According to him she
was a fraud of the highest order.

"Why do they want the book?"

"I can't answer that."

"Why did Houdini give me the book?"

"I can't answer that either."

"You can't, or you won't?"

"I'm not sure you appreciate the situation you're in. I am not
your enemy. This isn't about you or me or even Houdini."

"Then what is it about?" I felt an anger rising in me that I
wasn't sure I could contain.

Grigoriev's voice was soft and calm. "It is about competing
views of the world, a question of what is real and what is not."

"And what do I have to do with any of this?"

"No more or less than anyone. Perhaps you have yet to discover what is real and what is not in your own life." He swerved,
the momentum of the car leaning me away from him.

"The book is coded."

"It's a standard keyword code."

A keyword code. I knew a bit about these from the spy novels
I read as a kid. A word or phrase created a numerical value that

would allow a person to encipher passages of text. If the person receiving the garbled text knew the keyword, it would be a relatively simple matter to decode the text. "What's the keyword?"

"If I were to tell you and they were to find out, they would kill you."

They were already trying to kill me. Knowing the contents of the book didn't seem to make a difference. "I could destroy the book."

"Yes."

"I could just give it to them."

"Yes."

Perhaps if the Crandons had the book, they'd leave me alone. Though the incident with their thug probably wouldn't go overlooked. But giving them the book or destroying it didn't feel right.

"I didn't mean to punch Houdini," I said. I knew that the reason I had kept and would continue to protect the book was guilt.

"Didn't you? It didn't look like an accident."

"You were there?"

He said nothing, his eyes on the road. But he was right. The punch wasn't an accident. I may not have known why I did it, but my fist swung with intent.

"I didn't mean to kill him."

We had arrived back at my cheap hotel. He parked across the street and turned off the engine.

"Houdini was fond of saying that when he died, the spiritualists would declare the day a holiday. He may have underestimated their glee. All over the world telegrams and letters flew back and forth proclaiming victory. He was, for them, their greatest obstacle. They had tried to kill him before, and were actively trying to kill him now. There is no limit to what they will do in the name of their cause. Bear that in mind, Martin."

Grigoriev reached into his pocket and removed a letter. "This is for you. I collected it when you left New York."

I took the letter from him. It was indeed addressed to me, posted from Montreal. The return address was Clara's but the handwriting on the envelope wasn't hers.

"Thank you. What happens next?"

"Do we ever know what happens next? They will make a move, and we'll see where that leads us."

"I meant what happens to me."

Grigoriev smiled. "You should get some sleep. I'll be nearby, and will be in touch if need be. Just stay away from the Crandons for now."

I got out and watched him drive away. It was baffling how easy it was for people to find me. After all the precautions I'd taken, telling no one where I was, making no friends and keeping to myself, using a false name, and living completely disconnected from the world at large, it was simple for Grigoriev to track me and the Crandons to find me. Were Houdini's escapes so popular because people knew deep down that there was no way for anyone to escape?

I walked around the block to make sure no one was following me and then climbed the stairs to my fifth-floor room. Each thud of my feet was a thumping reminder of my exile.

The hair I had placed on my doorknob was undisturbed— another technique I'd read about. I opened the door and slipped inside. My hands were steady as I sat on the bed and tore open the letter Grigoriev had given me.

Mr. Martin Strauss,

Clara does not wish for you to have further contact with her. Given what you have done, I suggest you respect her wishes. As it stands I hereby discharge you of any further duty concerning her. You have disappeared, and you will stay disappeared. Should you contact her again I will bring down the full force of the law upon you.

The letter was signed by Clara's father.

I lay back on the bed and closed my eyes. What was I doing? What was I trying to accomplish? You don't abandon those you love, or those you could love, for nothing. Houdini had done it. And I had done it too. This elaborate game he had mixed me up in was just an excuse.

"It doesn't matter why you did it," my mother said, sitting on the bed beside me.

"Yes, it does."

"It only matters that it's done. It can't be taken back." She looked so young. Like she'd looked when I was a boy.

"Then there's no hope?"

She shook her head. "I didn't say that."

"Didn't you?"

She smiled and reached toward me. "Martin, dear Martin. Haven't you been listening?"

I stretched out to grasp her hand, but she was gone.

Houdini's book was hidden in the lining of my coat. I retrieved it and opened it to the first page. I'd looked at the letters many times before, but they remained as cryptic as ever.

QRQHRIWKLVLVUHDO
BRXUPHPRUBFDQQRWEHWUXVWHG
WKLVLVDOOUHDO

Gibberish. If there were clues inside, I wasn't going to find them, not without the keyword at least.

There was a bottle of whiskey on the floor beside my bed. I'd bought it the day before. I picked it up and stared at it. I could hide inside it, I knew. It wasn't an answer, but it was something. Things needed to stop. The confusion, the anger, the loss. The first third of the bottle charred. The second third tingled. An hour later, when I dropped the empty bottle on the floor and passed into oblivion, I felt nothing.

I stayed there for the next week, leaving my room only when it seemed like I would run out of drink. My routine was simple— any time a thought crept into my head, I drank it down. If my mother came to me, I drank her away. If a letter ended up in my hand, I drank it back into my pocket. My goal was to remain insensate, and for a while I achieved it.

One morning I woke up, on the floor, sober. I'd emptied every bottle I had, and while I didn't feel like having more, I didn't feel like changing anything either, so I pulled myself to my feet and made my way outside to find one of the local bootleggers.

It felt odd to be outside. Like I was in a foreign country where I didn't belong. I kept my head down for the first few blocks, but all I saw were parked cars, trees, grass, and the paving stones of the sidewalk. The farther I went, though, the more a feeling of alarm rose inside me. Something was off and I almost missed what it was.

I stopped walking. Grigoriev's car was parked about half a block back. I was sure of it. I should have recognized the unmistakable scrape on the passenger side door.

So he was still watching me. I hadn't expected any less of him. But still I stayed frozen on the sidewalk. Had I seen something inside the car? I felt like I had, like something was there that shouldn't have been and I'd somehow ignored it and kept on. It wouldn't be the first time I'd let my mind refute a fact.

It came back to me before I could actually see him. Grigoriev was inside the car, collapsed over the steering wheel. His face was obscured by his arm, as though he was sleeping.

When I reached the car I opened the passenger door and got inside. I pulled him back by the collar of his coat and he groaned. The front of his shirt was stained with blood, his hands and the car door handle coated with it. His face was drained of all color except for his lips, which were a pale blue.

"Who did this?"

He licked his lips, trying to speak. "John G. Nemesis. Findlay."

"Was it the Crandons?"

Grigoriev started to laugh but got nowhere, simply emitting a weak croak. "I told them you were a decoy. That you were always a decoy. I gave them a false book and keyword. That should buy you some time."

"What's in my book?"

"Most of it's a diary," he said. "At the end of it is a list of people who the spiritualists control and the means by which they're using them."

"What people?"

"You need to find him. He needs to know what's happened. This was not part of the plan." Grigoriev looked past me.

"I don't understand." I felt sick. A strong desire rose to be anywhere else but there.

"Forgive." His hand shook, and his eyes began to dart from side to side.

"Forgive who?"

"Forgive," he said. His eyes stopped moving. His mouth hung open. He looked surprised.

I raced out of the car and back toward my hotel. I didn't care if anyone saw me or was following me. It was as if I were an animal who had just caught sight of a predator, obeying only my instinct to run. I took the stairs to my room two at a time, unlocked my door, and slammed it behind me.

My room was a mess. I wasn't sure if this was because someone had ransacked it or because I'd been on a drunken binge for the past week. But the envelope containing what was left of the money I'd taken off the hired gun in New York was untouched.

I fell to my knees. Sweat dripped off my forehead and I watched it pool on the floor, soaking into the bare wood. I leaned forward and dry heaved.

My mother knelt next to me. "This is the last time I'll visit you," she said.

"Because of the drinking?"

"No."

"Because of what I did to Clara?"

"No."

"Then why?"

She looked old to me, older than I ever remembered her look-ing. Much older than she would have been. "It's how it works."

"I don't want it to work like this," I said.

"It doesn't matter how we want things to be. It doesn't even matter how things have been. Things are the way they are, and nothing can change the moment you're in."

I don't know how long I lay on the floor. It was dark outside when I was able to get up. I wiped my eyes clean and ran my sleeve across my mouth. I gathered my belongings and left, not bothering to collect the deposit I'd left with the hotel clerk.

The train station was deserted and I hadn't made up my mind where I would go. There wasn't anywhere left. I sought out a bench in a corner and replayed the last thing Grigoriev had said.

An idea seized me. In the spy novel I'd read, where a key-word code was used, each letter was given a number, A as 1, B as 2, and so on until Z was 26. With a keyword, you added up the relative numeric values of the letters of the word until you got a number. F-O-R-G-I-V-E, F as 6, O as 15, R as 18, until it all adds up to 82. Divide that by the number of letters in the alphabet and you end up with four letters left over. So the idea is that A would be written as D, the fourth letter of the al-phabet, with the rest of the letters transposed in the same way. It's simple, easy enough to decipher with or without the key-word. I made a chart that raised the alphabet by four letters.

I opened Houdini's book and looked at the first sentence. It made sense. I flipped to the back page, which was written in a hasty hand. After a few minutes the message was clear.

I had not killed Houdini because Houdini was not dead. And I knew where he was hiding.

MARTIN STRAUSS

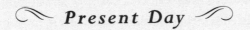

Present Day

"IT'S NOT GOOD NEWS," I SAY. ALICE SEEMS ACCUSTOMED to bad news—she betrays no shock or surprise.

I tell her the particulars of Dr. Korsakoff's diagnosis and ask if she has any questions.

"No, not really," she says.

This puzzles me. I have nothing but questions. The ice cream orderly is again lurking at the entrance.

"What's that guy's problem?" I say, the harshness of my voice surprising me.

Alice looks around. "Who?"

I point toward the hospital doors. "The ice cream man."

She looks at me like I'm a child throwing a tantrum. "He's not an ice cream man, Martin."

"I know that. He looks like one, though. He keeps coming out here and giving me dirty looks. We should go."

"He's just doing his job."

"Since when is staring at me his job?"

Alice begins to answer but thinks better of it. We're on the verge of a disagreement, and she seems to want to step back from it as much as I do. I don't know why I'm acting this way. There's an anger inside me, one I don't know what to do with. I will try harder to keep it in check. Especially around Alice.

We've been meeting regularly every few months or so since I came out of hiding. After that first meeting, where she tracked me down, it took me a while to work up the nerve to tell her my story. I couldn't tell her everything—I still haven't told her everything—but what I did say to her made me feel better. Just being around her seems to bring me a measure of peace. She's like me—she keeps to herself and isn't particularly forthcoming about her life. I enjoy her, though. She's the only link I have to the life I never lived. She's asked me a lot of questions about what I'm like, about my family, about why I am the way I am. Attempting to answer her has bonded us.

We watch the traffic lights on the street change from green to yellow to red and back to green. I can tell she's thinking, and I'm content to leave her to it.

"Do you know why I keep coming to see you?" she says, her voice so soft I almost can't hear her.

She's here for answers, I imagine. As I am the man who killed her father, she wants to know why, how. I want to tell her she was better off without him, that he wasn't anyone she'd have wanted for a father. It's hard to tell someone that their father was a horrible man. No, not hard. It's cruel. The truth is not the salve people make it out to be.

"You want to know what happened," I say.

"When I was about eleven," she says, "my mother took me to the beach. I'd never been before. We lived with my grandparents, who were not the sort of people who did such things. For a week before we went I asked her every day if today was the day, and finally her answer was yes. We took three buses, loaded up with towels and swimming suits and whatever else, it doesn't matter."

I haven't been to the beach in years, but when I was growing up, there was a swimming pond that all the town's kids would go to on hot summer days.

"When we got there, my mother spread out our blanket and said I could go swimming, but I didn't want to. Something felt wrong. I sat on the blanket and watched everyone else, kids building sand castles and swimming and running around, adults joining them or sunning themselves or talking. I couldn't figure out what was wrong, why I wasn't having a good time. My mother gave up trying to make me and sat reading her book.

"I want to be able to tell you a story about seeing a happy family with a mother and father and feeling sorry for myself, or maybe one where I went swimming and had trouble and some stranger had to save me because my father wasn't there, but nothing like that happened at all. I'd brought a small rubber chicken, a toy I was fond of, and at one point a dog picked it up and ran away with it. I didn't do anything, just sat there and watched it go."

Her neck is red and her shoulders are raised. She's looking off at a space where there isn't anything to see, the way people do when they're trying to remember something.

"I don't know what I expected to happen. But I know I

expected something—anything. And nothing happened. There was an absence of event."

An absence created by the loss of her father. An absence created by me. I wonder which is better, a parent who never fully existed or one who has haunted you through your life. Is the ghost of a real parent more or less than the imagination of an invisible one?

"What was it like? The absence." I am afraid of her response. She thinks before answering. I like that about her.

"It's like your life is a mystery. There are pieces of you that you don't know the origin of. They may be yours alone or you may be continuing a long history. There's a voice in your head and you don't know if it's yours or a stranger's."

"I'm sorry."

She smiles. "I know. That's not why I came today."

My head is buzzing. That damned tinnitus. She doesn't seem to understand that she doesn't know what really happened. I need to tell her. Maybe this will help her understand herself, or the voice in her head that might be her own. I'm making a mess of this.

"There's more, Alice. I haven't told you the whole story."

"I don't need to hear it," she says.

Another confabulation jumps out at me. I don't know why certain false memories are so persistent. It's a familiar one. I am sitting in a sparsely furnished room by myself. Above me a bare lightbulb hisses and ticks. There is a pile of boxes in the corner waiting to be unpacked. I am drunk, can taste my dry mouth. I have at some point been crying, but at this moment I am still. I am dazed by loneliness, futility, and the sense that while there was nothing I could have done to avoid ending up as I am, it was still my fault. The telephone rings, and I know that it is Clara calling, but I don't answer it. I can't. I sit there and feel myself get smaller and smaller, until I am certain I will vanish.

Now, recalling this moment that never happened, I want to make myself answer the phone. It doesn't matter why Clara's calling. Even if it is to scream at me, to berate me for all my failings and transgressions, it would be worth it to hear her voice. It doesn't matter that it's only my imagination.

"The past is the past," Alice says, and I remember where I am.

I'm not sure how to answer her. Nothing is in the past for me. Because I remember it in the present, it's in my head right now, though it's always reconstructed. And reconstruction can't be trusted. I can't be trusted. None of us can.

Houdini's audience saw an elephant disappear. That's what they remembered. They'd remember it moments after it happened, weeks after it happened, and years after it happened.

But Jennie the elephant never went anywhere. She went up a ramp into a box. The box was rotated a quarter turn and a curtain was drawn back, revealing an open circle with bars on it. Through this circle they were able to see the inside of the box and the backdrop on the stage behind the box.

Houdini was employing a trick that magicians had been using for a hundred years. It was a mirror. Jennie and her trainer walked into the box and stood behind an angled mirror that reflected the opposite half of the box and the background. They saw half an empty box and its reflection. That's all.

Because the audience saw Jennie go into the box, and they saw, or thought they saw, an empty box, what they reconstructed was a disappearing elephant. Something they knew to be impossible but nevertheless believed. It's what they wanted.

I know what I saw in Alice's father, what sort of man he was. He was a fool. He was a womanizer. He thought he loved his mother—what he really loved was how she made him feel about himself. When she died, he grieved not for her but for himself, for the loss of that version of the man he deep down knew he wasn't. He wanted people to think he was a brave man. At his core he was a coward. He betrayed the woman who loved him, and he betrayed himself. He was not fit to be a father. She might know all this already. But I have never told her. And before I am gone from myself, I need to tell her this, from my own mouth, in my own words. A confession.

"Alice," I say, "I have to tell you what really happened. It's important."

"I don't think it is."

If we have our three times, if there is the past, the present, and the future, then what purpose does the past serve? In the present we experience all sorts of situations, all of them requiring something of us. We need to react in a way that keeps us whole, keeps us from happily racing out into traffic. Without some sort of past, the present would paralyze us.

But does the past change who we are? It may change how Alice feels about her life, but not necessarily for the better. I could tell everyone who saw the elephant disappear in front of them at the Hippodrome that it was just a mirror and some clever physics, but would that make their lives better? Would the reconstruction of their reconstruction be more truthful or of more value to them? Because at the end of the past and the present is the future. It

never really comes but it's there all the same, this supposed place
we will someday get to. But the future is either our own death or
the existence of magic.

My mind is beginning to buzz again, and I'm in danger of
becoming overwhelmed.

"Martin?" she says, placing her hand on my arm. I flinch and
she pulls it back.

"I don't know," I say. My hands are shaking, and I'm speaking
in a voice I haven't used in a long time. I can't figure out what I
need to say. "I don't know what it will do. But soon it will be
gone. I can't keep these memories safe, that's what Dr. Korsakoff
has told me. And this story, it's your past. It's all I have to offer
you."

"Okay," she says. "I understand. Go ahead." There's that face
that is so reassuring.

"I don't know where to start."

She takes my hand. Her fingers are soft. "Start at the beginning."

I take a slow breath and let the buzzing in my ears subside. I
will tell her everything as I know it to be, and will not leave
anything out. She may not like what she learns, but I will have
to accept that as it comes.

"It is a constant struggle not to become the thing you hate
most," I begin.

MARTIN STRAUSS

⟨ *1927* ⟩

THE ANSWER WAS INSIDE A NONDESCRIPT BUILDING NES-
tled against the elevated train at the corner of Third Avenue and
48th Street in Manhattan. According to his book, this was where
Houdini was hiding.

It was a rundown building in a lower-class Irish neighborhood, the sort of place where he could blend in with a minimal
disguise. The people here would be too busy working to pay much
attention to a man who kept to himself and wore his hat low.

His leather book was in my inside pocket. I'd decoded each
and every page into another book that I hadn't brought with me.
It was mostly a list of names, some that I recognized, like President Coolidge and Prime Minister King, and many that I didn't.
After each name was a medium's name and a series of dates. None
of it made much sense until the final few pages. After reading, I
understood Houdini had amassed incriminating files on some of

the world's most powerful men, and he had faked his own death to stay a step ahead of them. The final line of the book was the address of this building.

I stood on the front steps, reached out, and turned the doorknob. It was unlocked, which surprised me, but then again Houdini likely wasn't much for locks. He knew better than anyone how little resistance they offered.

I stepped inside and closed the door behind me, trying to make as little noise as possible. The only advantage I had was that Houdini didn't know I was coming, or if he did, he didn't know when. On the ground floor was a sitting room and a make-shift kitchen, unwashed dishes mounded in the sink. There was a cup of coffee on the counter, still warm. A copy of the previous day's newspaper lay open at a small table.

There was a loud clatter above me, followed by the sound of muffled voices. My first instinct was to look for a place to hide, but then I remembered I'd come there for a reason and instead went to the staircase. The stairs were creaky and it took some effort to ascend them quietly. At the top was a door which was ajar. I peered in, apprehensive. All I could make out was a large stack of boxes and a wooden packing crate. I heard at least two distinct voices.

"You've made this all far more difficult than it needed to be," a voice said.

I pushed the door open a few more inches. A tall man with his back to me had one of the boxes open and was riffling through it. He was crouched down in the middle of the room, pulling papers out of the box with one hand, a revolver in his other hand.

I looked across the room and saw Houdini, thinner than

when I had last seen him. He was tied to a chair and his shirt was torn.

A smart man would have turned and crept back down the stairs and out of the building. Whatever was going on in that room meant that the people who had been looking for me were no longer interested now that they had Houdini.

I was not a smart man. I looked around the room for something to use as a weapon and saw, on top of one of several stacks of boxes, an ancient-looking pistol with an ivory-inlaid handle. As I stepped into the room and picked up the gun, Houdini saw me. He leaned forward in his chair and in a needlessly loud voice shouted at the kneeling man.

"Tell Wilkie that for every file in this room I have a copy hidden elsewhere. Unless I am released you'll never find where."

The man looked up at Houdini. "I already have my instructions."

Each step I took seemed like leaping a canyon. I knew I only had so much time to get to him before he saw me, but I dared not go too quickly for fear of making noise.

"You won't get away with this!" Houdini said.

The man laughed. "Of course I will. It happens all the time."

I gripped the barrel of the gun and swung the stock down hard onto the back of the man's head. He slumped forward and rolled onto his back, unconscious. It was John G. Nemesis, his face marred by a fresh scar from when I'd smashed him with the beer mug.

Houdini stood and shrugged off the ropes binding him like he was stepping out of a robe. He bent down, picked up a section of rope, and rushed toward Nemesis, rolling him over onto his stomach. In a few seconds he'd secured his hands behind his back with a series of knots so complicated I could barely make out how he tied them.

"Allow me to introduce you to Mr. Findlay, though you may know him by a different name."

I was unable to say anything.

Houdini was smaller than I remembered. "Forgive me, Mr. Strauss. I'm sure you're nothing if not confused. All will be explained in a moment. In the meantime, let's get our friend here more secure—people don't stay unconscious in real life for as long as they do in films."

We each took a shoulder and dragged Nemesis to the chair, where Houdini trussed him up as quickly as he'd escaped his own bonds.

"I'll have Grigoriev deal with him later," he said, standing back to admire his work. He turned to me. "I'm aware you and my Russian friend have met," he said. "I'm aware of all that's happened to you lately."

"Grigoriev's dead," I said.

He stepped back, shaken. "Are you sure?"

"I found him shot in his car three days ago."

Houdini went to the window and stared out. When he spoke, his voice was soft and desolate. "I underestimated them."

I took in the full scope of the room for the first time. There were more than fifteen boxes stacked against one wall next to a large fireplace. Next to that were six or so packing crates and as many or more traveling trunks with Houdini's name stamped on them. In one corner was a wood cabinet about three and a half feet tall with a sloping hinged lid. A hole was cut in the

middle of the lid and there was also one on each side. It looked
to me like it had been designed to hold a person. There were a
few other props beside it, including a milk can, and on the other
side of the room was the chair that Nemesis was tied to and another empty chair.

"You're alive," I said.

"Obviously."

"But you made the world believe you were dead."

"Houdini is dead."

"I don't understand," I said. "I don't understand any of this."

Houdini turned around. "No, you don't."

I looked at the gun in my hand. It seemed needlessly ornate.
"Is this thing loaded?"

"Of course it is."

I pointed it at him. "Tell me everything. Start at the beginning."

Houdini walked across the room to the empty chair. He pulled
it along the floor, away from Nemesis, and slumped into it. "All
right. It began with a lie told to Harold Osbourne in Garnett,
Kansas."

When he was finished Houdini rose from his chair and went to
the fireplace. He bent down and held a match to a pyramid of
wood and newspaper that was set up there, and in a few seconds
had a fire going. He opened the nearest box and dropped its
contents into the flames.

"What are you doing?" I asked. I'd lowered the gun while
Houdini was telling his story, but didn't want to put it down

with Findlay or Nemesis or whatever his name really was in the room, tied up or not.

"It's done," he said. "I've lost. It's time to disappear."

"You're already dead, as far as anyone knows."

He watched the flames as though hypnotized. "It is entirely possible for two seemingly contradictory things to be at once true. Houdini is dead. But Houdini was just an invention. He was never real. Wilkie knows Ehrich Weiss is alive, it seems."

He picked up another box and shook its contents into the fire.

"You have a daughter," I said.

My mouth was dry and the growing heat the fireplace was throwing into the room wasn't helpful.

"Her name is Alice."

Houdini said nothing. He didn't even acknowledge that I had said her name. I became angry. How could he just pretend something had never happened? That someone didn't exist?

"Why haven't you ever been a father to her?"

Houdini stared at me, his eyes dark.

"I was never cut out to be anyone's father."

"That's not a choice you get to make."

"Everything is a choice."

He reached into his coat pocket and pulled out an envelope. He strode toward me with it extended. As he got close I recognized my father's distinctive handwriting.

"Where did you get that?"

"You dropped it after you punched me. Take it."

I kept my hand at my side.

"Take it." He held the letter out, insistent. I took it from him, then crossed the room and threw it in the fire. I didn't want to read it again.

"You can deny it all you want," Houdini said. "That won't bring her back."

"I know that."

"The dead are gone. My mother's not coming back. Grigoriev's not coming back. Clara is not coming back."

I stepped back. He knew about Clara. How did this man know so much about my life? How did he seemingly know every terrible thing I'd ever done, everybody I loved? He had read the letter, obviously. He knew that it was from her, telling me she was sick, asking me to come and see her. And he knew that I had gone, had rushed to the hospital, but she was gone.

"Clara isn't dead." I swallowed, hoping that this was true.

"Isn't she? I think you know better than that." He said this with such condescension that I wanted to pull the pistol's trigger and shoot him.

"Bess isn't dead either," I said. "Except to you."

At the mention of Bess's name Houdini wilted. I kept at him.

"I went and saw her. She was returning love letters to the women who wrote them. She knows what kind of man you were."

Houdini remained silent.

"Why did you drag me into this?"

Houdini turned to look at me, his eyes watering from the smoke. "To buy me time."

"Time for what?"

"To protect her. You were always a decoy."

I took the book out of my pocket. "And this?"

"I slipped it into your pocket the night you punched me. They were supposed to take it from you weeks ago. It was supposed to be the last piece of the puzzle for them, the thing that would finally convince them they were done with Houdini. Do you really think I'd have put anything important in a keyword code? A child could crack one of those. But you got the better of our friend here."

Houdini returned to the fire. He fueled it with another box and retrieved a jerry can from beside the fireplace, unscrewed the lid, and poured what appeared to be gasoline onto the fire. A ball of flame momentarily threatened to escape the limits of the fireplace but subsided.

The man in the chair stirred. A moan escaped his lips, catching Houdini's attention. He put down the canister.

"You see this?" he said, gesturing to the fire. "It's over. I'm burning everything."

When he got no response, only a glassy stare, Houdini sprinted across the room. "That's how you want it to be, Findlay? You've spent a quarter of a century chasing me around, a lurking specter." He hit Findlay hard across the face with the back of his hand. Findlay's eyes rolled back and a trickle of blood ran down his chin, but he stayed conscious.

"I hand you and Wilkie a rube to uncover and you can't even do that," Houdini said.

"Grigoriev stopped me from going to the Crandons," I said.

Houdini turned and glared at me. "He shouldn't have done that."

Houdini returned to the fireplace and fed it more files. He picked up the gasoline again but didn't put any on the fire. Sweat poured down his face and his shirt was blackened and stained, but he didn't seem to notice the heat. He put the gasoline down and stepped away from the fireplace, moving toward the pile of remaining boxes.

"I'm sorry, Martin. I wish it didn't have to be this way."

I believed him. It seems odd to me now that I did, but he seemed sincere. How much does that matter? I wondered. Does being genuinely sorry for something make a difference?

Then I saw his right hand. He raised Findlay's gun at me and pointed it at my chest.

"What are you doing?"

He swung his arm away from me and pulled the trigger. The gun recoiled and filled the room with thunder. Findlay's chair fell backward and to the side. He aimed the gun back at me.

"I'm sorry, Martin. I don't want to do this. But you know everything. You're my last link to the past. Neither Houdini nor Ehrich Weiss can die as long as you're alive."

"Please don't."

He shook his head and sobbed, but he didn't lower the gun. I thought of Clara, and how I would never see her again. What would our life have been like if I had done something else in the next moment, anything else? Would we have married, raised kids, grown old? She would have come to depend on me to have answers, as someone who knew how to feel about what was happening. My children would have deserved a father who was capable of properly loving them. Standing there with a gun pointed at me by the most famous man no one knew was alive, I wished that I could have been that person. But I knew I wasn't. Punching Houdini hadn't ruined anything for me that I wasn't going to ruin on my own.

What happened next is a blur. It felt like we stood there for hours with him working up the nerve to pull the trigger and me trying to think of some way out. Then there was an explosion and the can of gasoline spewed forth an arcing column of fire. I still held the gun I'd used to knock Findlay out, and without thinking I raised it and shot Houdini in the heart.

He staggered back, blood seeping from his chest, and collapsed in a heap behind the boxes. A line of fire raced across the floor. If I didn't move quickly it would beat me to the door. Smoke was beginning to fill the room, making it difficult to breathe and see. I covered my mouth and nose with my arm and ducked low.

"Strauss!" Findlay called out. I should have ignored him and left but I didn't. I had only a second to react and instead of fleeing I made my way over to him. He was shot in the arm and one eye was swollen shut.

"Please don't leave me," he said.

I'd done a lot in my life that I wasn't proud of, but I couldn't leave him. I knelt down and tried to undo the ropes binding him to the chair, but Houdini's knots were too difficult for me. The fire had spread and was nearly at the door.

With a strength that surprised me I was able to pull Findlay upright, still tied to the chair. I tipped the chair back on two legs and dragged him across the floor. The fire had burned its way up the wall, and the boxes of files that Houdini hadn't burned in the fireplace were engulfed in flame. The smoke was so thick that I couldn't see the spot where Houdini had fallen. There was no question of stopping the fire now.

I pulled Findlay out the door and down the stairs, the legs of the chair landing with a thud on each tread. Findlay was quiet—

either he had nothing to say or he'd passed out. I focused on escape and survival. When I pushed open the front door, the building gulped in fresh air from the outside and glass showered the street as the upstairs windows blew out.

When we were safely across the street, I was overcome by a fit of coughing and fell to my knees. It took me a moment to recover, then I turned my attention to Findlay. He was awake but breathing heavily.

"Thank you," he said.

I suppressed the urge to cough again. "What now?"

"It's over."

"I just killed Harry Houdini."

"Didn't you do that already?"

"You saw me shoot him."

"You can't kill a man who's already dead."

He was right. I left him tied to a chair under the elevated train and walked away just as a fire crew arrived. It was possible they might be able to save the building. At the very least it seemed like they'd be able to prevent the fire from spreading. From the outside it didn't seem that bad—a little smoke was wafting out the second-floor windows, but otherwise the building appeared to be intact.

As I walked down Third Avenue toward Grand Central Terminal, I looked back and saw a man try to untie Houdini's knots, then give up and cut the rope with his pocketknife. I never heard from Findlay again.

MARTIN STRAUSS
∽ *Present Day* ∾

THAT'S IT. I'VE TOLD ALICE EVERYTHING.

She's listened without interrupting, her hands folded in her lap. There is sorrow in her posture but her face is calm, almost serene. I don't know what to make of this.

"I couldn't tell you before," I say. "I didn't want you to know what kind of man he was."

"I don't care about Houdini."

"I'm sorry," I say.

"I don't care that you're sorry. Why did you leave her?" She's not serene, she's angry.

"Clara?"

"Yes," she says, "you know, the woman you loved one moment and abandoned the next."

My head begins to ring again. "I don't know," I say. "Nothing happened right. I was overwhelmed and dealt with it in exactly the wrong way. I tried to make amends later, but her father told me never to come back."

"And you listened to him?"

"Yes." I shouldn't have listened to him. I should have gone back.

"Why?"

"Because it was what I wanted to hear. That I wasn't welcome, that the world had gone on without me."

"Did you love her?"

I pause. "Yes."

"Do you regret it?"

It doesn't matter whether I regret it. Life doesn't work that way. Once you've done something, it can't be undone. That only works in magic tricks. The rope cut into pieces made somehow whole again, the object that's disappeared reappearing. It's magic because we know that this doesn't really happen.

"Regret isn't a big enough word."

"No," Alice says, "I guess it's not."

I can feel her rage. Did I expect she wouldn't be angry? Why else would I have delayed telling her the truth all these years. It's possible that at any moment she's going to get up and walk away without looking back and I'll never see her again.

"My mother raised me by herself, Martin. She was lonely and she was betrayed. But she never became bitter. She was confused, if anything. Never understanding why she'd been abandoned by my father. It was as though there was something basic about human nature that she couldn't fathom. It eluded her, I believe, because it doesn't exist. There's no good reason she was left alone. It took me years to realize that I would never find it. But my mother . . ."

She's crying, tears running down her face. I reach my hand into my pocket and remove my coin. I show it to her, and she wipes her eyes and smiles a little. I transfer the coin from one hand to the other, throw it up in the air, catch it, and show it to her. I transfer the coin and throw it again. We watch it rise up, and for a moment I wonder if it will escape us both, somehow keep going upward away from here and into the unknown above us. Maybe Alice is wondering the same thing. But its ascent slows and then reverses, and the coin falls back to my waiting hand, tied to the earth by the same immutable forces that govern us all. I do the false transfer and mimic a throw with my left hand.

Alice places her hand on my right hand. She's stopped crying, but her face is blotchy and stained.

"She's dead, Martin."

"I'm sorry."

"So you keep saying."

But I am sorry. A grief envelops me, one that goes far beyond the bounds of normal empathy, even for someone I care for as much as I do Alice. I grieve for parents, and for parenthood. Being a parent is a monumental thing. You shape reality for another person. You cannot be an illusion. You cannot be paralyzed by the fear that you are an illusion. If you have done a bad job, or no job at all, what remains of you is proof that the world is an unfeeling place. If you have done a good job, what remains is the part of you that was magical.

A man walks by us, talking loudly on his cell phone. What do you say to a person who's lost her mother? It's a horrible thing to lose your mother. I know this as well as anyone. Now, in my old age, I can barely remember my mother. I have flashes of her, and I have an impression, but all that is left now is her faint reflection.

A memory isn't a finished product, it's a work in progress. We think that our minds are like a library—the right book is there somewhere if you can find it. A whole story will then unfold with you as the narrator. But our memory changes, evolves, erases. Moments disappear and are replaced and combined. What's left of a person after they're gone is a spirit of who and what they were.

This is where our pain comes from. Because we know this is going to happen. We feel it and it underwrites our mourning.

For all of us the future is an unmade promise. For the living there is the present and the past. The past is always moving, always changing, as the people we lose are transformed in us. The past is no place to live. But it's the only place the dead lived.

The spiritualists Houdini hated so much capitalized on these memories. Or at least that's what he believed. But the ghosts of our dead don't need to be used against us by mediums or fortune-tellers. We do it ourselves. We measure ourselves against ghosts. I've done this. I see that now. It's left me alone and remorseful. I've denied myself a life in the attempt to appease my flawed remembrances.

Alice reaches into her purse with her free hand and retrieves a small, leather-bound notebook. I recognize it as the book I write in to help me remember. Inside it is a square of newspaper. She hands it to me and I take it. Her left hand still grasps my right, so I hold the paper in one hand and squint to read the tiny type.

Clara Strauss: March 28, 1947–September 2, 2010

Clara Strauss passed away peacefully of natural causes at the age of sixty-three. Clara was born in Montreal, Quebec, where she lived and worked as a registered nurse. She is survived by her daughter, Alice, and predeceased by her parents, Isaac and Judith Weiss. No funeral services to be held.

I hand Alice back the obituary notice. I remember sitting in a waiting room, wanting to go inside, being told I was too late. I left everything too late. I had once woken up beside her on a cold morning, I had sat with her while our child cried, and I had left her. No, none of that is right. My confabulations are closing in. My head buzzes. I am dizzy.

I refocus on Alice. "There should have been a funeral."

She wipes her eyes with the back of her hand and returns the clipping to the notebook. "She didn't want one."

"Why not?"

Alice shrugs. "She didn't think anyone would go."

"Was she right?"

Alice thinks about this. "No. Lots of people would have gone. Everyone loved her. She just never believed they did."

"I think," I say, "it's important to put people to rest properly. I never went to my mother's funeral. I found out about her death a month after the fact in a letter from my father."

Alice nods. "I know."

I don't remember telling her this. But Dr. Korsakoff has warned me not to trust my recollections. I should heed his words.

"All these things you say about Houdini, Martin. The flaws, the way he treated people. You do know that you did all these things?"

"Yes, I know it. It's ruined me, and I've let it ruin me. I wish I'd known how to be better."

"You want there to be a moment. A grand mistake, like punching Harry Houdini, that is the cause of your leaving her. But there isn't."

Alice lowers her chin and turns over the hand she's been holding on to. She opens my palm and plucks out the coin.

I smile. She hadn't fallen for the trick at all; she'd detected the false transfer right away.

"Well done," I say.

Alice smiles back at me, and I realize that she looks a little like my mother. Funny that I've never noticed that before. "I'm my father's daughter," she says, and drops the coin into her bag.

"Then you know that magic isn't real," I say.

"Yes," she answers, leaning in to rest her head on my shoulder, "but I never stop wanting it to be."

I exhale and close my eyes. It's a sunny day and I'm here on a bench with Alice. It's not a picnic with my mother and father, and there is no packed lunch and there is no reassuring breeze, but it's just as good. Better maybe. This, I'm sure, is real. Maybe soon I'll have cause to doubt it, but for now there's no questioning it. I am happy.

"That dog that took your toy when you were a child," I say.

"My rubber chicken."

"Someone should have chased that dog down and got it back for you."

"Yes."

"I'm sorry I didn't do that," I say.

"I am too."

Her voice cuts through my tinnitus and my mind clears as though a strong wind has blown fog out to sea. I picture Alice and Clara sitting on a blanket in the sand, can hear the gulls screaming and the waves collapsing on themselves. I hold out the rubber chicken, still wet with the dog's drool, and Alice takes it from me, relieved and content. Clara hasn't seen me yet, preoccupied with something off to the side, but soon she'll turn and see me. She'll laugh as I wipe my hands on my pants and sit down beside them on the blanket.

"This doesn't make up for anything," Alice says.

"I know."

But she leans in closer, and I feel something shift. The past isn't gone, it never is, but that doesn't matter. The spiritualists were wrong and Houdini was wrong and I was wrong. I had to lose my memories for me to understand. Magic is believing in what we understand is not real because we want it to be. Magic is that tiny fraction keeping you from infinity. And this, right now, is magic.

The ice cream orderly strides through the automatic doors. He is intent on something. He turns and looks at me and taps his finger on his watch in a way that feels familiar to me. I can tell we've done this before and I understand that in a few minutes I will have to get up and go with him back inside the hospital.

But not yet.

Author's Note

Martin Strauss would have been intimately familiar with the major works related to the life of Houdini; particularly William Kalush and Larry Sloman's *The Secret Life of Houdini*, Kenneth Silverman's *Houdini*, and Ruth Brandon's *The Life and Many Deaths of Harry Houdini*. These texts were certainly invaluable to me, as were many others. The writings of Jim Steinmeyer are where I learned most of what I know about magic, and Greg King's *The Man Who Killed Rasputin* was an invaluable source of Russian intrigue. Houdini himself wrote many books on both magic and spiritualism, all of which give good insight into both their subjects and their author.

Where possible I have attempted to use both Houdini's and Arthur Conan Doyle's words, sometimes slightly edited. Lady Doyle's transcription of her Atlantic City séance with Houdini is one example; Houdini's speech to the audience containing

Martin and Clara in Montreal is another (though he didn't say those words in Montreal).

Most of what you read in these pages is made up, though many of the people did exist in one form or another. Regarding the descriptions of methods of magic, I make no claims of veracity.

I am indebted to Kevin Baker, Joseph Boyden, David Chariandy, Andrew Davidson, Jennica Harper, Lee Henderson, Nancy Lee, Keith Maillard, Diane Martin, John K. Samson, Timothy Taylor, Miriam Toews, John Vigna, Guy Vanderhaeghe, and Katherine Wagner for suffering various drafts and offering invaluable comments; to Taylor Brown-Evans for some terrific researching; and to John Cox of wildabouthoudini.com for help with an issue regarding locks. To Kevin Patterson and the Sea Mouse Writers' Trust: your hospitality is magnificent and helped me immensely. Thanks as well to all my colleagues at the University of British Columbia for providing me with the best place on earth to spend my days.

My editors and friends, Louise Dennys, Michael Heyward, Sarah McGrath, and Ravi Mirchandani, have made me happy to be a writer; my agent, Henry Dunow, is simply the best guy around. Thanks to Anne Beilby, Nina Ber-Donkor, Marion Garner, Anthony Goff, Liz Hohenadel, Amanda Lewis, Nicola Makoway, Yishai Seidman, and Sarah Stein. It is a privilege to work with each of you.

Lara, Katharine, and Margaret Galloway have seen me vanish while writing this book, and have worked hard to forgive me and let me reappear. I hope to repay their faith.

Steven Galloway lives in British Columbia and teaches creative writing at the University of British Columbia. He is the author of *The Cellist of Sarajevo*, which was an Indie-Bound and a Barnes and Noble Discover selection and has been chosen for community reads across the country.